TAU

Barbarians of Rome: Book Two

James Walker

Copyright © 2019 James Walker

All rights reserved.

ISBN: 9781670866356

DEDICATION

To Jenny, who always pushes me forward.
To my family, who always believe in me.
To Joan, my editor, whose efforts to improve my writing cannot be understated.
And to my readers, who make it all worth it.

CHAPTER ONE

Autumn, 357 A.D.

A stiff breeze blew toward the African coast. Tau sat on the stern deck of the Roman merchant ship as the broad sail bellied into the clear autumn sky. Ulrich was at his side, and they rested on the planks in companionable silence, enjoying the warmth of the evening sunlight as the day cooled. Seabirds had been following the boat since morning, a sure sign that they were nearing shore, and the ship's crew buzzed with anticipation.

A great brown dog dozed at Ulrich's side. Ulrich stroked its head absently. He had acquired two of the beasts in Gaul, a gift from the Auxilia commander, Eogan. They were Roman mastiffs, bred and trained by the Legions for battle. Ulrich's eyes were closed as he scratched the one named Thor behind the ears. Tau sat with his back to the rail and daydreamed about Ima, the Saxon girl he had met amidst the chaos of the German war. The last five days had been idyllic sailing through fair weather from Massalia to Hippo Regius.

"Sail on the horizon," called the steersman.

There was rustling from the cabin, and presently the merchant ship's captain appeared. He was a portly Roman named Gaius. A close friend of quartermaster Marius, a mutual acquaintance. He gave Tau an amiable nod and ambled to the side rail for a look.

Curious, Tau joined him. Sure enough, there was a dirty, gray sail on the southeastern horizon, a mere distant fleck on that radiant blue sea.

"It's square-rigged, single mast," Gaius grunted. He sounded unconcerned. There had been plenty of traffic along their route.

There was no reason to suspect any danger from yet another ship passing by on this busy shipping lane.

"An archaic design," Tau noted.

The triangular sails of the modern lateen-rigged vessels allowed them to sail against the breeze, while a square-rigged vessel was forced to row when the wind turned unfavorable. In fact, Gaius's lateen-rigged vessel had only a couple of oars, just for maneuvering in port. Removing the rowing benches also allowed a smaller crew and much more room for cargo. Gaius shrugged and went back to his cabin.

The gentle rocking of the boat lulled Tau to sleep. The sun was lower when a bustle of activity on the deck woke him again. He stood to find Ulrich leaning on the larboard rail alongside Gaius. The strange ship was close now, only a mile away and closing fast. The wind had shifted, coming nearly directly from the south, bringing with it the smell of land, and the square-rigged ship was riding that southerly breeze. It steered as though it meant to cut across the merchant ship's bow.

"That's a slave galley," Gaius observed. There was tension in his voice.

"I don't like it," Ulrich growled, and one of the mastiffs growled with him.

The crew of Gaius's ship was small, only six men, and they all crowded onto the deck, watching.

"It is probably no threat to us, but I have not lived this long by taking chances," Gaius said. He addressed his helmsman. "Take us off course, Drausus. We'll make port at Saldae. Hold the boat as hard to the southwesterly tack as she will stand."

The helmsman nodded and leaned on the steering oar. The sail fluttered and went slack as the boat turned straight into the wind. The ship's momentum carried it through the turn, and the sail, with its diagonal spar, rotated on the mast until it caught the breeze on the opposite tack. Two of the crew went to tighten the loose clew to hold the sail taut to the wind.

The ship was now running southwest, a right angle from its previous course southeast, and the strange ship was being left behind, unable to turn its primitive square sail so close into the wind.

"Just as I feared," Gaius said, his voice tight. The stranger's crew furled their useless sail and a bank of oars sprouted from the galley.

They began to row, giving chase.

Tau took a close look at the stranger. It was a single-deck galley, longer and leaner than Gaius's merchant vessel, low to the water with ten oars per side pulling powerfully against the waves. A long, wicked ram, tipped with bronze, shone in the sun, slicing just beneath the surface of the water. The gleam of sunlight on dull metal betrayed the presence of chains and shackles among the rowers. There was no doubt that this was a slave ship. Tau found that he was grinding his teeth. He had spent years as a galley slave, pulling an oar on just such a ship.

Despite hard rowing, the galley was unable to catch the merchantman as the lateen-rigged vessel raced upwind. A group of men stood frustrated in the bows of the enemy ship. Naked swords gleamed in their hands. Gaius touched the clew line, checking the tension of the sail and nodded, satisfied.

"If the wind holds, we will lose them by sunset. By then we will be near landfall and either make the port of Saldae or find a Roman patrol boat," he said.

The captain looked at the mast. The ship's flag bore the symbol of a golden orb encircled by a laurel wreath, designating the ship as a tax-paying subject of the Roman Empire. Gaius ordered a new flag run up the halyard—a solid square of red—universal symbol of distress at sea. The enemy ship flew no flags.

Ulrich gave Tau a meaningful look then entered the hold. Tau followed, descending through a hatch and down a ladder. Their belongings were piled beneath their hanging cots in the corner, and Ulrich unwrapped his heavy armor from its oiled sheepskin. He handed Tau his swords, and Tau pulled on his chainmail while Ulrich donned his steel cuirass and hefted his massive battle axe. Armed and armored, they returned to the deck.

The merchant ship had already doubled the distance from the slave galley, but the tension on deck was palpable. Their own ship was at the mercy of the fickle wind, while their pursuers were not. Any slackening in this breeze, and the gap would close, and none onboard doubted the hostile intentions of the slavers.

Gaius served a dinner of smoked fish, dark Roman bread, olive oil, and diluted wine. The crew spent an anxious evening, splitting time between trimming the sail and gazing at the enemy, who showed no signs of breaking off the chase. Just before sunset, land was finally visible on the southern horizon. Gaius held his course, sliding along close-set to the wind, and the sun dipped below the horizon. The stars sparkled, filling the sky from east to west, and a full moon rose high into the cloudless sky. Once Tau's eyes adjusted to the dark, the moonlight seemed almost as bright as full day, and he watched the mountainous coast of Africa loom larger and larger as they drew near. The enemy galley faded into the darkness, becoming lost among the soft whitecaps of the gentle waves.

Around midnight the wind stopped. The sail, which had been as tight as a drumhead, fluttered and lay slack, and the world fell deathly silent. All the crew was on deck, and Gaius restlessly paced the stern platform. Tau stared back in the direction they had come but saw no sign of the galley.

"We could take down the mast," Tau whispered. "We would hide better against the horizon."

Gaius shook his head. "No," he hissed. "I want the sail to be ready if the wind starts back up. Our best bet is still to make for Saldae."

They waited, straining all their senses staring into that dark night. The boat rocked gently on the rolling sea. The only sounds were the soft splash of water on the stern and the muffled footsteps of the crew as they paced the deck. Tau tried to estimate the distance to shore. They could not be more than a mile from the rocky beaches of that barren coast. Far to the west Tau could see the orange glow of torchlight on the land.

"Is that Saldae?" Tau asked, indicating the faraway lights.

Gaius nodded but did not respond, too nervous even to speak.

Suddenly a new noise broke in on the night, and Tau's heart skipped a beat. When it restarted it was running a little faster. He could hear oars striking water—the rhythmic pulse of the pirate galley. It was drawing closer. Tau stared astern, but nothing was visible in the darkness. The sound grew louder, and a darker shadow moved against the dark sea. Finally, it resolved into the form of the enemy.

The pirate galley approached the Roman merchantman. They knew their prey was helpless, and they began lining up for their attack. Rather than come from directly astern, they circled, angling to drive their bronze ram into the merchantman's flank where the deck was lowest. Tau looked to Gaius, but the captain seemed frozen in fear.

"Oars," Tau shouted. He pushed two of the seamen toward the maneuvering oars in the waist of the ship.

"Pull away. Give us enough headway to steer. Drausus, keep us pointed directly away from them. They may still ram us, but we can take some of the force out of the blow. Gaius snap out of it! I need you to find me a lamp and a pot of something flammable. Lamp oil, pitch, whatever you have. And hurry!"

The men were grateful to have leadership, and they jumped to their tasks. The two sail trimmers stood nearby, both sturdy Phoenicians from Massalia.

"Grab whatever weapons you can find and join us on the stern," Tau told them. He turned to Ulrich, who looked fierce with his big axe and two equally fearsome dogs. "Ready to repel boarders?" Tau asked.

Ulrich's teeth were bared, and they gleamed white in the darkness. "Just like old times, my friend," he said with relish, and Tau grinned.

CHAPTER TWO

If they could keep the merchant ship's high stern platform facing the attackers, they would have the advantage of height when the enemy tried to board. Drausus and the two rowing seamen were doing a commendable job of frustrating the galley's attempts to ram their flank.

After two more tries, the galley finally gave up on circling and came straight on. The distance closed rapidly. An armed mob of pirates stood on the bow platform of the enemy ship. Tau counted least a dozen men who carried short, curved swords. They had no visible armor, just long cloaks against the night's chill, and Tau wished he had a bow and arrows. A good bowman could have slaughtered these pirates at this range, but unfortunately, they had no bows. All they had was Tau, Ulrich, and two nervous seamen with fillet knives who huddled close behind.

The galley gained speed as it approached. The oars rose and fell in unison, and the bronze-tipped ram gleamed in the moonlight as it slid beneath the waves. The dark-clad pirates began extending a boarding ramp. The angled wooden boards would reach the level of the merchant ship's deck, but Tau estimated that the ramp would not quite top the stern rail. The enemy would be fighting uphill.

"Ahum, Danel," Tau yelled, addressing the two seamen who manned the oars. "Good job, but we are done rowing. Bring two buckets of seawater to the stern. Quickly. And arm yourselves however you can."

Tau did not look back to see if they complied. He drew his two, long, straight swords. They hissed as they left their scabbards, a familiar and comforting sound. Ulrich looked stoic as he hefted his big axe. His dogs stood flanking him, patiently awaiting orders. The buckets of seawater were brought, and at the same time, Gaius appeared with a clay pot of lamp oil in one hand and a lit lamp in the other.

With one last sweep of oars, the slaver plowed into the merchantman's stern. There was a splintering sound as the ram punctured the hull below the waterline, and the boat jolted violently. Tau steadied himself against the sudden blow, but Gaius was not so lucky. The portly man fell over with a thump.

"Water!" Tau yelled, because the attackers, three abreast and swords drawn, were charging up the steep ramp. Seeing only a couple of defenders, they yelled in triumph in a language that Tau did not recognize. The seamen dashed their buckets on the slick wood, and the enemy was forced to slow to keep from slipping. Tau could not place their ethnicity or allegiance definitively. They were fair-skinned men who wore their long dark hair in braids that they bound behind their heads. Perhaps they were Greek.

Tau backed one pace away from the rail. As the first pirate reached the head of the ramp, Tau stabbed his swords at the pirate's grasping hands, forcing him back. Ulrich struck a man with a right-handed swing of his heavy axe, and the blow threw the man from the entangled vessels to splash into the water below. Two more men filled his place. They might slow the enemy, but there were too many following behind. The pirates would soon overwhelm them.

"Gaius, bring me the oil," Tau ordered.

"I can't. I dropped it, and it rolled into the hold," Gaius responded. His voice came in winded gasps.

"Go get it," Tau insisted. "It is our only chance. Hurry!"

To Tau's right, a pirate had shimmied off the ramp and around to the side rail. He balanced there while Danel timidly stabbed at him with a short knife. The pirate parried the feeble blow and cut back, slicing open Danel's forearm with a curved sword. In his pain, the seaman dropped his fillet knife. Tau stabbed the pirate in the chest with the sword in his right hand, but the blade did not pierce. It grated hard against the pirate's bony sternum. The pirate howled in pain, lost his grip on the rail, and fell backward to splash into the water below.

While Tau was preoccupied, two pirates climbed the rail astern. Ulrich was surrounded. He fended off attacks from three sides. A man to Ulrich's left had sneakily climbed around the side of the boat, hanging low from the rail, and leapt up behind Ulrich, thinking to stab him in the back. But Ulrich saw him coming. Even while swinging his axe at another man on his right, Ulrich gave a command to his dogs. The word was in Latin, the language the dogs understood, and they responded instantly. One grabbed the attacker's ankle and pulled with fearsome strength, throwing the man to the deck. The second efficiently ripped out the man's throat, making not a sound.

A thrown spear flashed from the crowd of pirates and caught Danel in the chest. The young seaman fell, screaming in pain. Ulrich and Tau were shoulder to shoulder, backing and hacking at the advancing enemy as they fought desperately to avoid becoming surrounded.

"Gaius, where is that oil?" Tau asked, trying to keep the panic from his voice.

"Here, Tau," Gaius said from the cabin. Tau saw that he held the clay pot again as well as the lamp.

"Good, stay close to us," Tau said. He turned to his friend. "Ulrich, let's drive these pirates off our boat." Ulrich grinned, and they charged.

Six pirates had made it onto Gaius's vessel, and Tau and Ulrich tore into them. Tau's dual longswords had a longer reach than the enemy's short curved blades, and he used that to his advantage, keeping just out of range and stabbing and slashing as he moved forward. Ulrich was a whirling machine of death. He ignored the blades that glanced off his armor. His axe flew as he slammed into the enemy. In moments, four pirates were dead, two had fled back over the rail, and the stern was momentarily clear of enemy. More pirates were clambering up the ramp, but they hesitated in the face of this devastating counterattack.

Tau sheathed his left-hand sword and held back an open hand. "Gaius. Give me the oil." He closed his hand on the handle of the heavy clay pot. Then, he froze as a new threat appeared.

The foremost pirates had shuffled aside in deference to a huge man who pushed his way to the head of the ramp. He appeared to be the biggest warrior among them. He was seven feet tall, built of heavy muscle, and he wore a gleaming bronze circlet binding his dark hair. Scars marked his pale face, and there were white streaks in his long, braided beard. He smiled with an evil competence as he cocked a throwing spear on his right arm, dark eyes staring into Tau's.

The distance was so short the pirate could not miss, and Tau knew that he would die. In panic, Tau threw himself to the deck as the giant's arm came forward. The wind was driven out of him when he hit the wooden planking, but the spear missed him by mere inches. There was a cry of pain, and Tau looked back to see that Gaius, still clasping the glowing lamp, had been struck in the belly with the spear. There was a shocked look on the merchant captain's face as he sank to the deck, wooden shaft protruding from his crumpled form.

Tau was overcome with rage. He leapt to his feet and rushed the big pirate. The man tried to draw a sword from his belt, but it was too late. One of Tau's blades flashed up to slice a gash from the pirate's face, blinding him and making him recoil backward in pain.

Tau dropped the point of his sword and slid a foot of cold steel between the pirate's ribs. The man coughed blood and fell, collapsing onto the ramp.

Tau mounted the rail. He threw the clay pot of oil onto the enemy ship, and it shattered, spraying the fluid in all directions. The oil covered the men on the boarding ramp, it smeared the deck of the galley, and it splashed across the nearest rows of slaves at the benches.

Ulrich and his dogs held the pirates at bay while Tau went to Gaius.

"Thank you, friend," he said crouching, but Gaius did not hear him. His eyes were tightly closed in pain. Tau gently removed the lit lamp from the captain's clenched hands. He turned and held the flame aloft.

Tau felt red hot rage flash through him. "Do you want to die?" he howled at the pirates. "Do you want to be roasted in your own flesh? Get back you bastards! Back!" They did not have to speak Latin to understand Tau's meaning. The pirates dropped their weapons and backed away. Dripping of the pungent fluid, they held their hands in the air and pleaded in an unfamiliar tongue, begging not to be burned alive.

But even as he made the threat, Tau knew that he was bluffing. There were two-dozen poor souls chained to the benches. Killing the slavers would mean killing them too. For many years he too had been a slave, made to row on a ship very much like this one. Life as a slave was agony, but Tau would not be the one to take their lives from them.

Terrified, the enemy retreated before his threat. They gathered their wounded, an order was shouted, and the galley's oars backed water. For a few strokes nothing happened as the two boats were stuck fast, then finally, the galley slaves gave a great heave. With a groaning and tearing of timbers the ship leapt away.

A slave in the nearest row of benches stood. Somehow his shackles had failed, and he shrugged free of his chains. He sprinted toward the bow of the galley. One of the pirates made a halfhearted attempt to grab him, but the escaping slave spun away, danced past the party on the deck, and dashed up the retreating gangway. The boats were ten feet apart, but the man leapt the growing distance. His fingertips snatched safety on the merchant ship's flat planking, clutching the deck just below the high rail.

The slave ship did not return for their runaway. They continued rowing into the darkness. The escaped slave heaved himself up, clambered over the rail, and found his feet on the deck. He was tall and thin with a distinguished, angular face and long blond hair. He was wearing only a sackcloth shift. He looked emaciated and haggard, but his eyes were bright and flashing.

"Ulrich. Tau." The strange man said in a familiar voice. "How lucky I am to run into the two of you all the way out here."

Tau was stunned, and Ulrich was speechless. The man who stood before them was Ejnar, Serpent of the Waves.

CHAPTER THREE

The crew spent the next minutes taking stock of the situation. Gaius was the most badly hurt; blood welled from the deep spear wound in his abdomen. A spear blade had gone clean through Danel's shoulder, and while painful, it was not life threatening, so Tau tasked him and Ahum with tending to Gaius and staunching the flow of blood from his terrible wound. The other seamen were unhurt, so Tau put them to work bailing. The boat was taking on water fast. Ulrich and Tau descended to the hold and found a barrel-sized hole through which the sea was rushing in. They tried to block it with crates and pieces of lumber, but the water gained fast. In moments the cold seawater came up to their knees.

"Sailcloth." Ejnar said. He had followed the companions down into the dark hold. He held a lamp and eyeballed the damage. "Fold a patch of sailcloth and tie it on from the outside. It is called 'fothering.' It will slow the leak."

Ulrich looked at Tau, and Tau shrugged. It was a desperate situation. Old Drausus the helmsman showed where the extra sailcloth was stored, and Ejnar deftly fashioned a patch, taking the four-times folded linen and tying long ropes to each of its four corners. They went to the stern, and Ejnar gave the free ends of the ropes to Drausus. Then, with no hesitation and still holding the makeshift patch, Ejnar dove out into the inky blackness, long ropes trailing behind. He splashed into the ocean and swam beneath the hull.

Tau tied a safety line to the stern rail and lowered himself down the outside hull of the ship, but Ejnar did not need his help. Ejnar had already found the breach, and his head was underwater while he held the patch to the big hole. Drausus and a seaman tied the ropes forward about the ship's hull, holding the cloth in place, and Tau and Ejnar returned to the deck.

Descending again to the hold, they found that the fothering was working. The rush of water had become a trickle, and by bailing they could just keep up with the inflow. Tau returned topside.

There was the faintest breeze picking up, and Drausus instructed Ulrich in the proper luffing so they could sail nearer the wind. When Tau returned to the night air, he found that his friend was frowning.

"You look troubled, friend," Tau said, knowing him well. "Something on your mind?"

Ulrich's voice was low. "What do you want to do with Ejnar? Should we kill him?"

Dark as it seemed, the thought was not far from Tau's mind. Before Ulrich had rescued Tau from slavery, Tau had been shackled to a rowing bench on Ejnar's ship. Ejnar had been a slave master then, and Tau's oar helped carry the pirate and his Frisian crew on raid after raid along the frigid northern sea. Tau had been sold into slavery before his eleventh birthday, and Ejnar had been only the latest in an endless string of cruel masters.

Tau thought of the indignities he had suffered: the crushing hopelessness, the nights close to death from the cold, and the pain of the beatings. He remembered the agony of near starvation, of pulling an oar with bleeding hands, of boils from the hot sun, and of the chafing of rough iron shackles. Tau bore many scars from that time, and he rubbed his wrists absently.

Tau thought about Ejnar. Unlike many slavers, Ejnar was not a sadist, but he was cold and calculating. Tau remembered fellow slaves, good men, no different than he, who had wasted away on the benches with no protection from the unremitting exposure to the sun and rain, heat and cold, illness and despair.

Despite all the suffering, Tau could find little anger in his heart. Killing Ejnar would not bring back those lost years; it would not save the lives of his enslaved brethren. Killing Ejnar did not promise justice, only revenge and more pain.

Tau made up his mind. "No. I think not," he said. "He proved useful in saving this ship. He has earned some mercy for that."

Ulrich nodded his head. "He was your slaver. It is your decision," he said. "Besides, we can always kill him later." He touched the handle of his axe and turned away.

The immediate danger was over. The ship was no longer sinking. Wind began to fill the sail, and they made for shore.

Dawn broke as they reached port, revealing Saldae as a low-flung city of tan adobe and Roman brick. An aqueduct ran to the mountains in the west, and a marble amphitheater dominated the city center. The morning sunlight lit the distant peaks of the snow-capped mountains that hung in the distance, and Gaius was dying. Despite the earnest ministrations of Danel and Ahum, he had lost too much blood, and his breathing turned agonal and harsh. Drausus steered the boat for the nearest dock, but Gaius was dead before they made the quay.

A Roman officer boarded as they docked. He was the harbormaster, a tall, severe-looking man who introduced himself as Martinus. He greeted the crew formally, hands clasped behind his back and announced that he would be collecting the customs duties on the boat's trade goods. He frowned when he saw Gaius's body and the haggard state of the crew. Drausus explained what had happened while Martinus inspected their papers.

Martinus was stoic. "I am sorry for your loss. Illyrian piracy is on the rise along the African coast." The officer counted the coins that constituted the ship's docking fee and made notes on a wax stylus.

"Why are there no patrols?" Drausus demanded. "I was led to believe that the Empire had extinguished the criminal elements of the Mare Nostrum."

Martinus shrugged. "There are not enough ships to patrol Our Sea. The fleet has gone east, drawn into the war with the Persian empire. The final trireme of the Saldae station was called away just last month."

"The war with Persia is foolishness," Drausus responded, his voice bitter. "Rome has failed its people."

"Politics is not my field," Martinus answered. "But I have shipwrights for hire if you require assistance with repairs. I will return when you have finished unloading your cargo. You may rent space in warehouse number four." The officer climbed off the boat and walked back up the dock, hands clasped behind his back.

"What will you do?" Tau asked Drausus.

The old man sighed. Tau knew he had been friends with Gaius for many years. A deep pain wrote itself across Drausus's face.

"This ship now belongs to Gaius's eldest son, who lives in Italy. I will oversee the sale of this cargo and use a portion of the proceeds to repair the hull. After that I will make sure the ship returns to him." He looked at Gaius's body where it lay on the deck. Danel had covered it with a cloak. "And Gaius wished to be buried at sea. I will take him out into deep water and do it properly." He nodded to Tau. "Thank you for your assistance. We would have all died at the hands of those pirates had you and your friend not been aboard."

Ulrich and Tau gathered their things and left. They walked up the quay, Ulrich's two dogs trailing close behind. But when they got to the end of the planks they stopped and turned. Ejnar was following them. Ulrich stepped forward and crossed his arms on his chest. Ejnar could not come any closer because the dogs blocked his path. They did not growl; they did not snarl or bare their teeth; they simply stood protectively between the stranger and their master. Ulrich watched impassively.

"What do you want, Ejnar?" Tau asked.

The former pirate smiled, flashing white teeth. Tau could tell he was trying to look friendly. "Gold, women, and a fast ship. That is all I've ever wanted."

"And how do we play into your schemes, slaver?" Ulrich asked in a low voice.

Ejnar's held out his hands in a supplicating gesture. "Listen," Ejnar said. "I'm just a man down on his luck. I have nowhere to go, but you know how good with a sword I am. I can help you."

"And what do you want in return?" Ulrich demanded.

"Just a percentage, of course." Ejnar smiled again. "A percentage of whatever loot we might happen to come across."

Tau considered Ejnar. He looked thinner than the last time Tau had seen him. He had suffered in his time at the oar. A scruffy beard covered his face, and scars from a whip marred his arms and shoulders. His skin, once fair, was tanned to brown, and his only clothing was a rough piece of sackcloth that dangled to his knees. He was barefoot. Tau noticed then that he was shivering in the cold.

"How did you get loose from your shackles anyway?" Tau asked.

"I picked the lock. It was a cheap Corsican model. Child's play once I had a scrap of loose iron." He sounded proud of himself.

"And how did you like being a slave?" Tau asked. His voice had grown very cold.

Ejnar did not respond. His face fell. He looked at the ground and seemed to shudder from more than just the frigid air.

Tau stared at him for a long moment. Ulrich shifted restlessly. Finally, Tau made up his mind.

"You may come with us, Ejnar," Tau said at last. "On one condition. You must swear to whatever gods you believe in that you will never enslave another soul as long as you live. You will never own a slave, you will not trade in slavery, you will not permit others to profit from slavery on your behalf." Tau drew his right-hand sword and held it level at Ejnar's chest. He was fully ready to drive the blade into the man's heart if he felt the ex-pirate was playing him false. The steel was still flecked with dried blood.

"Swear on your life," Tau demanded.

Ejnar's eyes looked into Tau's, and Tau thought the man might cry. "I swear it. I swear to Odin," he said fervently. Tau was still not sure if he could believe him, but he sheathed his sword.

"All right, let's go," Tau said.

CHAPTER FOUR

Tau, Ulrich, and Ejnar walked into the harbor town of Saldae just as the town began to wake. Past the two-story Roman warehouses of brick and stone, the paved road opened into an oval marketplace. Stalls were being stocked, and shutters were being opened as merchants prepared for their day. The town seemed to be a mix of cultures: fair-skinned Romans in brightly colored tunics set up wares alongside tan-skinned Berbers with long, full beards and elegant wool and linen robes. In the center of the plaza was a sight that made Tau stare. Like an inverted cataract, a vertical pipe shot out a clear jet of water, the stream cascading into a perfect arc to splash into an ornamented marble pool ten feet across. The sound of splashing water filled the air.

Ejnar saw Tau staring and chuckled. "It's called a fountain," he said.

"Yes, but how does it work? What shoots the water… up?" Tau asked, transfixed.

Ejnar pointed into the distance. A tall aqueduct of Roman stone rose out of the town. It ran in a straight-line due west, toward the faraway mountains. When it left the edge of the town, it was only two stories tall, but as it traveled across the distant countryside, the aqueduct soared to tremendous heights, scraping the sky on elegant sets of stone arches.

"The aqueduct takes water from a lake high in the Atlas Mountains. The fresh water supplies the town, and when it is routed through a narrow pipe, it maintains the energy, the vital force, it has gained from its long fall from the heights," Ejnar explained.

"Another marvel of Roman engineering," Tau concluded.

Ejnar was shivering, and Tau began to feel sorry for him. He set down his rucksack and from it pulled an extra set of leather trousers and a fine leather hunting jacket that had been dyed green as camouflage in the woodlands. The Romans might think of sleeves as effeminate and pants as barbaric, but Tau preferred being warm in the winter to such petty gallantry. He held the clothes out to Ejnar.

Ejnar made no move to take them. "I don't need your charity," he muttered.

"It hurts me to see you suffering. Just take it," Tau responded.

Ejnar sniffed, taking the gift grudgingly. He was still barefoot, but the only pair of boots Tau owned was the one he wore. They moved on as Ejnar tugged the trousers over his bare legs.

On the right-hand side of the plaza was the public bath, and Tau made note of it for later. For now, he just wanted to find an inn and take a rest after a sleepless night. At the head of the plaza, a soldier guarded the open archway to the town's tall stone amphitheater. He nodded a greeting as Tau approached, and Tau asked if he could recommend accommodations in the city.

"Go to the Amula Aereus." The soldier said. "It is run by a friend of my sister's. It's beyond this road on the left side of the street. Tell them Florentius sent you."

Tau thanked him, and they moved on. They passed the amphitheater and soon found the inn. A banner showing a bronze basin hung proudly above a white-painted wooden door. Shallow stone stairs led to a stately, two-story house of Roman brick with decorative marble facings. Tau knocked, and a young woman opened the door. She was wearing a cheerful orange tunic and smiled from beneath a mop of unruly brown hair.

"We are travelers looking for an inn," Tau explained.

The young woman stepped back to let them in, then stopped when she saw Ulrich's two dogs.

"I'm sorry," she said, "but you cannot bring those animals inside. They will ruin the fine rugs. Come this way."

The young woman stepped outside and skipped down the stairs. She led them around the corner and down a narrow alleyway. She opened a steel gate into a courtyard behind the inn. In the courtyard was a lush garden fed by pipes carrying rainwater from the roof. A dozen brightly colored fish swam in a small pool of clear water.

She shut the gate behind them. "The dogs will be safe here," she said.

She crouched to greet the big dogs. Normally reticent with strangers, the ferocious war-beasts responded to the young woman with unabashed happiness, panting and wagging their tails appreciatively as she scratched each behind the ears.

"What are their names?" she asked.

Ulrich was fond of his dogs and seeing them happy made him grin. "The brown and black one is named Thor, and the black and brown one is Loki," he answered.

The young woman blinked at that, trying to decide if Ulrich was being facetious. She looked closely at the two dogs. They were nearly identical, big, broad chested beasts with drooping jowls and dark fur. One was, ever so slightly, darker than the other, and the woman pointed at that one.

"Loki?" she asked.

Ulrich chuckled. "Yes."

Reluctantly, the young woman pulled herself away from the happy animals and led the way through a back door of the inn. Inside, a woman with graying hair napped in a chair facing the window. There was a small entryway, a table cluttered with papers, and a staircase leading to the upper level. The young woman turned and addressed her guests.

"My name is Yael, and this is my cousin Delia. Welcome to the Amula Aereus. How many nights will you be staying?"

Tau introduced himself and his companions, and he explained that they only needed to stay one night. Yael showed them an upstairs room with three straw-filled mattresses, and they agreed on a price. Clear, clean water from the city aqueduct was freely available from a cistern in the courtyard, and Tau drank deeply from it, then used a rag to carefully clean his swords and wipe the salt spray from his chainmail armor. Ulrich stepped out, headed to the market to find fresh meat for his dogs. Ejnar left as well, but Tau was exhausted. He flung himself on one of the mattresses and fell asleep.

When Tau awoke it was past midday, and he was ravenously hungry. He found Ulrich fast asleep on the next mattress, but Ejnar was gone. He looked out the window of the small room to see the dogs dozing in the courtyard, lying in a sunny patch near an olive tree. Tau strapped on his sword belt and exited the room, closing the door quietly so as not to wake Ulrich. Heading toward the stairs leading to the ground floor, Tau rubbed his face to shake off sleep. He reflected on his journey.

Over past year, he and Ulrich had traveled across Germania, crossed into Gaul, met a Caesar, joined the Roman army, and defeated the Alemanni. They avenged the loss of home and family and brought down the great warlord Chnodomar. At the end of it all, Ulrich had returned to the northern sea and found his birthright, the Saxon kingdom of Bremen, destroyed by war. Naught was left but ash.

But Tau's home was the empire of Ghana, south of the windy dunes of the Sahara Desert. Tau was the true prince, and he would return to reclaim his kingdom. He would be sitting on the throne now had he not been betrayed by his stepmother, sold at the age of ten to pull an oar on a Takrur galley. Tau remembered the golden city of Koumbi Saleh, whose beauty surpassed any he had seen in all the world.

Lost in thought, Tau was startled when Yael suddenly appeared at the base of the stairs.

"Hi, Tau. How was your rest?" she asked cheerfully.

Tau composed himself. "Good to see you, Yael. I slept well, thank you."

Tau crossed the entryway and let himself out the front door. A cart full of barrels rumbled down the street, drawn by two shaggy donkeys. A family of white-clad citizens chattered jovially while they waited for the cart to pass. The driver of the cart waved at a woman who leaned from a second story window. The city was alive with people, and Tau stepped onto the street and began walking toward the plaza, thinking to spend some coin on a fresh meal and a much-needed bath.

Tau heard footsteps behind and turned to find that Yael was following. He paused to let her catch up.

"Are you and your friends mercenaries?" she asked.

Tau raised an eyebrow. "What makes you think that?"

"Your swords," she said, pointing at his waist. "And that Saxon's big axe. Those are serious weapons for mere travelers or pilgrims."

Tau's twin swords were beautiful, finely crafted weapons that he had won the same day as he had won freedom from slavery. Celtic symbols chased serpentine patterns along iron hilts. Wavy shadows on the double-edged blades traced where the steel had been folded again and again in its forging. They were Frisian in make, and while the forged steel of Roman swords was more durable, he had seen no swords to match these in balance or elegance. They had been stolen from him once, taken by Chnodomar and his Alemanni, but Tau had recovered them after the battle of Argentoratum. They had become extensions of Tau, and he felt naked without them.

"We are not mercenaries," Tau responded. "Just travelers. But tell me about yourself, Yael. Where are you from?"

She told her story readily. Yael had been born in Saldae and was now nineteen years old. While her parents had travelled half the world before opening the inn, she had hardly been beyond the city walls. She longed for adventure, to sail the seas and scale the mountains, to see exotic beasts and experience the cultures of foreign lands. But her parents said the world was too dangerous, so she stayed home and read books instead. She had learned to speak half a dozen languages, and she filled her days collecting stories from travelers as they passed through town. Her parents had died of a coughing sickness last winter, and she, with her cousin Delia, were left to run the inn alone.

They wandered the market as they talked, and Tau's nose led him to a stall that sold roast lamb. The meat was turned on a spit over a low flame and smelled of rich meat and spices. He gave the Berber merchant a Roman coin and received two great slices of the stuff, served on the flat leaf of a date palm as a makeshift platter. Tau ate with his hands, pleasantly surprised to find that the lamb had been spiced with cumin, giving the lean meat earthy and nutty tones. Roman food was grand in its own way: predominant with bread, fish, oil, and cheese, but meat was never a very large part of a Roman meal, and Tau felt the Romans were always stingy with their spices. This first meal in Africa felt like coming home. His senses felt sharp, and the ground under his feet in the dusty marketplace felt familiar and somehow…right.

Tau sat on the edge of the fountain and enjoyed the buzz and hum of activity in this lively city. Yael sat next to him, eating olives from a small clay bowl as they lapsed into a companionable silence. The Atlas Mountains stood tall in the south, and Tau knew that his destiny lay over those snowy peaks, across a great desert, and to a city of gold. Suddenly, he wished that Ima were here to see this, to taste the African meat and breathe the African air. But she was half a world away now. Silently, Tau cast a prayer to the ancestors that he might see her again.

Eventually Tau broke the silence. "Yael, my journey takes me over those mountains and far across the desert. Do you know where I could find a guide to lead me on my way?"

Yael frowned in thought. "The best guides over the mountains would probably be the Gaetuli. They live in the Atlas and raise horses, grazing their herds on the southern slopes. They come down from the heights to sell spare beasts before the cold weather comes, but they have all returned to their homes for the winter." She paused to toss an olive in her mouth, chew, and spit the seed back into the small bowl she carried before continuing. "The camel caravans of the Garamantes would be able to take you across the desert, but they have been strangely absent. They used to come all the way to town, but nobody has seen them for many years, and nobody knows where they have gone."

"So, is there no one who can take us inland from here?" Tau asked.

She shook her head. "Not that I know of. You can try asking around with the local Berbers, but Saldae lives primarily on sea trade and exporting grain to Italy. Not many people venture into the Atlas Mountains."

Tau sighed. He thanked Yael and took his leave. He made his way to the baths. They were split into two large concrete and marble buildings, one for men and one for women, both busy with people. Tau entered the proper door and found an enormous marble pool, kept filled with clear water from the aqueduct. The broad space was well lit by hanging lamps and bordered by cushioned benches. Dozens of men lounged and talked and bathed. It was a cold day, but the bath water was pleasantly warm, heated as it entered the building by a fire that was carefully tended beneath the lead pipe connected to the stone aqueduct. Tau undressed and washed off a week's worth of salt spray, bilge water, and sweat.

Tau was pleased to find that his skin color was not shocking here. For years he had been an oddity and an outcast among the fair Europeans, most of whom had never seen a black man. Africa was unsurprised by his dark skin. He asked around, but nobody knew of any Atlas guides or caravans going over the mountains. The townspeople were sociable and pleasant and seemed to enjoy talking to an outsider, but Tau found himself no closer to an answer than he had been before. Tau spent an hour in the bath before dressing and returning to the square. He found Ulrich in the market, hungrily devouring a whole roast chicken while Thor and Loki waited patiently nearby. Tau felt a surge of fondness for his friend, who had always shown him such unconditional kindness.

"Good?" Tau asked, and Ulrich grinned back through a mouthful of food. Tau filled him in on what he had discovered so far. They traded ideas for a while until a hubbub across the plaza revealed that a show was starting in the amphitheater. Roman shows were, of course, free, so they joined the queue and climbed the stairs to find seats among the high, stone benches.

The first show was an acrobatic exhibition with the actors dancing, leaping, twirling, and jumping between tall wooden posts. The second show was a situational comedy, mostly centered around romance, miscommunication, and unfortunate timing for the hero. Tau and Ulrich found themselves laughing along with the audience at the clever acting and well-timed slapstick.

It was near dinnertime when they left the theater. Tau and Ulrich were in high spirits, but nowhere nearer to a plan for the next leg of their journey.

"It's all right," Ulrich said, slapping Tau on the back. "Let us get some supper, rest tonight, and figure it out tomorrow."

Tau agreed, and they bought some food from the market: a shank of spiced roast lamb, a handful of fresh figs, a flask of olive oil, and two loaves of dark Roman bread. Ulrich bought fresh pork for Thor and Loki, as well as a sack of smoked pork for later. They carried their haul back to the inn. Ejnar was there, and Yael too, and they shared the food in the courtyard and talked until after sunset. Yael had a voracious appetite for stories, and Tau was happy to tell them, speaking of the Legion, the Emperor's cousin Julian, the barbaric wastes of faraway Germany, and the hated Alemanni and their leader Chnodomar. Ejnar was still barefoot, but his long, yellow hair was now washed and bound, and his beard was neatly trimmed; he began to look again like the proud pirate that once terrorized the northern sea.

Eventually, they wound down for the night. Yael excused herself and the companions mounted the stairs to their room. From instinct, Tau slept with his swords cradled in his arms and his back to the wall.

CHAPTER FIVE

Footsteps in the night brought Tau bolt upright. The noise came from just outside the door. Many men were climbing the stairs, but their heavy steps were slow and deliberate, like they did not wish to be heard. The sound of hushed, unfamiliar voices filtered from the hall. The jangle of weapons in belts was unmistakable. Tau went to the window and threw open the shutters to flood the room with moonlight. He drew his twin swords and nudged Ulrich awake who sprang to his feet and snatched up his axe.

Tau noticed that Ejnar's bed was empty.

"Where is Ejnar?" Tau asked.

"He's gone. The bastard must have deserted us," Ulrich snarled.

The door burst open, and nine swarthy men with braided black hair rushed in with weapons drawn. Tau instantly recognized members of the slaver pirate crew. They wore dark cloaks and carried curved swords. Blue and black tattoos covered their cheeks, outlined their eyebrows, and traced curves that got lost in dark hair and full beards.

The first man to enter died on Tau's swords. Tau slashed his leftmost blade across the pirate's face, spraying blood on the whitewashed plaster wall, while his right-hand sword drove deep into the man's stomach. The intruder slumped forward, but Tau was forced backward as the next man shoved into the room. Tau tried desperately to drag his sword loose, but he was driven into the corner before he could wrench his blade free of the glutinous flesh. He was surrounded, and the enemy pressed close.

Meanwhile, Ulrich's first overhand axe stroke cleaved into a man's head, but somehow the man kept coming. The man's skull had slowed the blow from driving deep enough to kill him, and the pirate, with a berserk energy, dropped his own sword and grabbed the handle of the axe. He pushed Ulrich back into the other corner, and by the time Ulrich had wrestled away from the dying man, he was surrounded as well. Thor and Loki, sensing something amiss, began to howl, but they were helpless to assist, caged in the yard beyond the window.

"What is going on?" Came a small, sleepy voice from the hallway.

Tau shouted a warning, but it was too late. A pirate stepped away and came back with Yael. He held the young woman by the hair and his sword was at her throat. The pirate began to speak in an angry voice, but in a language that neither Tau nor Ulrich could understand.

"Yael, can you understand what he is saying?" Tau asked, trying to keep his voice calm.

White showed around her wide eyes, and her voice shook. "He is speaking Greek. He says that you two must die," she said.

"Why must we die, Yael?" Tau asked.

"He says because you killed his leader," Yael said. Tears flowed from her eyes, but she continued dutifully translating. "He says that it is a matter of honor. He says it is his pirate code to avenge his fallen comrade."

Tau did not respond. He scanned the enemy. The man to his right was young and held his sword awkwardly. Tau knew that he would be easy to dispatch. He could slam aside his defense and stab his sword into his unprotected chest. If Tau did that, he would only have two opponents between him and Yael, but the man to his left had a wary, competent look in his eyes. Tau would have to let his guard down and he had no armor. There seemed to be no choice. He gripped his swords tight as he prepared to launch himself at the enemy.

Suddenly Yael stumbled, free of the pirate's grasp. Her former captor bore a distant, vacant stare. His sword clattered to the floor, and he fell forward.

Ejnar stepped into the room. He drew a blood-soaked blade from the dying pirate's back. He wore a vicious grin and, quite suddenly, the tables were turned.

Tau attacked. He ignored the young pirate on his immediate right. That man stood frozen with shock and indecision. The man on Tau's left twisted a curved sword toward Tau's face, but Tau's blade found him first, coming up into his groin while Tau's offhand sword parried the slashing blow. As the pirate fell, another took his place, pushing his way past his fallen comrade to hack at Tau's raised blade. Tau parried his attacks and Ejnar stepped forward to stab this enemy in the back.

Ulrich put down two of the men that faced him with flashing swings of his axe. Only two pirates remained standing. They dashed for the window. Tau let them pass, and they leapt through headfirst, falling the ten or so feet to the courtyard below. Ulrich drew a deep breath, and Tau knew he was going to order the dogs to attack the terrified men. Tau put a gentle hand on Ulrich's shoulder, and Ulrich refrained from giving the command. Thor and Loki, who stopped howling when they saw their master appear in the window, watched the two fleeing men climb the fence and disappear into the night.

A wounded pirate groaned, but Tau ignored him.

Ejnar was grinning. "You must have thought I'd abandoned you. You should not have feared. I heard them coming. They made so much noise stomping up the stairs. I slipped out the window and got behind them." He flourished his bloody sword.

"How did they know where we were?" Ulrich asked aloud.

Ejnar rolled his eyes dramatically. "Oh, I don't know, Ulrich. Maybe they asked around town where the black man with the swords and the big, axe-wielding barbarian were staying. This isn't the Metropolis."

Yael climbed to her feet. "Oh, God," she breathed. "Delia!"

"She is fine," Ejnar reassured her. "The pirates walked right past her bedroom. I woke her up and sent her out to fetch the guard."

Ejnar crouched and began looting the bodies. There were six corpses in the small room and one wounded man, who clutched his groin and moaned pitifully. Ejnar was checking boots. When he found a pair he liked, he set about tugging them off their dead owner.

Tau looked at the wounded pirate and sighed. The man was curled in pain and oblivious to the world. "That one is still alive. Yael, see if you and Ulrich can find the wound and put pressure on it. Try to stop the bleeding. I am going to go find a medic."

Tau left the house just as a Roman officer arrived with two soldiers. Tau recognized Florentius, the same Roman who gave the travelers directions the day before.

"What happened?" Florentius demanded.

"Pirates," Tau answered. "Greek slavers who attacked us at sea and came to finish the job. The citizens are safe, but one pirate is wounded. He needs a medic."

The officer rapped out orders. One soldier turned and jogged away, going back the way they had come; the other entered the house. The officer turned back to Tau.

"Soldier Lucanus will bring the medic. You are Tau, I presume. Citizen Delia briefed me on the situation," he said.

"Yes, I am Tau," Tau responded, then he had a sudden cold realization. "More than a score of pirates attacked us at sea. Only nine entered the house." The officer's eyes narrowed as he realized what Tau was saying.

"There must be more of them nearby, and their ship as well," the Roman officer concluded.

He strode inside and called up the stairs. "Soldier. Report."

The legionnaire reappeared at the head of the stairs. "We have one wounded man and six corpses, Centurion," he answered.

Florentius betrayed no surprise at the body count. "Stay here and guard the house," he commanded the soldier. "There may be more enemy about."

The officer turned back to Tau. "We will raise the garrison and search for the boat."

"They may have also attacked the merchant ship we arrived on," Tau said. "With your permission, I wish to check on their safety." The officer nodded, and Tau turned away. He ran down the street, across the market, and toward the harbor.

Gaius's ship was still there, but there were no lights and no movement on the boat. "Drausus?" Tau shouted as he boarded, "Ahum, Danel?" There was no response, so Tau crossed the deck and descended into the hold. There he found Drausus and the other four sailors hiding in a wooden shipping crate. They were unharmed. The pirates had been there, they said, but they had heard the pirates coming and had hidden until they went away. Tau, relieved, returned to the inn.

Roman soldiers removed the corpses and carried away the surviving pirate for treatment and questioning. A guard was posted at the inn door, and Yael and Delia did what they could to clean the room of blood, though the stench was pervasive. Apologizing for the trouble, Tau gave Yael and Delia a generous handful of coin. The rest of that night was blessedly uneventful. Tau awoke in the morning feeling rested, and he sought out the Roman centurion for advice.

Florentius looked none the worse for wear despite a sleepless night. The garrison had searched the coast but failed to find either the fugitive pirates or the pirate ship. Tau asked about crossing the mountains.

Florentius shook his head. "You are unlikely to find a guide or a caravan at this time of year, but perhaps you would not need one. The road south is safe enough for one such as yourself. There are villages in those mountains," Florentius provided a vague wave of his hand. "And the locals have enough fear and respect for the Empire not to molest travelers. Just go south. The desert is very big. You cannot possibly miss it."

Ulrich had no argument against that plan, so they loaded up on supplies. They stuffed their packs with bread, olive oil, smoked meat, and flasks of water with which to cut a bottle of concentrated wine. Ejnar was convinced that he would get rich if he stuck with Tau and Ulrich, so Tau bought Ejnar a rucksack and made sure he carried his fair share of the load. The former pirate had a pirate's falchion thrust in a sword belt, and he wore a black cloak looted from one of the dead enemies. Tau noticed that his pride appeared to be recovering rapidly.

The three left the town, Ulrich's two big dogs loping behind. They followed a paved stone road that led through olive groves and past empty fields of harvested wheat. Dry stalks rose above bare, brown earth, from which dust lifted into the scattering gusts. The sun was bright in the east and shone onto a cool, windy day while dark storm clouds brooded on the western horizon. Ulrich wore his heavy steel armor and slung his massive poleaxe across his back. Tau pulled a woolen coat over his jangling chainmail and wore woolen trousers against the wintery chill. He wrapped a scarf around his mouth and nose as protection against the thick dust that blew off the fields.

They went south through the coastal plain. By afternoon the road led into foothills and left the farmland behind. As they rose above the dusty air Ejnar broke the silence.

"You know," Ejnar pointed out, "those are my swords that you are carrying."

"Oh?" Tau responded. He drew one of the blades and held it up. Intricate Celtic designs chased themselves over guard and pommel. Tau's finger traced the organic waves of the pattern-welded steel.

"You want this sword back?" Tau asked. He lowered the blade to point its gleaming tip at Ejnar's belly.

Ejnar laughed disarmingly, "I just wanted you to know where they came from. They were my spares. I had half a dozen like them crafted by Halfdan, the greatest smith of the North Sea. They are yours now. You won them when you burned The Red Serpent."

His words brought to Tau's mind the vivid memory of that great ship, turning in the current as the flames consumed its tall sails.

Ejnar drew the weapon he had taken from the pirates, inspecting it casually. The falchion was a short, single-bladed sword made of soft iron. Its broad blade widened from the handle to the tip, point curving backward from the cutting edge.

"This weapon is rubbish," he sighed. "It is a tool for hacking, not fencing. There is no finesse in such a blade." Ejnar glanced at Ulrich, about to comment derisively on the qualities of axes, but Ulrich's savage glare changed his mind. Ejnar stopped smiling. Ulrich had been walking a bit behind Ejnar who noticed the Saxon now held his weapon loose in his hand. Ejnar carefully sheathed his weapon and swallowed uncomfortably.

"You talk too much," Ulrich growled.

The companions walked on, traveling deeper into the hilly country.

CHAPTER SIX

They walked until dusk. The road took them southwest, ascending through a wide valley where the mountains stood like massive sentinels against the darkening sky. The sun settled red into a horizon filling with forbidding black clouds. The wind blew from the west, and it brought with it the earthy smell of rain. Tau estimated that they had covered nearly twenty miles. That was enough for one day. They left the road and picked out a campsite, finding a small depression in the rocky hillside that would hide them from casual view. A stone outcropping blocked most of the wind, and the slope of the ground would keep water from pooling when the inevitable rains came. They disassembled their packs, the wooden frames doubling as tent poles, and threw up a shelter of leather tarpaulins. They unfurled their woolen bedrolls, shared their food, and settled in for the night.

Tau took the first watch while Ejnar and Ulrich slept. An hour after dark, with storm clouds roiling overhead, the rain began to pour. Tau sat under the awning of the tent and watched the lightning flash across the mountainous land. This was truly a beautiful place. From where he sat, he could see all the way back to the Mediterranean Sea. The Roman town of Saldae was a pinprick of mingled torchlight far below. The mountain peaks were low where the land met the water then grew ever taller and more majestic as they flowed inland. On the other side of the valley a family of gazelles huddled for warmth. They were a couple of miles away, but well-lit by the intermittent lightning. Tau was passing the time by trying to count the animals when he noticed movement on the road.

Tau peered into the blowing rain, trying to decide if his eyes were deceiving him. There it was again, a dark shadow, working its way uphill along the paved causeway. The stranger was coming slowly, a dark, cloaked figure, and he appeared to be alone; a lone traveler, moving in the stormy night. Tau sat very still, knowing that the shelter was well hidden, tucked down as it was below the skyline. Tau assumed that the traveler would pass by, but he was wrong. At Tau's feet was the hump of a hill that blocked his view of the road, and the mysterious traveler disappeared behind it. Tau waited for him to reappear further up the road, but he did not. Tau waited longer. The stranger was nowhere to be seen. He must have either stopped on the road or turned into the hilly countryside below. Tau buckled his swords around his waist and slipped out into the rain. He was immediately soaked through, but his wool and leather kept him warm as he moved downhill, circling far away from the road, crouching low to hide his outline against the scrubby hillside.

It took Tau only a moment to find the stranger, who had moved a few paces from the road and was crouched on the muddy ground. Tau touched his swords as he approached. The stranger slumped to the ground; legs crossed beneath him. Tau waited. Nothing happened. The stranger was just sitting there, soaking in the freezing rain. Finally, curiosity overcame Tau's wariness.

"Hey," Tau called softly. "Hey, you. Who are you?"

The stranger leapt back onto the road, eyes searching the foliage. Tau stepped into view with his hands raised.

"It's okay," Tau said. "I am not a brigand. Just a traveler."

Tau stepped closer, then stopped. "Yael?" he asked, surprised. "Yael? What are you doing here?"

The girl was shivering. "Hi, Tau," she said. "I've come for the adventure."

Tau led the girl back to the tent. Ulrich and Ejnar were fast asleep. It was too damp to build a fire, so Tau wrapped Yael in his woolen bedroll for warmth.

"It's your linen clothes," he told her. "Cotton doesn't keep you warm when it gets wet. Always travel wearing wool or leather or fur."

She huddled in the blankets, but already looked more cheerful. Loki, a light sleeper, roused and padded silently over to the girl and flopped down, resting his heavy head in her lap. His brown eyes considered her thoughtfully as Yael stroked the big dog's ears.

"I brought bread," she said, producing a basket from her robes.

Somehow, she had kept the sweet golden loaf dry despite the downpour. She had even brought a small clay jar of honey. Tau could not help smiling even as he chastised her.

"You can't be serious about coming with us," he said. "What about the inn?"

"I sold my share of it to Delia," she said, holding up a purse that jangled with coin.

Tau sighed. The rain poured down on the tent, running off the lanolin-infused fabric in great glistening drops. Each teardrop of water scattered moonlight as it fell. Tau stared into the night. He remembered a boy, running wild through a golden castle and dreaming of journeying the wide world, of exploring deep jungles and chasing the wind on the open seas. That boy's childhood was stolen from him, but here was someone who shared that dream. She was naïve, but her eyes were bright, and her face was alive with curiosity. Tau said nothing, but Yael watched his face soften, and she grinned.

"So, it's settled then!" she said happily.

Before long, Yael went to sleep curled in a mountain of blankets. Tau kept watch until midnight, then roused Ulrich. Seeing Yael's sleeping form in their midst, Ulrich raised an eyebrow at Tau.

Tau shrugged. "She is a grown woman; she can make her own choices," he said.

Ulrich considered for a moment, then shrugged.

"She knows languages. It might be useful to have an interpreter," he said.

Tau found the warm, dry spot that Ulrich had vacated and went to sleep.

CHAPTER SEVEN

The rain stopped before dawn, and the sun rose on a wet world. Water ran in rivulets down the shrub-laden slopes. Yael, wrapped in a heavy woolen robe, was chatting with Ejnar when Tau awoke. Ulrich scanned the horizon. They devoured a breakfast of golden bread and smoked fish, then broke camp. Their journey took them ever higher into the mountains along the smooth Roman road. By midday they came across a broad space that had been cleared of trees and bushes. It was a place of terraced earth, yellow grass, and fields marked with lines of rough stone.

"This is a Gaetuli settlement plot," Yael said. "Their towns are seasonal. As winter approaches, they abandon their trading posts near the Roman shore and retreat south." Her eyes shone with interest as she explored the empty ground.

"But I don't know where they go," she added.

"Perhaps they have not gone far," Ulrich interjected. He pointed to the west.

On a high ridge on the other side of a deep chasm, two horsemen sat. The distance was too great to make out detail, but Tau could see the strangers were swathed in long cloaks and mounted on tall, dark horses.

Tau felt uneasy under those far-seeing eyes. The earth was still and quiet. The only movement in that stark, empty landscape was the slow-wheeling glide of a falcon that was almost lost in the cloudy sky. The wind rustled through the shrubby growth, and Loki rubbed against Tau's leg, letting out a low, ominous growl. Tau glanced down and petted the big dog, soothing him, and when he looked back up, the horsemen were gone. He looked to Ulrich who was peering at the far hills, his eyes narrow. The Saxon's hand gripped the handle of his axe.

"We should keep moving," Tau said, shaking off a sudden chill. There was a long day's travel ahead of them, and he was hoping to find some friendly nomads among these high peaks. They would need guides if they were to cross the great desert that lay beyond the mountains.

Past the empty settlement, the Roman road ended. Its flagstones gave way to a rough dirt track. They followed the steep path of packed earth that wove its way ever upward. After a few hours they reached a high ridgetop, and the land fell away before them. The path led down into a deep sunlit valley of dark green woods where the brilliance of a blue mountain river rushed.

Tau turned to look back the way they had come. From this distance, the town of Saldae was invisible, but he could just make out the outline of the high Roman aqueduct as it ran west along the coast. The sky above was cloudy, but the faraway sea was dazzling with sunlight. Ejnar crossed his arms and sighed.

"I miss the sea already," he said wistfully. "There is no thrill like riding the waves."

"What is it like?" Yael asked.

Ejnar turned his charming smile on the young woman. "My lady, it is like soaring through the sky while taming a wild beast. The wind is your direst enemy and your dearest friend, while the ship rolls like a lover and the rigging sings like sirens. And when the journey is done, you arrive on the most distant shores to walk the most exotic lands."

Tau noted with some unease that Yael was entranced by the tall pirate. "Where is the wildest place you have sailed?" she asked.

"Oh, gods," Ejnar breathed. "I have been far north and seen entire landscapes of floating ice, where the whales herd in swarms and a mere careless flip of a giant tail can doom an entire crew to the icy depths. I have been west to the burning lands of fire, where the very earth trembles as the titans of creation wage war with the ancient frost giants. But the strangest lands I have seen are to the east. In the sands of the Nile there is a civilization that predates time itself, one that was old when the frost giants were thrown down by Odin and where wizards built monuments that scrape the very sky. The great sandy cities of the Pharaohs were already falling into decay when the founders of Rome were being raised by wolves."

Ulrich was unimpressed by Ejnar's boasting. He turned away and started down the long path toward the swiftly flowing river. Tau followed, and Ejnar and Yael came along behind, still talking enthusiastically. Tau caught up with Ulrich, and they walked together for a long time in companionable silence. They were moving from the thin, cold air of the high ridge into the warm, wet atmosphere of the valley. As they approached the trees, the sun, though far from setting, slid ever lower into the western peaks, and great shadows of mountains fell across the path.

Just before they entered the cover of the trees, Tau thought he saw movement across the valley. Burned in his mind was the haunting image of a faraway horseman. A rocky outcropping stood off the path, and Tau scrambled up it for a better view, steadying himself against the stones as he peered over the treetops. The valley was empty. There was nothing there.

Ulrich stood at the foot of the rock formation. His arms were crossed as he looked up quizzically.

"It's nothing," Tau called down. "Just my imagination."

He shook himself and climbed back down. By this time, Yael and Ejnar had caught up, and they all entered the woods together. It was a loose stand of oak, pine, and cedar that shaded a thick undergrowth through which small animals rustled. Birds chirped in the trees, and a chatter of unusual howls and cries reached their ears. The cacophony of noise was piercing and strange but somehow familiar.

"Monkeys," Yael said cheerfully. She pointed off the trail to where a family of the animals was cavorting. Most were clustered on the ground, but a few had climbed the lower limbs of nearby trees. All were gazing curiously at the interlopers. A tiny baby clung to its mother's back. Its dark eyes were wide.

"Macaque monkeys," Yael added. "I've seen drawings but never a live one. They used to live along the coast too, but they fled from the cities. The farmers drove them from the fields as pests."

"I wonder how they taste," Ulrich commented.

"One should not eat monkeys," Tau responded, feeling the ghost of an old memory. "My father told me that." He watched the furry little animals whose faces were so very close to human. There was something ineffably wise in their knowing expressions.

"Why not?" Ulrich asked.

Tau shook his head. "I don't know. I don't remember why. I just remember that you should not," he said. But seeing the intelligence in the animal's eyes he knew he could never willingly hurt the curious, little beasts.

The companions moved on. The path led toward the sound of rushing water and opened onto a shallow ford. The river spread over smooth, flat stones, and though it was as wide as a Roman city block, at its deepest point the water was no more than calf deep.

Looking up, Tau could see through the thinning clouds that the sky was bright and blue, but all around the land lay in the shadow of the western mountains. Across the river was a rocky beach, and the dirt path continued into the woods beyond. The water was cold. They removed their boots and hitched up their trousers for the crossing. Skin would dry, but cold, wet clothes were dangerous. In the failing light, they made camp above the steep bank on the other side. They pitched their tent and unfurled their bedrolls on the rocky ground.

They ate the last of Yael's bread, and Tau was grateful they had it. Already his taste buds rebelled against the dry smoked mutton. He wondered if he might try to hunt a mountain gazelle.

"Are you worried about those horsemen?" Ulrich asked.

The question was directed at Tau, but Ejnar answered instead. "They were probably just shepherds," he said glibly.

Ulrich was unconvinced. "I saw no sheep," he said. His dogs sat patiently as he fed them smoked meat.

Ejnar shrugged. "Whoever they are, they would be fools to attack us," he said, patting the falchion at his waist.

"That thing is a toy," Ulrich grunted.

Ejnar looked downcast. "I know," he admitted sourly, then he brightened. "I'll just kill the next person who attacks us and take his sword," he concluded.

Ulrich made no response, and the conversation died. Tau munched on a piece of dry mutton. He washed down the meat with wine diluted with clear river water.

"No sense speculating about it," Tau concluded. "If they are friendly, maybe they can help us. If they are hostile, we will keep our weapons visible. Hopefully they will be sensible enough to realize that they would lose more than they would gain if they attack. We will keep nightly watches as usual."

That settled the discussion. They bedded down in the twilight.

Tau took the first watch and began his shift by patrolling the fringe of woods along the shingle. The noise of the monkeys had gone. It was replaced by the buzz and hum of a thousand exotic insects. Tau looked up for the stars but was disappointed by a dense cloud cover that had moved in from the west. He heard a noise and turned to see Yael leaving the tent. She walked to where he stood at the edge of the wood. It was a cold night, and she wrapped herself in her woolen cloak. Her brown hair tumbled about her shoulders.

"Having trouble sleeping?" he asked. She gave a smile in response but said nothing.

They stood at the tree line, and a huge moth fluttered into sight. Its opalescent wings were a hands-breadth wide and flashed in the moonlight.

"I'm glad I came," she said. The moth disappeared into the dark foliage.

Tau remained silent.

"What do you think of Ejnar?" she asked. Tau hesitated, caught off guard by the sudden question. "I think Ulrich hates him," Yael added.

Tau chuckled. "Oh, I don't think Ulrich's feelings are that strong. If Ulrich really hated him, Ejnar would already be dead."

"But what do you think?" she persisted.

"He's a thief," Tau responded. "He's a pirate and a slaver. He was even my slaver once. I pulled an oar on his ship for many seasons. I fantasized about strangling the bastard with my own manacled arms more than once." He paused, thinking about those awful years before he continued. "But more recently, he was also a slave, and he suffered cruelly. I have sympathy for him."

"Do you think he is a good person?" she asked.

"Probably not." Tau sighed. "But I don't really know. I've been surprised before."

There was a long pause, and she pulled the cloak up to cover her unruly hair before she turned back toward the tent.

"He is handsome, though," she breathed to herself as she walked away.

Just then the first snowflakes began to fall.

CHAPTER EIGHT

Two hours later, Tau sat alone. His back was to the tent as he faced out into the night. Snow was falling, and the night had grown quiet. Tau was slumped and fighting heavy eyelids when he heard a noise. He sat bolt upright, and the noise came again. A muffled thump came from the tree line, and Tau stood, touching the hilts of his swords. There was a long moment of silence as he stared into the darkness. With a shuffling of the tent flap, Thor and Loki padded out. They sniffed the air and rubbed against Tau's legs as they, too, peered out into the night.

The squeak of leather and the snort of a horse confirmed Tau's suspicions. A horse and rider were out there. The sound came from just beyond the clearing, within the edge of the wood. It could not have been more than fifty feet away. Tau ducked into the tent to shake awake his companions.

"We have company. There is a horseman in the woods," he whispered, and returned to the night. Ulrich and Ejnar rose and grabbed their weapons. They joined Tau, and together they crouched in the silence of the dark clearing as the snow fell.

The moments stretched into minutes, and the minutes stretched on. Tau did not know how long it was before he began to doubt that he had heard anything at all. Eventually, Ulrich grew tired of waiting. He led the way cautiously to the woods, axe held low, then he pointed at the ground. There were fresh hoof prints, clear in the new snow.

"Just one rider," Ejnar noted. He crouched, inspecting the ground. "And it looks like he went south."

"He's scouting us," Ulrich said, and Ejnar nodded.

"Still, we should stay camped here for tonight," Tau said. "It would make little sense to travel in the dark. We would be as likely as not to run into a trap blundering about in the snow."

"And we do not know that they mean us any harm," Yael piped up. Her voice was muffled behind the cloak that she had wrapped about her face against the cold. Only her bright eyes showed from the folds of woolen cloth. "The Gaetuli of the Atlas have been a peaceful people for generations."

"If it is the Gaetuli who are watching us," Tau responded.

The night was chill, so Tau collected dry driftwood from the riverbank and started a fire to warm his hands. He did not worry about giving away their location, since whoever roamed this high valley already knew of their presence. Meanwhile, Ulrich used his axe to cut down a tree that grew at the wood's edge. He joined Tau and Ejnar at the fire to share its warmth, dragging five feet of newly hewn yew log along with him.

Ulrich embarked on a new project with customary single-minded determination. Using his axe and newly crafted wooden wedges, he quartered the log. He split these quarters lengthwise, preserving the heartwood, to produce four yew staves. With his knife he shaved them carefully, and choosing one, began the process of crafting a bow.

Yael, at Ulrich's instruction, cut a strip of fabric off her linen dress and began pulling apart the fibers. Trusting his friend to keep the watch, Tau curled up in the tent under a blanket and fell asleep.

Tau woke at dawn to the smell of cooking fish. Ejnar had managed to catch five yellow trout from the river, and he was roasting them over the small fire. Tau walked to the river and washed his face, rinsing his sleep-stale mouth with the clean water. It was a beautiful wintry day. A fine layer of glistening white snow frosted the trees. The snow on the ground was melting under the rising sun, and the sky was bright blue and clear. Tau turned at a rustling sound across the river and saw macaque monkeys peering curiously from the undergrowth. He smiled at them and returned to the fire, taking a proffered fish on a stick from Ejnar.

Ulrich, clad in his heavy armor, was demonstrating the new bow and arrow to Yael. In his hands was a short hunting bow, staff cut from the yew heartwood and bowstring braided from the linen fibers of Yael's dress. He had whittled arrows from green wood and fletched them with more strips of cloth, stiffened with wax. He handed the bow to Yael, then walked to the fire. He grabbed a fish and munched on it as he spoke.

"She needed a weapon," he explained. "The wood is green. It lacks power, but I made more staves." He indicated the three smoothed yew rods that rested near the fire. "As the wood dries, the bows will become stronger. The missiles are simple, but good enough to practice with, and we will keep an eye out for flint and feathers, so we can make better arrows."

Yael nocked an arrow and drew. Ulrich had taught her well. She anchored the string below her chin, trembling a bit from the effort but steadying as she focused on her target: a tall cedar twenty paces away. She released, and the arrow flew true, bouncing from the tree's bark. Its crude wooden point had been unable to penetrate, but the accuracy was impressive. She was a natural archer.

"Nice shot," Tau called. Yael turned and beamed. She had hemmed Tau's borrowed robe, making a neat tunic of the rough wool. The light blue linen of her dress showed at the garment's collar. She looked vibrant and pleased with her new skill.

"Ready to move out?" Tau asked Ulrich. He nodded, and Ejnar kicked dirt onto the fire. They packed up the tent and started south, following the trail that wove away from the river and through the evergreen woods. The going was easy across the level forest floor, and the day grew pleasantly warm. The monkeys, chattering in the trees, followed curiously. It was not long before the path began to climb upward, and by midmorning, they were exiting the woods, leaving the noisy macaques behind.

The mountains ahead loomed tall and forbidding. A high wind blew white ice off the ragged peaks, and the path led ever upward, visible as a dark line amid the melting snow. The four companions walked until evening but, to Tau, it felt as though they hardly moved against that broad, still landscape. The mountains sat impassive, ancient, and uncaring of the presence of man.

They stopped to make camp on a rocky outcropping off the trail. The path was leading them into a high pass between two stark slopes where the rough foliage gave way to empty ground and glassy ice. Tau turned back to see that the woods were now a distant smudge against the valley's floor. It was an incredible vista with the green valley lying between two opposing ranges of high mountains. In that humbling landscape, Tau felt like an ant, crawling slowly along the great world's surface.

"I don't see any horsemen," Ulrich noted.

They pitched the tent. The snow started again that night, and the cold wind flapped the loose corners of the leather tarpaulin as they huddled for warmth. In the morning, the snow was thick on the ground, and the path was almost hidden beneath the dense whiteness. The sun shone weakly through a cover of thin, high cloud, and a light feathering of snow continued to fall. They were cold, they had slept poorly, and all that was left to eat was hard, dried meat and grainy travel bread. They donned what extra clothes they could. Ejnar and Yael wrapped blankets over their clothes. Ulrich wore a fur cloak over his armor. Tau clasped his woolen cloak over his chainmail.

They spoke little and focused on keeping moving, trudging through a foot of loose snow. The pass still led upward, running between two high peaks.

Yael's voice was hopeful as she raised it against the rising wind. "It we can just get over this range of mountains, we'll find the green lands of the Gaetuli. They raise their horses and graze their herds on the fertile slopes between the frozen peaks of the Atlas and the dry wastes of the Sahara."

Tau could not find the energy to respond. The snow fell thicker, and the wind picked up. Tau's face and ears were bitterly torn by the wind's malice, and the frozen slush filled his boots and found its way into the collar of his cloak.

Ulrich had been leading, but he stopped. He raised a hand of warning.

"Did you hear that?" he asked. His dogs, who had been following in the path through the snow made by his leather boots, slid forward to flank him, ears perked and forward.

Tau stood still, snow whirling around his ankles, and listened. The only sound that came to his ears was the howling of the wind as it raced through the icy pass. Ulrich did not move. He was as still as a stone golem, unflinching even as a vicious gust threw the hood back from his head. The wind was making Tau's eyes start and tear as he stared into the empty whiteness of a blizzard. Ulrich slowly unlimbered his great axe.

Tau felt a soft form move against his side. Yael was there, eyes wide. She was shivering. Tau put his arm about her shoulders and drew her closer. Her shivering stopped as she looked up at him. Ejnar stood close behind, his hand on his small falchion, and for once, had nothing to say.

Suddenly, there was a low rumble, more felt than heard. It seemed to come from all around.

"Avalanche?" Yael cried, taking a step back.

"It is no avalanche," Ulrich answered.

With a growl, a monster emerged from the blowing snow.

CHAPTER NINE

The monster stalked from the heights. A shaggy black mane stretched back from a snarling visage of long white teeth and predatory orange eyes. Long claws, needle sharp, extended and retracted from four massive paws as the beast crunched its way through the snow.

"A lion," Yael breathed in awe.

"To the rocks," Ulrich said, pointing to the left. The pass ran along a vertical wall, and the companions moved toward it. Tau's heart pounded in his chest. There was something terrible and primal in those implacable, amber eyes as the beast drew closer. A fear gripped him. It was not unlike the terror of half-forgotten nights on a faraway sea, chained to the bench of a foundering ship as it broached, and the sea rushed in. What use was the courage of man against the pitiless force of nature?

The cliff's face was steep and rocky, and Ejnar, half running, reached it first. It was not tall, twenty feet at most, and handholds were plentiful. He climbed it swiftly, pulling himself hand over hand with his customary grace.

"There is a flat plateau up here," he called back when he reached the top. "It's empty. Quickly! Climb on up."

The beast advanced slowly. Ulrich stood before it but was edging away as it approached. His dogs were on either side of him as he stood with drawn axe. Tau went with Yael to the cliff face and its promise of safety. She was trembling again, and he guided her hands onto likely holds.

"Climb," he urged. "I doubt that beast can follow us." He turned back to join Ulrich, but Ulrich waved him away.

"Follow her," he commanded. "Make sure she is safe."

Tau turned and obediently began scaling the wall of rock. His mind felt muddled as it fought against terror. Yael was already halfway up, and in moments, she and Tau joined Ejnar, crouching in knee-deep snow. The plateau vanished into the whiteness behind.

The growl of the beast filled the air. The monster was only five paces from Ulrich, who stood with his back against the cliff face below.

"Come on," Tau called to him.

"No," he said, "I will not abandon Thor and Loki."

Tau swore. Of course, Ulrich would not leave the dogs. Tau should have known that, but the fear had fogged his mind. He considered leaping back down to stand with Ulrich, but the fall would probably break his legs. He crouched and began to scramble back down the rocks. Meanwhile, the fight began.

Thor and Loki, ever protective of their master, sprang into action. Within moments they had the beast encircled. With a low howl they attacked from right and left simultaneously. Loki's strong jaws clamped on a massive forepaw, and Thor, snarling, went for the monster's face. But, formidable as the mastiffs were, they were dwarfed by the massive size of the beast. The monster contemptuously slapped Thor aside. It was a massive blow, and Thor was flung through the air, disappearing into a snowdrift at the base of the cliff. The monster lifted his other paw, and Loki dangled from it, jaws still clamped tight. The beast drew Loki in, opening its mouth to reveal a mouth of dagger-sharp teeth. Ulrich charged.

Ulrich held his axe high as he ran at the monster. He roared his barbarian rage as he swung his axe at the creature's head. The beast saw the weapon coming and hopped backward, letting the axe slice uselessly through empty air. A hard shake of the monster's forepaw flung Loki free, and then Ulrich faced the beast alone. The monster crouched low on its four paws and bared its long teeth. It shook snow from its dark mane and roared. The noise shook the valley itself.

Then the beast struck. Ulrich seemed motionless in the face of that blinding speed. A right and then a left blow was delivered in nearly the same moment, batting Ulrich back and forth. Then one blow, delivered with a paw larger than a grown man's head, spun him around, and another struck him low on the body. Ulrich was thrown backward, landing with a dull thump at the base of the cliff.

Tau was halfway down the cliff, but he found that his body would no longer respond to his commands. Terror filled him at the approach of the implacable beast. He gripped the rocks spastically as he looked on. Loki was drawing himself slowly to his four legs, but he looked cowed and stunned. There was a shifting in the snow where Thor had landed, but the dog did not emerge. Tau watched helplessly as Ulrich lay motionless, crumpled at the cliff's foot. The creature advanced, all feline grace and primal fury. It was Yael who sprang into action.

She had strung her bow during the brief fight, and she had an arrow nocked on the string. She stood tall on the edge of the precipice and showed no fear. She drew the string and released in a quick movement, and the arrow flew true. Tau watched the missile glide toward the terrible animal's neck and felt a sudden surge of hope. But the simple wooden point was blunt. The arrow glanced harmlessly off the beast's thick mane. It ignored the impotent attack and took another step toward the prostrate Ulrich.

Tau released his grip. He scraped against the rocks on the way down. It was a long fall, and he crumpled when he landed. A jolt of pain shot up his legs; he ignored it. He ignored, too, the advancing monster and scrambled to where Ulrich lay.

Tau thanked the ancestors because his friend was still breathing. He felt tears of relief slide down his face, freezing instantly in the frigid air. He rolled Ulrich onto his back. Ulrich groaned, but his eyes did not open. Tau looked up to find that the beast was only a pace away. Its huge whiskered face filled the world. It licked its lips, and Tau held his friend. He no longer felt any fear.

Then the beast stopped. Its ears flicked to the left, and it turned away from Tau and Ulrich. It looked back down the pass, the same way that the companions had come. For a long moment nothing happened. The blizzard raged, and the blinding snow fell. The beast growled as it peered into the whiteness.

Suddenly a ball of fire burst from the veil of snow. It arced through the air, falling toward the lion's flank. Tau saw that the object was a lit torch, and the beast leapt away. The torch extinguished itself harmlessly in the snow. The animal howled in a mixture of anger and fear. Three riders on horseback emerged from the whiteness. They were carrying long spears, and each brandished a lit torch. The lion turned to face them and growled. Its ears were flat, and it bared its teeth. The horsemen waved their torches as they rode forward, and quite suddenly, the lion had had enough. It spun and vanished into the snow.

The horsemen rode slowly toward the companions, but Tau looked down at his friend.

Ulrich's eyes were open.

"Are you all right, friend?" Tau asked softly.

Ulrich nodded. "I think so," he said.

Ulrich put his hand to his torso. Low on his armored cuirass was a small dimple. It was barely a crease in the steel armor, but it showed where the beast had struck him, ripping his fur cloak as it did so. Ulrich grimaced with pain.

"I think I broke a couple of ribs," he noted. "How are Thor and Loki?"

The dogs were all right. Loki walked to where Thor was buried in the snow and helped dig him out of the deep drift. Loki licked his brother's face, and both animals padded over to where Ulrich lay. Loki nuzzled his master's hand, and Thor sniffed his head, burying his snout in Ulrich's dark hair.

"I think they're fine," Tau said, and Ulrich smiled. He grunted in pain as he sat up.

"Hey, Tau," Ejnar called down from the cliff top, "there are horsemen here."

"I know," Tau called back, as three riders approached. They were speaking to each other in a language Tau did not understand.

They had found the Gaetuli.

CHAPTER TEN

It would be more accurate to say that the Gaetuli found them. In addition to the three that faced Tau and Ulrich, three more rode up the trail, and six appeared beyond Yael and Ejnar at the plateau's top. Yael spoke the Berber language, so she interpreted as the horsemen led the companions through the pass.

The Gaetuli explained that they had been tracking the strangers since they entered the mountains. The horsemen were polite, but firm in their insistence to escort the companions through their territory. Tau realized that their horses, which had looked so tall from a distance, were smaller than the great warhorses of the Romans, and were draped in leather blankets against the high-mountain chill. The riders were tan-skinned Berbers with dark beards and were clad in close-fitting, leather tunics. There were small, leather shields strapped to their backs, two or three long spears strapped lengthwise along their mounts, and short swords buckled around their waists.

The horsemen rode ahead, behind, and beside the companions; moving slowly to allow them to keep up. Ulrich's injury slowed his pace, so one of the riders lifted Ulrich onto his own mount and led the beast on foot. Tau was surprised to find they did not use saddles or bridles. The only tack of any kind was a single rope, tied low and loose on each animal's neck. The Gaetuli seemed to communicate with their mounts through gentle nudges with their knees or with softly spoken words. Ulrich, unused to riding bareback, clung tightly to the rope with both hands. He winced with each step that jolted his wounded ribs, but he did not complain. They continued moving up the pass through the blizzard.

"They must have followed us this whole time, but why? Why were they tracking us?" Tau asked Yael.

She passed the question on. She spoke to the leader of these men, a man in his early thirties who rode at the head of the column. His skin was creased and lined by weather and sun, but his dark brown eyes were kind, and they gazed from a strikingly handsome face. He rode comfortably, sitting on his horse with both arms crossed across his chest. It was a long moment before he answered with a few short words.

"He says that things will be explained later," Yael interpreted.

Tau felt a hand on his shoulder and turned to see one of the Gaetuli leaning over him. The rider was a young man with bright eyes and a ready smile. He offered down a piece of dark meat. It was a thick hunk with a gamey taste that Tau soon realized was smoked horse. Tau nodded his thanks and chewed gratefully. He was tired and cold, and the meat was welcome. The rider nudged him again and pushed two more pieces into his hands, indicating the two mastiffs that trailed dutifully behind their mounted master. He smiled when Tau fed the dogs, who wolfed down the food without a pause.

Tau trotted back to the front of the procession to walk alongside Yael. She had been speaking to the leader in Berber, and she wore a surprised look on her face.

"What is it?" Tau asked.

"He says that lion was not the only one stalking us," she said.

"What do you mean?" Tau asked.

"Atlas lions do not typically attack humans. They only do so when the winter hunger gets the better of them. They are the biggest predators in the world, and that was the male of the pride. The males are big and strong, but they do not deal the final blow. Two females were waiting for us atop the plateau. They were stalking us, closing in for the kill."

Tau was surprised. "Really? I saw nothing."

She shook her head. "Nor did I."

Tau let that sink in. While their attention was focused on the enemy in front, invisible death had been closing in from behind. He shivered.

Eventually they crested the height of the pass, and the ground began to slope back down. Tau could see nothing through the all-pervading whiteness of the driving snow, but he trusted the Gaetuli to lead the way. Finally, the snow began to lessen and then cease altogether as they left the blizzard behind. As night fell, Tau could see that they were leaving the heights, and another valley lay before them. A dense cloud cover slid overhead to hide the light of the moon and stars.

A thinner layer of snow crunched under Tau's boots as the Gaetuli led them off the beaten path. A patch of undergrowth hid a flat campsite laid with smooth stone. A cold stream ran nearby from which the horses watered. The leader dismounted, leaving his horse untethered to graze in a stand of grass. He spoke to Yael.

"He says we are welcome to make camp here among his men. We will travel again at dawn," Yael translated.

"Why are they helping us?" Ejnar asked suspiciously.

"He says they help all travelers that are not poachers," Yael responded. "His task is to drive away poachers from Rome, but it is good for trade to help travelers. He says that more will be explained in the morning. He says now is the time for rest not for questions."

Tau unpacked his gear. The Gaetuli riders moved to help Ulrich dismount, but he waved them away and leapt down on his own, landing with a pained grunt. Tau helped him unbuckle his heavy armor while Yael and Ejnar pitched the tent.

Thor and Loki, having eaten and drunk their fill, were oblivious to the night's chill as they splashed in the cold stream and ran in the nearby pasture. One of the younger horses joined the play, rolling its long body on the ground and pawing the air with its hooves. A young horseman guffawed and patted his horse's belly as it played.

Soon enough the tent was set up, and the bedrolls were laid out inside it. The Gaetuli had made their own camp adjoining, throwing up four simple yurts. The yurts were elegant cones of leather supported by long poles. The companions' low tent looked ramshackle in comparison.

Yael inspected Ulrich's chest and found that two ribs were, in fact, broken. Fortunately, they were not displaced, and his lung was not punctured. She bandaged him tightly with the remaining strips of linen from her dress, and the pressure seemed to relieve much of his pain. Tau laid down and allowed the exhaustion to drag him toward sleep.

But Ejnar was full of restless energy. He walked among the Gaetuli horses, now tethered to staves to keep them from wandering off in the night. He inspected hooves and teeth, patted withers and looked intently at the Gaetuli spears and swords. He wore a smile and an interested look, and even without speaking the language, his charisma won him license. The Gaetuli humored him, drawing their short iron swords and showing their long spears for his inspection. Eventually he wandered back to the tent.

"Their iron work is good, and they make a sharp edge, but their blades are too soft. They would break were they to strike against good Roman or Frisian steel," he said. "But the Gaetuli horses are fine beasts. I wonder how many pieces of silver it would take for one of the savages to part with one. I grow tired of walking."

"Whose silver would you use?" Ulrich growled. "It will not be mine."

"Sleep now, boys," Yael admonished. "You can fight more tomorrow."

Then sleep overcame Tau. In his exhaustion he did not dream.

CHAPTER ELEVEN

The next morning the sun rose on a clear, wintry day. They had made it to the southern slopes. In the foreground, the mountains transitioned from snow-covered rock to dry scrub, and finally, to lush, grassy land, still green despite the lateness of the year. Tendrils of the Atlas stretched beyond in steep, rocky ridges, terminating far in the distance, and there, on the world's far edge, was the suggestion of a great flat plain that could only be the Sahara itself.

While the Gaetuli were striking camp, Tau and Yael went to talk with their leader. The man sat atop his horse contemplating the slopes. He turned his piercing gaze to consider the outsiders as they approached.

"We mean to cross the Sahara. Our journey takes us to the Empire of Ghana," Yael said.

The Gaetuli leader, whose name was Gulussa, nodded. "I assumed that one was of Ghana from the color of his skin," he responded. "There are only two tribes who cross the great desert, the Tuareg and the Garamantes. The Tuareg, the blue nomads, are an ancient people with knowledge of the secret paths, but they do not accept outsiders. You will not be permitted to travel with them. If you wish to cross the Sahara, you must do so with the camel caravans of the Garamantes, the modern city-builders of the deep sands and hidden oases."

"How do we find them?" Yael asked.

"They have a port of call two days' ride to the east. They come to trade camel wool, metals, and gems in return for leather and Roman goods brought from the north. The next caravan will come at the turn of the moon."

"Could you lead us to this place?" Yael asked.

He nodded. "Yes. And you and your companions will stay in our village until it is time to go."

"Thank you," Yael said.

Gulussa inclined his head, then rode away without another word. Yael and Tau worked their way back to the tent across the rough ground.

"I suppose are fortunate the Gaetuli are well disposed toward us," Tau said.

"The Gaetuli are reputedly peaceful," Yael responded. "There is an old history of conflict with Rome, but there has been no trouble in centuries. Trade is profitable for all, and Rome has ceased attempting to expand into the mountains. It is live and let live."

Tau said nothing. The Gaetuli seemed hospitable now, but he wondered what would happen to him if he tried to leave the path they had set for the outsiders. They carried a lot of weapons for a peaceful tribe. The Gaetuli were superficially friendly, but Tau suspected that something dangerous lurked beneath the surface.

"Yesterday, Gulussa said something that I could not translate exactly, but I think they believe in Karma," Yael broke the silence.

"Karma?" Tau asked.

She smiled. "It's something I read in a book that came from far in the east. It is the belief that the world is in balance. So, if you are good to people then the world will repay you, perhaps by others being good to you."

"That seems a nice way to see the world," Tau said. And naïve he thought but did not say.

She shrugged. "My parents believed in it. When someone was in need, they would bring them in and feed them and clothe them and send them off again without charging any payment."

"They sound like good people," Tau said.

"They were," she said, but her smile could not hide the sadness in her voice.

They packed up and moved out that morning. The Gaetuli led on paths that crisscrossed the hills. The younger horsemen, enjoying the mild day, cut on and off the narrow lane, jostling each other as they leapt boulders and raced up steep, rocky slopes. Gulussa made no effort to restrain them. They were comfortably in home territory. Thor and Loki ran with the horses until they got tired and loped back to their master, chests heaving and tongues lolling.

They descended the heights to roam east along the low, grassy fields. The Atlas Mountains reared high to the left, while to the right, the green gradually gave way to bare rock and dry plain.

Ulrich limped along bravely, but he leaned on his axe handle as he plodded along, trying not to wince with every step. He had shrugged off a horseman's offer for a ride and Ejnar's offer to help carry his gear.

"I get the feeling you do not like me," Ejnar said, sounding hurt.

"I do not like or dislike you, Ejnar," said Ulrich brusquely. "I do not care about you either way."

In the silence, Ejnar glanced at Tau.

"Are you sure you want to cross the desert?" Tau asked. "You could turn back now."

Ejnar shrugged. "Any journey that ends in a chest of coin is a worthy one."

Tau sighed. "And how do you expect to get rich from this? Just how do you see that happening?"

"I know exactly what is going to happen," Ejnar said, smile returning. "During this journey I am going to save your life many times, so by the time we get to Ghana you will be so grateful you will give me enough gold to buy me a whole fleet of ships. Ghana is lousy with gold. I am certain you will not mind parting with a few hundred pounds of the stuff."

Tau could not resist a chuckle. It was clear that Ejnar actually believed what he said. But Tau found himself shaking his head. He had no idea what they would find when they reached Ghana. Tau's stepmother would probably try to kill them all the moment she found out that Tau had returned.

"You seem very optimistic," Tau said.

"Of course!" Ejnar responded. "The gods smile on me. I have filled Valhalla with brave warriors, and I have entertained Odin with sword, song, and sacrifice. I have never lost, and I never will."

Except, Tau reflected, that Ejnar had lost. Only recently Ejnar had been a slave. The gods must be capricious. He kept his thoughts to himself.

"I am glad that I came, Tau," Yael said, touching his arm. In the warmer air, she had shaken off her wool cloak, revealing her lithe form in a close-fitting tunic.

"I have seen the Atlas lion," she continued, "and the horsemen of the Gaetuli. I wonder what we shall see next." She smiled, and perfect white teeth showed between full lips. Tau swallowed hard and looked away.

"After this adventure, lady," Ejnar interjected, "you can come ride the waves with me. I can show you seas that swarm with whales the size of islands and foreign lands with such great beasts that have yet to be named by man."

Yael's attention went to Ejnar, and Tau watched her cheeks fill with color as she looked at the tall, handsome pirate. Tau's heart fell. He distracted himself with thoughts of Ima, the blonde Saxon girl who had stolen his heart. He wished for the hundredth time that she had come on this journey.

The Gaetuli ate from their saddles as the sun crossed its zenith. As the companions walked, they chewed on their stores of smoked meat and drank from their flasks of water and wine. They reached the village in the early evening, coming visible from a steep ridge that opened into a secluded valley. Until then, the dusty paths were the only evidence of human habitation, but now a full Gaetuli village lay before them.

Hundreds of horses populated the scene. The animals filled the fields, grazing from the short grass and drinking from a small river that coursed across the valley floor. Five boys rode among the herd on ponies, themselves watched over by two grown men on full-sized mounts. Alongside the river was the village itself. It consisted of a group of yurts. These were much like the tents the horsemen carried to travel, although many times larger. A stand of unfamiliar crops, protected from the grazing herd by a wooden fence, grew in a depression alongside the water. The plants were thick and bushy, but Tau was sure he had never seen their like before.

Gulussa led the way into the valley. The riders dismounted and allowed their horses to join the herd, watched by the boys on ponies. The women of the village came to greet their men, and Gulussa took the visitors to meet the chief.

The chief of the tribe was a man named Massyl, and he was Gulussa's father. He looked weathered, although he could not have been older than fifty. Unlike the Romans, these men lived outside and aged quickly. Their skin was tanned and lined from years of sun and wind. Chief Massyl met the visitors before his tent and bowed deeply to them. He asked them to wait while he disappeared back into his tent to speak with his son.

His wife, a younger woman in a fine linen tunic which was dyed a brilliant shade of purple, brought a basket of freshly cooked horse meat, clean water, and a roasted green vegetable that Yael called asparagus. The Gaetuli apparently had no use for chairs or other furniture, so the companions sat on the ground while they waited. Yael went to Ulrich to check his bandage.

"I'm fine," he grunted, but removed his cloak dutifully. The bindings had loosened during the day's travel, and she tightened them. He winced with pain.

Yael had been a talented healer, taught by her mother to tend guests at the inn and often members of the community. She palpated his ribs then put an ear to his chest and listened. When she was done, she delivered her verdict.

"The ribs are shifting a bit. They must be broken both in front and in back. But your lungs are intact. You must continue taking deep breaths despite the pain or else the bones will not set properly," she told him.

Ulrich grunted his thanks.

Meanwhile, Ejnar was preening. Rather than sit in the dirt, he propped himself up on his pack. It was a warm day, so he wore his cloak loose like a cape. He spent the time fastidiously picking nettles from its dark cloth. Tau lay back, glad to be off his feet after another long day's walk and closed his eyes. He was dozing when Massyl reappeared. The chieftain beckoned the visitors into the tent.

Camel hair rugs were spread on the ground, and father and son sat cross-legged. They invited their guests to do the same. The tent, large enough for a dozen men to stand, was bright and airy, with a cleverly designed weather-awning above an open roof that allowed air and light in but would stay dry in rain. The rugs were padded with horsehair mattresses, and a set of copper plates, a rare luxury, rested on a rack nearby.

"My son tells me you are travelers, set on crossing the great desert," the chief said, Yael interpreting.

"Yes, lord," Tau responded. "And we thank you for your hospitality, as well as for your son's timely guidance through the mountains."

He waved a hand. "Do not call me 'lord.' I am merely the head of my family, and we are no great family among the Gaetuli. Now, I am curious about your quest. Tell me, what brings you Romans so far from Rome?"

"We may journey from the provinces of Rome, but we are not all Romans," Tau responded. "This is my friend, Ulrich. He is a Saxon warrior from the far north, and I am Tau, of Ghana. The goal of my journey is to return home to my people. That is why we must cross the desert."

"And your other companions?" Massyl asked.

"I am Ejnar." The pirate spoke for himself. "In the heroic songs of my people I am called the Serpent of the Waves, and I am the greatest shipmaster of the North Sea. My companions look to me for protection on their noble quest."

The chief blinked. Ejnar's bombast was not lost in translation. He nodded politely while Gulussa hid a grin. Massyl then turned to Yael. Yael spoke to him directly. Tau did not know what she said, but she was an honest soul, and he imagined she gave an accurate account of herself. When she finished, Massyl nodded then turned to address Ulrich.

"I also understand you met the king of the mountains, the great Atlas lion," he said.

"It was only due to your son's intervention that we survived," Ulrich answered.

"Yes, he told me the story. You are fortunate. Few meet a hungry pride and survive. I am also glad to hear that the beast was not hurt. They are majestic creatures, and their numbers dwindle year by year. Before long they will be only a memory."

A heavy silence followed his words. There was sadness on his face, and Tau felt as though he could feel the man's sentiment, projected through those pained eyes. Indeed, the world must become an emptier place if such a beast were to disappear. Massyl shook his head, clearing the melancholy, and turned back to Tau.

"If you are headed through the desert, then you must know of the war," he said.

There was a long silence. Tau frowned, all eyes were on him, expectant.

"What war?" he asked.

The chief sat back, considering his response. Finally, he did at length. The melodic timbre of his Berber tongue rose and fell as it filled the quiet space within the tent.

"There has come," he sighed, "like voices on the wind, whispers of a great war between the city builders of the Garamante desert and the proud warriors of the Ghana nation. The dark men beyond the Sahara's southern edge hone their blades and swarm in their spear-wielding hordes, howling their war cries torn from the throat of the deep, lost jungles. The dun men of the deep sands ride forth to meet them in their rumbling chariots of war. Thousands perish, wetting the dry earth with blood."

"I do not understand," Tau interrupted. "In my childhood the Garamantes and the nation of Ghana were friends. From where does this feud arise?"

"Rumor says that a queen arises in Ghana," Massyl responded. "That she speaks to the spirits of the earth, and they tell her to unite the vast continent under the true children of Africa. She conquers the lands of the Garamantes and slaughters all that oppose her." His voice grew low. "It is even said that she has brought forth the people of the jungle, the naked beast men of the far Congo, and they ride into battle astride the great black panthers of the dark morass."

Tau frowned. A war would be terrible. The Ghanan empire of Tau's childhood had depended upon the trans-Saharan trade, and it was only the camel caravans of the Garamantes that made that trade possible. Time and time again, Tau's father, the Emperor Kayode, had underscored the importance of that friendship. What use, after all, were the deep gold mines of Ghana if they could not trade the precious metal for Roman tools and Sassanid silks? War with the Garamantes would isolate Ghana from the north, crippling the Ghanan trade economy. Only total conquest of the Sahara would make war with the Garamantes viable. Kayode would never countenance such a thing. If Tau's stepmother wanted this, Tau wondered at her audacity, or her madness.

Ulrich turned to Tau. "What does this war mean for us?" he asked.

Tau had no answer. In the silence, it was Massyl who spoke.

"Getting home may be more difficult than you expected," he said.

CHAPTER TWELVE

Tau, Ulrich, Yael, and Ejnar settled in with Massyl's tribe to wait for the camel caravan to arrive. Tau stood atop a ridge and gazed into the desert. The featureless emptiness stretched into a blue horizon. A midday moon hung low in the west. He imagined the caravan, which must be traveling even now, dusty camels plodding, massive hooves throwing up dust with every tortuous step on that hot, dry earth.

Gulussa and his men left at dawn the next day. They rode north, resuming the task of patrolling the Atlas passes. The village was a hub of regional activity. Riders came and went from all points of the compass, passing news and restocking supplies. Tau realized that from his tent Massyl maintained a wide net of scouts, roaming hundreds of miles of mountainous land. Tau wondered why a small tribe like the Gaetuli required this much protection.

Before noon, Massyl sent for Tau and Yael. They met the Gaetuli chieftain at the edge of camp. He sat on a dun horse, spears on its flank, short sword strapped about his waist. Mounted, Massyl looked lithe and strong, competent horsemanship belying his advanced years.

"I want to show you something," Massyl explained to Yael. "What I will show you is for you two alone. Ulrich attacked the Atlas lion like a fool, while that man Ejnar froze in terror. Only you and Tau stood before the beast without fear. You are worthy."

Yael and Tau glanced at each other but said nothing. Tau felt vaguely ashamed. He had been terrified before the lion. Yael opened her mouth to say something, but then shook her head and stayed silent.

A pair of Gaetuli boys brought horses from the village.

"Come," Massyl said. "Mount and follow."

Tau clambered onto the proffered horse, which was not easy as the animal had no saddle or tack. Once on its back, he clung to the animal's neck to steady himself. He glanced over to find that Yael was being helped up by one of the boys. Once seated, she spoke to the horse gently and tried to look confident. She patted her mount's neck and grinned at Tau.

With a nudge of Massyl's knee his horse started off. Tau and Yael's beasts followed obediently. Tau quickly learned that the easiest way to ride bareback was to sit straight upright and hold on with his legs as the horse trotted along. The two Gaetuli boys mounted ponies and followed close behind.

Massyl ascended the eastern slope of the valley, the path leading through a series of switchbacks as they climbed the steep slope. At the crest, Massyl stopped and looked back into the valley.

"What do you see?" he asked his guests.

"I see tents," Tau said uncertainly, "and a valley."

"I see a people that live on their horses," Yael offered.

Massyl nodded. "You both see rightly. Tents and Horses. We had cities once, but now we take no such risks. If danger comes, we pack our tents and flee."

Massyl sighed. A gust of wind rustled the undergrowth and his horse raised its head, scenting the breeze. But Massyl's attention was elsewhere, his eyes distant.

"Our Numidian ancestors were great warriors, heirs to a vast empire and bearers of the standards of Carthage. But defeat has left my people cowed. For years we were safe on our sheltered slopes. Now rumor of war stirs the land. King Hiarbas warns that the time approaches when we will have to fight once again."

"King Hiarbas?" Tau asked. "The Gaetuli have a king?" Yael translated his words.

"Of course, we have a king. We are not savages," the chieftain answered.

Massyl led on. They rode across the ridgetop then turned north and climbed toward the mountains. They entered a region of broad basins and verdant fields. A line of green hills sheltered this place from the dry winds of the Sahara, and the valleys were dotted with low forests and narrow rivers that flowed down from the heights above. They crossed another valley, rode through a wood in which macaques howled and chattered, and stopped at the edge of a high plateau. They overlooked a broad green basin. The blue ribbon of a stream fed a glimmering pool of clear water.

Another Gaetuli rider was already there. He sat on the ground, a pair of horses tethered nearby, and was smoking three fish over a small fire. He seemed unsurprised to see Massyl and merely nodded as he approached. Massyl stood his horse close and they spoke in quiet voices.

"What are they saying?" Tau asked Yael.

"'They are still there,'" Yael interpreted. "'The big one is guiding them further south,'" she said.

"Who are 'they'?" Tau asked. "I don't understand. What are they talking about?"

Yael shrugged.

Tau spotted movement on the opposite crest. Another Gaetuli rider rode his horse on that far ridgeline. The distant rider waved at the group, and Massyl waved back.

Massyl turned back to Tau and Yael. "This is the reason that my tribe is here. We are the protectors."

"Protectors of what?" Yael asked.

Massyl pointed down into the valley. Near the river something moved. Something huge and gray.

"Of the last family of elephants," he said.

There were thirty-four of the great beasts, and they grazed at the river's edge. They were good swimmers, and they waded in two or three at a time, driving through the river's current with their trunks held high above the churning water before returning, dripping and snorting, to the shore. They were all ages. The eldest was a massive bull with tusks twice the length of a fully-grown man, while half a dozen calves ran along with the herd, their smaller legs pumping to keep up with their tall, stately mothers. There was much affection among the animals, greeting each other with touched trunks and spraying water as they played at the river's edge.

"They are beautiful," Yael said.

"Yes," Massyl said, and there was profound sadness in his voice. "And when I was a child the hills were filled with them. My mother would give them asparagus, and they would bring her juniper by the cartload. They are gentle creatures. But every year more hunters would come from the Roman lands. We would find elephants dead in the valleys, piled by the dozen, with their ivory tusks cut from their skulls and their corpses left to rot."

He shook his head violently. "Our king decided that they must be protected. Throughout the Gaetuli lands, hunting was forbidden, but not all the families could be trusted, and the Romans brought gold and wine and promises, and some of Gaetuli would kill the beasts themselves, bringing the ivory to the Romans in their coastal cities."

A great, black ibis soared overhead, its white bill gleaming in the evening sun. Massyl paused to watch it pass. It banked and settled into the treetops at the river's edge.

"A good omen," he murmured to himself.

He spoke again. "The sacred Gaetuli duty to protect the elephants was passed to my father. He proved his loyalty when a band of Roman mercenaries tried to drive us from these hills in pursuit of their precious ivory. In his time there were two families of elephants left." He waved his hand at the valley. "Now there is only one."

"What happened to the other family?" Yael asked.

"Our friendship betrayed them," Massyl said sadly. "We lived among the elephants and when the poachers came, the elephants ran toward them instead of away. They were too fond of people, and they had no fear. Unsuspecting, they went to their deaths." There was a deep pain in his eyes.

"Now we stay away. None are allowed to approach the elephants. If the beasts get too close to our homes, we jab them with spears and throw stones and drive them away. They have learned to fear us. To fear people. Now, if the Roman poachers slip past, the elephants will run and maybe they will survive."

Massyl looked at the sky. "Come. Evening falls, and it is time we returned home."

They turned their horses and rode away.

CHAPTER THIRTEEN

Massyl said that the Garamante caravan would arrive in a week, to sail the waves of the great dunes to make landfall upon the grassy Atlas shore. The companions spent the intervening time, each in their own way, recovering from the trek across the heights. For Ulrich, this included repairing the dent the great Atlas lion had put in his armor.

The cuirass Ulrich wore he had forged himself, using the skills and knowledge passed down by Wiglaf, the blacksmith who raised him. The armor was called Lorica Segmentata, and it was the same design as the heavy armor of the Roman Legions. He disassembled its overlapping segments and placed the dented piece on a smoothed mound of hard clay. The steel was darkly patterned from the case-hardening process. The dent that marred its surface was about the size and depth of a man's cupped palm. Tau watched curiously.

"This is cold forging," Ulrich explained. "Working cold steel is risky. It brings a danger of weakening the metal, so it must be done very carefully. Ideally, I would heat the piece until it glowed bright red before reshaping it, but without a forge I have no choice." He produced a tiny hammer and began gently tapping the dent.

"How long will it take?" Tau asked.

"Perhaps two days," Ulrich said, fully engrossed in his careful tapping. "The metal has not just been bent—it has been stretched. To retain its hardness, it must be compressed without being upset. Next chance I get I will re-anneal the entire segment."

Tau left him to his work.

Yael spent the days practicing with her short bow and writing in her journal. She had brought a sheaf of dry parchment, a box of thin reeds, and two pots of black ink.

"I will make a book about our adventure. There is a voracious appetite for stories in the Empire. There have been no stories of the Gaetuli since Jugurtha, centuries ago, and when we cross the desert, I will be the first since Tacitus to write about the tribes of deep Africa," she told Tau excitedly.

Ejnar spent his spare time swindling the Gaetuli. Tau found him on the second day trying to trade a handful of worthless quartz for a pot of purple dye. The old woman patiently shook her head at his persistent bargaining, but somehow the next morning found him striding about the campsite wearing a calf-length woolen robe, dyed a brilliant and gaudy purple.

Meanwhile, Tau worried. After they crossed the desert, what then? What might they find when they got to Ghana? What would the war mean for their journey? He went to consult with Ulrich the morning after a sleepless night.

Ulrich was nonplussed. "What use is worrying if worrying does not get you any closer to the solution? Fate governs the broad strokes. Preparation to act takes care of the rest."

"A war between Ghana and the Garamantes could close the trade routes and make our journey impossible," Tau mused.

Ulrich smiled. The tapping of his hammer was a steady cadence. "Conflict brings opportunity," he said. "Perhaps the war will be to our advantage."

Tau was not so sure. An eagle wheeled in the evening sky and he thought about omens. His father had begun to teach him to read them, but he had been taken away before he could finish learning. He remembered that there was meaning to be found in the flight of birds and the patterns of falling stars in the night sky. But as hard as Tau tried, he could not recall his father's words. The eagle dived, plummeting out of sight behind the eastern ridge.

Ulrich paused in his work to look up. "We just have to go and find out what fate has in store for us," he said.

Finally, on a cloudless night when a haze of dust billowed across the empty plain, the camel caravan arrived. It was massive. It slid from the darkness like an uncoiling snake, endless, tremendous, moving soundless toward the green shore. The meeting spot was marked with a pattern of burning torches and paved with flat stones for unloading the tons and tons of cargo that flowed northward. Tau attempted to count the camels. The throng shifted and moved, and he lost count again and again. But by mentally dividing the caravan into sections, dividing those sections again, and counting fast he made a guess.

"A thousand," Tau breathed. "There are at least a thousand camels in that caravan."

Massyl was unperturbed. "Of course," he said to Yael. "It takes at least a thousand camels to cross the desert. Only the Tuareg nomads can cross with less. Everybody knows that. Come. Follow me. We will arrange your passage."

Massyl led the companions into the thronging crowd that was possessed with a busy and efficient energy. Groups of women filled casks with water from a nearby stream and boys laid out forage for the camels. The beasts looked dusty and tired, and their humps sagged. They ate and drank with vigor as the caravan's men busily unloaded their wares.

Each Garamante family seemed to specialize in a different commodity. Tau saw loads of raw salt, gemstones from the deep African jungle, and items of fine metalwork. There were exotic animals: brightly colored birds in cages, monkeys of a dozen varieties, and small yellow cats that came from somewhere far to the east.

Hundreds of Gaetuli streamed from the mountains to meet the caravan. They were representatives of dozens of villages that carried the trade south from Rome and west from Persia. They brought barrels of wine and casks of olive oil. They bore Roman pottery, bolts of silk from the far east, and baskets of tea and spices that would go to enrich the mysterious desert cities of the Garamantes.

Massyl weaved through the burgeoning market, angling toward a particular family of merchants. The family consisted of two men, two women, and four boys, all busily unloading wares, tending to their camels, and pitching tents. They, like all the Garamantes of the caravan, were dressed in pale woolen robes and wore woolen hoods. Their faces, uncovered, were hard and pale in the moonlight.

Massyl spoke to the eldest man while Yael interpreted for the benefit of Tau, Ulrich, and Ejnar. After a formal greeting, Massyl introduced his charges.

"These are travelers," Massyl said. "They have come from Rome and wish to buy passage across the desert."

The man placed his bundle on the ground and inspected the

outsiders gravely. "Where are they going?" he asked Massyl.

"To Ghana."

The man's eyes narrowed. He held Tau's gaze. Tau looked into a weathered face of high cheekbones, a wide nose, and shocking blue eyes.

"Are you allied with the black demons that are burning our cities?" He asked.

It took Tau a moment to realize that he could understand the man's words. The man was speaking Soninke, the language of Ghana and the tongue of Tau's childhood.

"I know nothing of any conflict between our people," Tau answered. "I have been away for many years. When I left, the Garamantes were long friends of Ghana."

He gave Tau a long, measured look, then turned back to Massyl.

"Can they be trusted?" he asked.

"I believe so," said Massyl.

"And we will pay in good Roman coin," Tau offered.

The man shrugged, looked between Massyl and Tau, and then bowed.

"My name is Idir," he said.

And the next phase of the journey began.

CHAPTER FOURTEEN

The caravan did not linger long before returning to the desert. The camels were tended and, as evening fell the next day, they made preparations to depart. The family that would be guide and protector to Tau and his companions consisted of Idir and his brother Hadir, accompanied by their wives and by Idir's four sons.

"Your life depends on your camel," Idir lectured. "It must eat before you eat. It must be groomed before you bathe. You make sure it sleeps soundly before you doze off, and you tend to it first thing when you wake. If your camel falls ill, you will die in the desert."

Tau, Ulrich, Yael, and Ejnar were each lent a beast and were given instruction in mounting the tall creatures, commanding them to sit before climbing into the broad saddle cleverly arranged about each camel's high hump.

"If you get separated from the caravan, you will die," Idir continued. "If you become caught in a sandstorm, you will die. If you do not follow my instructions immediately, you will die. Do you understand?" Idir spoke mildly but insisted on payment in advance. A small fortune of coin, mostly consisting of the golden solidus of Constantine, emptied from Tau's coin purse. It was very nearly all the money left to him and Ulrich from their time with the Legion.

"It seems ominous that the first word I learn of an African language is 'die.'" Ejnar quipped.

Ejnar grinned but looked nervous, perched precariously on the camel's high back. Ulrich, grunting with bandaged ribs, straddled his beast stoically. Thor perched behind him, tongue lolling from his open mouth, eyes bright in the moonlight, while Loki climbed into Tau's saddle, his big body slung across his legs. The dog nuzzled

Tau's hand with his wet nose, panting happily as Tau scratched his head. Meanwhile, Yael shone with excitement, and Tau smiled back at her. He tried not to look down, for the ground fell away to an alarming distance when the tall animal stood.

The caravan was organized with the precision of a military convoy. Even before the sun set, half a dozen scouting parties vanished over the southern horizon, questing ahead to make sure that the next watering place would be viable. The caravan would have to refill its stock of water many times during the trip, and Idir explained that the oases were often untrustworthy. The main body of the caravan moved out in three columns with the workload divided up by family. Idir's group carried extra tents, while another carried water, and others hay and other foodstuffs. Each had a specific task when making camp, and each was dependent on the others for survival. It rivalled the high level of efficiency Tau had experienced marching with the Roman Legions.

They rode into a plain of rock and dust. The night was moonless and cooling rapidly. Heat rose in waves as the arid land gave up the warmth of the day.

"Where are the rolling sand dunes I've always read about?" Yael asked. The land was flat and dry without a grain of sand in sight.

Idir's wife laughed. She was a handsome woman who looked at least forty, a good ten years older than her husband. Her name was Tauda. She slowed her camel to ride alongside Yael.

"All the foreigners want to see the dunes," she said. "In truth the dunes are only in small regions of the great desert. The vast majority is this, the Ténéré, what we call 'the loneliness.'"

They left the mountains behind, and 'the loneliness' stretched on all sides. Tau's mind quailed before the desolation. Even hidden in the teeming throng of the convoy, the emptiness seemed to surround him. It was beautiful and overwhelming and as terrifying as being cast adrift in the ocean.

"But you will see the dunes as well," Tauda continued. "They shift in the deep ergs, the sand seas, beyond the far horizon. Crossing them will be the most dangerous part of our journey."

"How long is the trip?" Tau asked, realizing that he had neglected to ask before now.

"It is two thousand Roman miles from edge to edge of the great desert," Tauda explained. "The caravan will travel twenty miles each night, so you can expect to be on the camel for one hundred nights. Plus, we will stop for water at several of the oases along the way and take final supplies at the city of Abalessa. The total trip will take four months, more or less."

It was a shocking number. Tau glanced at Ulrich who made no response.

"What does it matter?" Ejnar commented. He was sitting cross legged, quickly becoming comfortable on his steadily rocking mount. "On the North Sea deep winter consumes four months of every year. That is time spent indoors, bored witless, bundled around a fire and living off the autumn's harvest. At least here we might have some change of scenery."

But for days the scenery did not change. Each morning they made camp, sheltering in tents from the unrelenting heat of the desert sun. Each night they packed, saddled the tall camels, and rode into the darkness. They moved steadily south across the endless plain as the stars wheeled above and the Atlas faded behind.

"How do they know where they are going?" Yael wondered. It was the third night of the voyage, and Tau was shifting uncomfortably in his saddle, trying to find the right balance between the soreness of his left buttock and the growing pins and needles of his right thigh.

"I have no idea," Tau said.

"They use the sand and the stars and the rocks," said one of Idir's sons. The nine-year-old boy had hopped down from the camels to scramble between rocks as he kept pace with the convoy. He danced between the tall camels' pacing legs to scramble up into Yael's saddle.

Yael smiled at the child. "You have lots of energy tonight, Idlis," she said.

He grinned back and leaned over to pat the camel's head; it blinked appreciatively.

"So," Yael pressed, "the caravan navigates using sand and rocks?"

"Yes!" the boy exclaimed. "And, if you are really good, you can navigate using rocks alone. I know my papa can." Idlis stood up, balancing on the camel's saddle and waved back at his father. Idir rode at the rear of our group. He was too far away to hear the conversation, but he benevolently waved back at his son.

"Don't tease them, Idlis," Tauda said. "And sit down. You'll fall and crack your head." She turned to Yael. "If you are curious, the navigators ride at the head of the caravan. Perhaps they would explain if you asked."

"Let's go then!" Idlis exclaimed, he twisted in the saddle to sit in Yael's lap. "I'll take you to the front of the convoy. Hang on."

The boy slapped the camel's flank, clicking his tongue as he did so, and the camel obediently broke into a run. Tau watched Yael cling to the saddle as the beast raced ahead, breaking from the orderly lines to intersect with the faraway van. Thor and Loki, catching the fun, howled to one another and raced off after them.

Tauda laughed. "Don't worry. My son is an excellent rider. Yael is safe in his hands."

In a few hours, Yael and Idlis returned. Yael was flush with exhilaration and tailed by the two tired but contented dogs. Thor rejoined Ulrich, and Tau reached down and helped Loki back to his usual place in the saddle. The dog was breathing heavily, and he licked Tau's palm once he was settled. Tau retrieved his water flask and let Loki lap clean water from his cupped hands while Yael recounted what she had learned.

The Garamantes did indeed use sand and rocks, as well as stars to navigate the vast desert. Tau had seen stellar navigation before. On their crossing of the Mediterranean, the friendly Roman sailors had pointed out the constellations that kept them oriented. The Garamantes added another layer of precision. By measuring the height of the North star from the horizon, they could calculate their latitude.

In addition to celestial navigation, the Garamante navigators had access to a compendium of knowledge that was passed from generation to generation. Landmarks, invisible to untrained eyes, filled the horizon for the knowing observer. Even the sand changed in color and composition in distinct, well-understood ways if one knew the desert.

Yael stayed awake nearly the whole of the next day, busily writing in her journal to capture the knowledge. Exhausted, Tau slept.

In that week, the journey began to take on a surreal, timeless quality. The Garamante caravaneers were a reserved, quiet people, and an easy silence pervaded as the camels' hooves plodded ever deeper into that great, flat nothingness.

Finally, as another night of travel gave way to an early dawn, a group of scouts was seen riding back toward the caravan. Word made its way down the lines that the oasis of Waraglan was near. The brightening sky revealed a low line of mountains barring the path ahead. A few hours later, the caravan crested a low rise, and the oasis came into sight.

In the midst of the vast wasteland, a forest of verdant green hid. It lay in a bowl bordered on all sides by steep, rocky cliffs. The caravan descended the slope into the secret haven, finding a wide shallow lake of salty tasting, but potable, water amid a grove of date palm trees. The caravan stayed for only one day, but in that time, sacks were filled with sweet dates, and water casks were topped off to the brim.

"Prepare yourselves," Tauda said. "Tomorrow we begin the crossing of the Grand Erg. Yael, you will finally see your sand dunes."

CHAPTER FIFTEEN

The next twilight found the camels riding through a narrow defile. Dark rock towered high on both sides. Eventually the path found a flat plateau, and the Grand Erg, that ocean of sand, rose to blot out the horizon. The dunes towered in massive waves. They looked in the moonlight like a turbulent sea, frozen at the height of a great storm. A steady wind carried blinding sand off the shifting crests, and Tau wrapped his woolen cloak protectively about his face.

The crescent moon slipped behind the crest as the caravan flowed into the shadow of a massive dune. The wind stilled in the giant dune's lee, and Tau could remove the cloth from his eyes. They passed in near silence through an alien landscape. The camels' hooves were hushed by the softly flowing grains. The only sound was the hiss of sand as it tumbled down the slopes and was blown in thin tendrils, like smoke, from the faraway heights.

They plodded steadily on all that night and the next and the next until the nights began to run together. Tau could not say how many days it was into the journey when he was awakened by a tiny lizard, not four inches long, that swam into his tent as if the sand were water. It poked its head above the grains, gazed about impassively, then dived back into the fluid medium, never to be seen again. Perhaps it was that same night, or perhaps it was a week later, that a herd of rodents, hopping and scampering on their hind legs, dashed through the convoy in the twilight, dodging lithely between the camels' heavy footfalls, pursued by a yellow fox with large ears, which hardly took notice of the caravan as it chased its prey into the falling darkness.

It was also during this dreamlike, flowing, endless time that Ejnar and Yael flowed into each other. Ejnar had swindled, or perhaps charmed, his way into ownership of one of the tall yurts the Garamantes used, and that is where he and Yael made love. The bloom of naïve, young ardor was bright on her face, which to Tau was as charming as it was heartbreaking.

Another day stood out in memory. Soon after pitching camp on a cool morning, a darkness was seen growing in the east. A wall of blackness approached, stretching from horizon to horizon, swiftly blotting out the rising sun. The Garamantes rushed to make all fast. Tents were attached one to another with ropes, and all was weighted down with the heavy cargo unloaded from the camels. The camels themselves were led into the tents and made to lie down while the tent flaps were tightened. Despite his weariness from the night's travel, Tau could not contain his curiosity. He waited outside until the last possible moment, watching the storm approach. The great billowing mass of dust and sand filled the world, stretching far into the heavens, dwarfing even the titanic dunes and barreling down with inconceivable speed.

He ducked into the tent just before the storm struck. With a roar of sound, it slammed into the huddled caravan with tremendous force. It howled and whirled, sand battered the leather tarpaulins, and the convoy shivered as the temperature fell. In a few hours, it was done, and Tau emerged into an orange haze of hanging dust. Two of the smaller tents, nearer the leeward side of a massive dune, had been partially buried and were obliged to be dug out, but no men or beasts had been lost. The caravan had weathered the blow, and the journey continued.

Three weeks after entering the erg, the caravan reached the far shore, the end of the sea of dunes. The blowing sand gave way to a steep upward slope and a flat plateau. This place was called the Tademait, and it was a perfectly level and windswept expanse of rock. It was an austere and forbidding landscape in the daytime, but by night the burning sun gave way to an unparalleled brilliance of stars. The horizon fell away, and the gleaming points of celestial light reached all the way down to the earth's rim. The constellations wheeled in their stoic, perfect, spheres.

The moon passed through a full phase as they moved across the Tademait Plateau. Tau developed saddle sores, which burned, ached, and then, slowly, healed. Ulrich's ribs knitted, the companions learned to speak rudimentary Berber, and the dogs grew thoroughly bored. Yael and Ejnar kept each other entertained in clandestine meetings at camp during the day and rode close in whispering confidence at night. Throughout it all, the convoy moved in its timeless, endless, implacable way, and Tau learned to doze sitting in the saddle, lulled to sleep by the steady sway of the camel's stride.

Finally, the peaks of the steep Ahaggar Mountains heaved into sight. They began as dark shadows, perceived only by the low-hanging stars they blocked. By day they were knifepoint monuments of black craggy rock, stabbing into the sky from the arid landscape. The convoy's stores were growing low, but Idir and Tauda were unconcerned. A palpable excitement was growing among the Garamantes. Talk, which had died to a minimum during the past weeks, was rising to an expectant hum. Abalessa, the desert city, was just over the horizon.

The next night, the caravan crested a ridge and entered a paradise. Vast fields swayed with winter wheat, still green and rich from their seeds' long sleep. Groomed orchards of fig trees bordered an elegant paved road, and vineyards graced the higher slopes. It was a haven in the middle of the desert. In the midst of the cultivated fields rose a great city of marble-sheathed stone. Orderly streets cut between two- and three-story, stone houses, complete with high terraces and fired-clay roofs. The only feature that belied the place's non-Roman origin was the absence of a defensive city wall, which would have been sacrilege to any Roman citizen, war minded as that race tended to be.

The caravan's arrival had been anticipated, and a great crowd awaited, thronging a broad, paved square that abutted the outer ring of homes. A cheer greeted the tired travelers, but tradition guided the caravan through its timeless ritual of tending the camels before all else, though the beasts now drank fresh, clear water that flowed openly through clean stone troughs. The caravaneers unloaded their cargo and pitched their forest of tents. Only once these duties were done did they greet friends, take drink, and embrace family.

A festival began as the sun rose that morning. The men and women of the caravan were replete with coin from their trade with the Gaetuli, and they showered their wealth on the city. Merchants flooded the plaza. Fresh meat and vegetables were ambrosia to the hungry caravan, as was wine, ale, and fresh baked bread.

The companions were forgotten amid the amiable chaos. Tau stood with Ulrich, Yael, Ejnar, Thor, and Loki, feeling stunned in the clamor after so many weeks of silent, meditative travel. Ejnar was the first to regain his wits. He bought roast lamb, fresh bread, and a deep red wine from a passing merchant. Used to smoked meat, dried vegetables, and stale water, the rich food was overwhelmingly wonderful. Tau forced himself to eat slowly, savoring every morsel as it passed his lips.

"What now?" Yael asked eagerly. "Shall we explore the town?"

Tau hesitated. "Let's ask Idir how much time we have."

Tau found the caravaneer perched on a dismounted saddle watching the tired camels. The beasts were lying comfortably on the sandy ground, having eaten and drunk their fill.

"Idir," Tau called over the din. "How long until the caravan moves out again?"

"Five days," he called back, holding up a hand with out-splayed fingers to emphasize the point. "We stay in Abalessa for five days then continue south to trade with Djenné-Djenno and Gao."

Tau turned back to Yael. "I think we have plenty of time to explore the town," he said. She smiled with such evident joy that Tau could not help grinning back.

Taking their few belongings, the companions entered the city of Abalessa. Decorative marble arches crowned the entrances to the town, through which wide roads ran. They walked along the central causeway, handsomely paved with broad, smooth stones between tall, elegant houses of brick and stone. The city was clearly very old. Many ages of construction coexisted, sometimes in single structures. Ancient bricks made up the lower layer, which was topped with handsome walls of granite or plaster and capped, in places, with gleaming polished marble. It gave the buildings a charming, albeit mottled, appearance.

Abalessa bustled with activity. The Garamante city folk were small of stature, even by Roman standards, with the men being no taller than the women. They were otherwise apparently of the same tan-skinned, dark-haired, but often strikingly blue or green-eyed Berber stock as the Gaetuli. It was a prosperous city, with most inhabitants wearing fine, brilliantly dyed woolen or cotton robes. Small camel-drawn chariots worked their way through the foot traffic along the broad streets.

Social stratification was evident. Tau saw that many of the richer residents had black slaves who followed with heads bowed as they carried goods for their owners. A group of robed men and women, all wearing a distinctive shade of blue, dodged into a gutter to allow their betters to pass, party to some subtle clue of caste that Tau could not quite discern. Curiously, the adult men in this lower caste had their faces shrouded in cloth. Only their eyes were visible.

"That head covering is called the tagelmust," Yael said. "It is worn by the men of the Tuareg. The Tuareg are Berbers, like the Garamantes, but they build no cities. They are the desert nomads. It is said that once a blue man of the desert reaches adulthood, no stranger will see their face again. The tagelmust is why the Tuareg are called 'the people of the veil.'"

The blue-robed Tuareg huddled together wherever they went, but their presence grew less frequent as the companions approached the center of the town.

The sun was halfway to its zenith, rising in a clear blue sky, but the day was pleasantly temperate, with a continual cool breeze wafting through the town from the east. The sun shone off polished marble and glistened off the flowing water that filled the desert city. Water was present everywhere. Cisterns marked street corners from which men and women filled pots and flasks. Camels drank from freshly filled troughs scattered about the public areas. Tau even noticed a separate sewage gutter. It was covered with an iron screen and discreetly carried wastewater through a back alley. Abalessa's water flowed through a system of stone pipes that ran, ever so gently, downhill from east to west.

They made it to the center of the town where they beheld a plaza. In the middle of the open square was a round pool. The pool was shallow, but about ten feet across and gleaming with fresh clear water. It, too was filled by a gentle trickle from a small stone pipe, rising, so it seemed, directly through the stone slabs of the plaza itself.

"Where is all this water coming from?" Yael wondered aloud.

"I could not begin to fathom," Tau said. There was no river, there was no lake nearby. He raised his head to scan the horizon. In no direction could he see an aqueduct like the Romans would have used. Beyond the green fields was dry desert plateau. Somehow these people had brought clear, cold water right out of the middle of the desert.

"They've dug wells probably," Ejnar offered.

"Wells wouldn't explain the water pressure in the pipes," Yael pointed out.

At this point Ulrich gave a huge yawn. Catching it, Tau could not help but yawn too. The weariness had caught up with him. They had been riding all night and had pushed wakefulness far into the morning.

"Well, wherever the water is coming from, I would wager the source will still be here tomorrow. We can investigate later. I am exhausted. What do you say we find an inn and get some rest?" Tau said.

Yael smiled. "I would love to sleep in a bed after all those weeks sleeping in a tent."

"I would be happy sleeping in a barn," Ulrich interjected, eyelids drooping from weariness. Thor leaned sleepily against one of Ulrich's legs, and Loki gave a yawn, stumbled, then shook himself, blinking.

The first and the second places they checked, both elegant, well-furnished inns near the city center, were completely full. It seemed that there was limited vacancy in Abalessa with the caravan in town. Just when Tau was about to suggest they give up and go back to their tents, Yael caught sight of another inn. It was a smaller, townhouse affair, tucked into a back alley some way off the main part of town. Its sign was a painted banner showing a thin green plant covered with purple flowers and bore the Berber word for "inn." It seemed welcoming enough.

Tau pushed open the heavy wooden door to find a cozy, well-cushioned entryway. They were greeted by an elderly Garamante couple. Even after more than two months among the Berbers, Tau's grasp of that language was still rough, so he let Yael run the proceedings. She spoke to the innkeepers and then passed coin from her pouch.

"Come on. They have only one room left, but I'm sure we can all squeeze in. They said they will find some extra bedding," she said.

Tired beyond all reckoning, Tau let himself be led up two flights of stairs to a spacious room with two beds. Two spare mattresses were found and laid out on the tiled floor. The dogs swarmed in ahead and tried to claim one of the mattresses only to be pushed gently aside by Ulrich, who flopped down gratefully in their place.

The dogs piled on after him and began to doze. Tau sat on the other mattress and pulled his leather boots off. He was glad he had not bothered to don his chainmail, because he doubted he would have had the energy to tug it over his head at this point.

"Did anybody notice any guards in this town?" Ejnar asked, settling himself into one of the beds.

"No, I didn't see any," Yael said. "No guards, no town watch, no militia of any kind."

"And no walls," Ulrich muttered, half asleep already.

"Well, they wouldn't need any," Tau answered. "They are a thousand miles from any enemy. The desert is their defense."

Ejnar gave the slightest narrowing of his eyes. "A clever man," he said, "would travel ten thousand miles if there was gold to be had."

Tau opened his mouth to respond but then remembered he was tired. He closed his mouth and went to sleep.

And that night, Ejnar was proven right.

CHAPTER SIXTEEN

Tau woke to the sound of screams. He sat up; the stricken noise fresh in his mind. He was at first uncertain of what he had heard, but seeing that his companions had been woken too, he knew it had not been a dream. Confused noises filtered through the plaster and stone walls of the inn.

Tau stood and pulled his chainmail shirt from his pack then donned it over his worn leather tunic. The links were slick from the protective beeswax. He strapped his familiar swords around his waist while Ulrich began fastening on his heavy steel cuirass. Yael went to the window and threw open the shutter.

With the shutter open the noises of the night were clearer. There was yelling and shouts. Tau joined Yael at the window. The street was empty. Nothing could be seen below except darkened houses and shops. The soft glow of a hanging lantern cast a pool of yellow light at the corner. The clamor seemed to be coming from the south side of town. Men and women howled with pain and outrage into the night. Every now and then the sound was mixed with a triumphant bellowing, the scream of a horse, and the splintering crash of breaking wood.

It was coming closer.

"Is there a fire?" Yael asked.

The window was facing south, and being on the third floor, had a view of the dark horizon over some of the lower-lying buildings in town.

Tau shook his head. "I don't see any smoke, any glow of flames," he responded.

Lamps were being lit in the houses across the street. A family of blue-robed figures, clutching sacks and bags, huddled together as they rushed up the street, fleeing from the growing noise.

Ejnar scoffed. "This is no fire. Don't you know the sound of a raid when you hear it?"

The pirate stood at the door, curved falchion in hand. He had somehow found the time to install heels into his boots to make himself look even taller, and he wore a purple woolen cape over a white-painted leather tunic. Ulrich hefted his axe, his profile brutal and forbidding in his blackened steel armor. Yael strung her bow and strapped her arrow bag across her back. Tau touched his twin swords for luck.

"Finally. Some action. I was getting bored," Ejnar said.

"What do we do now?" Yael asked.

Thundering hoof-beats rang on the stone road. Tau leaned out the window to see another family, this one in fine white and yellow linen, hurry down the street. There were six of them: one man, one woman, three young children, and a black slave. Hampered by baggage, they stumbled down the road. Tau saw panic in their flight; they were being pursued. Three dark figures on horseback gained on them. Tau recognized the pursuers, for they were men of his own nation.

The warriors of Ghana were a proud caste of a proud people. The strongest boys of the best families were brought before their lords. They were tested in single combat before they could be called warriors. Warrior men were proud to have warrior boys, and they, in turn, prided themselves on mastery of the leaf-bladed spear and leather shield. The greatest warriors could make the air sing with the shimmering speed of their whirling, stabbing blades. The bravest showed their courage by going into battle bare-chested and without fear.

These men were warriors of the highest calling. They were naked above the waist, black skin bared to the cool night air, and they wore golden circlets around their necks to boast of their wealth and status. On pure-bred Arabian horses, they bore down on the fugitives, hooting to one-another in Soninke as they charged.

The black slave dropped the fleeing family's baggage and turned. He raised his hands in the air, greeting the advancing black warriors with open palms. He even gave a small hop into the air, although whether this was from joy or fear Tau could not tell.

Tau did not know what the slave expected would happen, but he likely did not expect to be clubbed to death. The lead rider, disdaining the use of his blade, twirled his spear as he rode past, smashing its wooden haft into the side of the slave's head. A spray of blood flew into the air, and the slave fell. The second horse, unable to avoid the body, landed a running hoof on the fallen man's chest. There was a crunch of splintering bone as the slave's ribcage caved into a mess of shattered bone and gore. The horses, missing not a beat, continued at a gallop.

In another instant they caught the fleeing Garamante family. Their bloody work began. Spear blades stabbed into unprotected backs, necks, and faces. The woman tried to cover her child with her body, but a quick swipe of a spear knocked her contemptuously aside, and the child was speared too. The warriors, hollering in triumph, continued down the street, disappearing into the darkness. Six corpses decorated the bloody flagstones.

"Those were Ghanan warriors," Tau whispered into the sudden silence.

"It seems the rumors were true," Yael replied. "And the war has reached us already."

"Let's get out of here. We need to get moving," Ejnar said impatiently.

"And go where?" Ulrich asked. "There is no fortress in this town. There are no walls or ramparts. There is nowhere to hide. But this inn is made of stone." He thumped the hard tile with his axe haft to emphasize his point. It gave a sharp, metallic ring. "If we are under attack, this inn is a good place to make a stand."

Ulrich walked out the door. Thor and Loki were close behind, and Ejnar followed after. Tau went to follow but paused for a thought.

"Yael," he said, "Why don't you stay up here and cover us from the window? With that bow, you would do more good from a decent vantage spot."

There was a flicker of fear across her face, but with a slight tightening of her lips, she nodded.

"I don't want to kill anybody," she said firmly. "But I will do what is necessary to protect my friends."

Tau extended his hand. Yael grasped his forearm in the handshake of Rome.

"Thank you," he said simply, then turned and left the room.

The inn's ground floor was in chaos. Two families of Tuareg

hastily gathered their belongings while a third was already halfway out the front door. Tau shouted for them to stop, but it was too late, they disappeared into the night.

Ulrich pushed past the nearer families and ran out the door after them.

"Come back!" Ulrich yelled. In his excitement he realized he was speaking in German. "Stop!" he called in Berber.

The fleeing family did not hear Ulrich's warning, but their headlong flight slowed when they saw the carnage of the corpses that littered the eastern end of the street. Ulrich sprinted to get in front of the panicking family. He held his axe sideways, blocking their path.

"You fools are going to get yourself killed. Go back in the house. Now," he ordered. They gazed at him dumbly but did not move.

"Circum," he commanded his dogs in Latin. Thor and Loki heeded, circling around the terrified family with heads held low and teeth bared. Like sheepdogs, they herded the terrified family back to the inn.

The family went inside, and Ulrich followed close behind. Two dozen men, women, and children now filled the rooms of the lower floor. There would be no room to fight with all these people here. They needed to be moved if there was to be any chance of defending this place.

"All of you. Upstairs now. Clear the entryway," Ulrich commanded. They stared at him with wide eyes.

"Illa via," Ulrich told the dogs, pointing at the stairs. Dutifully, the two big mastiffs advanced. Their paws were spread wide, and they fixed the nearest Berbers with their intense brown gaze. The Berbers backed away, instinctively shuffling backward up the stairs, protesting all the while but unable to match the implacable force that drove them out of the room.

The sound of hoof-beats filled the front street.

CHAPTER SEVENTEEN

Ulrich turned, hefting his axe. He did not bother to close the front door; he merely filled the doorway with his massive armored form. Four riders appeared at the end of the street, while two other warriors dismounted to ransack a nearby house. Fresh screams betrayed their grisly work. When they noticed Ulrich, the Ghanan riders stopped and considered their new foe. The sky was just beginning to lighten in the east, and a fresh gust of cool wind rustled through the town.

"Look at this one," said the lead rider in Soninke, leveling his spear.

"Is he a Roman?" asked a second.

"He must be. Look at his armor," replied the first.

"No Roman carries an axe," argued a third, "and he's much too big to be a Roman."

"It matters not," said the first. "That cuirass will hang on my villa wall."

The lead warrior attacked.

Ulrich had not understood the exchange, but he was ready for a fight. As the horse galloped forward, Ulrich stepped into the street to meet the charge. The warrior thrust his spear, aiming for a sudden killing blow, but Ulrich moved with ferocious speed. His up-swinging axe knocked aside the reaching spear then continued to hack off the attacker's arm at the elbow. The warrior tumbled from his horse, howling in pain and clutching at the bloody stump.

The remaining warriors were stunned speechless for a moment, then without a word, they dismounted. On foot they advanced together. The men who had been sacking nearby houses came to join them. The fallen warrior was screaming in pain, and the second man spoke.

"Hush, Mbaneh," he commanded. "Remember who you are. Staunch the bleeding. We will tend to you after we have slain this one."

Five warriors advanced on Ulrich with leveled spears, then with a whispered command, two disappeared into the narrow alley between the inn and the next building. They were flanking their enemy. Tau noticed that the inn had a back door. It was closed. He moved to it and waited.

Three warriors stood before Ulrich and threatened him with their spear-points. Their spears were a real threat, as Ulrich did not have enough reach with his axe to kill one before another could slice into him. He stepped forward and swung his axe, but the warriors danced out of range before returning to threaten him again. There was an open window that flanked the door that Ulrich blocked. Leaving his companions to deal with Ulrich, one of the three warriors moved toward the opening.

That warrior did not see Ejnar waiting for him just inside. Ejnar stood with his back to the wall, sword held high. As soon as the man began to climb through the window, Ejnar grabbed the man's spear with one hand. With the other, Ejnar's falchion sliced down into the man's neck. The wound fountained blood as the warrior fell back into the street.

When the warriors' attention flicked to their falling companion, Ulrich attacked. He lunged forward to slam an armored shoulder into the man on his left, knocking him to the ground. He swung his axe at the other. The warrior was too quick, and he leapt back out of Ulrich's range. Ulrich stepped forward to press the attack, but the downed warrior was not yet out of the fight. He thrust his spear between Ulrich's legs, tripping him, and Ulrich fell to hands and knees.

Ulrich's attackers leapt to their feet and raised their spears, but Yael saved Ulrich's life. She shot an arrow from the window above. The missile drove deep into the rightmost warrior's chest, and the man fell before his spear could find Ulrich's face. Ulrich rolled into the other warrior's legs and wrestled him to the ground. He planted his knee in the man's stomach, driving the wind from his lungs.

At that moment the inn's back door shuddered from a heavy

blow. Tau stepped back just as a spear blade pierced the wooden planks. Another blow, and the door burst inwards, revealing the last two warriors brandishing spears.

Ejnar threw the spear he had taken. It whistled an inch from Tau's face and caught the nearest warrior in the thigh. The man fell to one knee with a curse. The second warrior rushed into the doorway, driving Tau back with three lightning-quick stabs. Tau dodged the first, parried the second, and the third he slipped past. Tau was within the spearman's range and under his guard; the warrior was defenseless against Tau's twin swords. His eyes widened in surprise as those flashing blades came up. Tau killed him quickly. The first slash cut into his stomach and sliced open his viscera; the second slid between ribs to pierce the warrior's heart.

By this time, the other warrior had pulled Ejnar's thrown spear from his leg and was limping away down the street. He was retreating, so Tau did not follow him. Tau pushed closed the shattered back door and blocked it with a nearby couch.

Ulrich pulled his opponent into the house. The warrior was not wounded, but he gasped from the blow Ulrich had delivered to his diaphragm.

"Go get the other one," Ulrich grunted to Ejnar, indicating the wounded man that lay, clutching his amputated arm, in the street.

"Don't order me around like a peasant," Ejnar responded, offended.

"Go get the other one, please," Ulrich amended. His face was dangerous. Ejnar sniffed but complied.

Ejnar and Ulrich sat their prisoners in the corner of the room. Ulrich's man tried to stand, and Ulrich slapped him gently.

"Stay," he commanded. The prisoner glared at him but remained sitting.

The wounded man was pale. He clutched the stump of his arm at the elbow, but blood oozed between his fingers. Tau snatched a bolt of cloth from the discarded belongings on the floor and held pressure on the wound, but it was no good. The artery was shredded, and blood darkened the cloth.

Yael descended the stairs. Seeing the blood flow fail to staunch, she took action. She crossed the room and picked up a wooden chair that leaned against the far wall. She smashed it against the carpeted stone floor. It took her a few hard swings to splinter the wood, but soon she had broken away the seat and separated one of the chair's legs. She went to the wounded man and used the chair leg to tighten the cloth into a tourniquet about the man's upper arm. The blood flow stopped.

Tau thanked her and she nodded back gravely.

"Now," Tau said. He spoke in Soninke, addressing the defeated warriors. "Who are you, and who do you serve? What do you want with this town?"

"You speak their language?" Ejnar interjected.

"Of course," Tau replied. "Soninke is the language of Ghana. It is the language of my home."

"I am Masireh," answered the uninjured warrior, "and this is Mbaneh, my brother." His voice was proud and defiant.

"You are of Ghana?" Tau asked.

"We are of the golden capital of Koumbi Saleh," the man responded. "And we serve our god-king Kabu, son of the mortal Kayode and the immortal Kansoleh, herself scion of the goddess Asase Yaa."

"Asase Yaa?" Tau asked. He had not heard these names in years, but the memories came. Kabu was his half-brother, ten years his junior. Kansoleh was his stepmother, his father's second wife, and Kayode was his father's name, himself the Emperor of Ghana. The warrior's words spoke of Tau's past, from before he was betrayed and sold into slavery.

"Asase Yaa?" Tau repeated. "The earth goddess?"

"Yes," said Masireh. "The Earth Mother has sent Kansoleh and Kabu to lead us to glory."

"And Kayode, the Emperor. What of him?" Tau asked. His father's name felt strange on his lips.

"They say that Kansoleh consumed him. That she partook of his flesh on the new moon and from it saw visions of our glory," the warrior said.

Tau frowned. He had never heard of any such ritual. Cannibalism was not a part of the rites of Asase Yaa. Tau wondered if that was something that Kansoleh would have made up.

"Kayode is dead?" he asked.

Masireh shrugged. "It is said that Kansoleh killed him last year. The throne is her son's."

"So, you serve Kabu, the new prince," Tau concluded.

Mbaneh, the now-armless warrior, was beginning to rouse. He kicked his brother, who was about to respond.

"Don't tell the enemy everything you know, brother," Mbaneh said. His voice was tight with pain, but he held his chin high. "You," he said, addressing Tau, "tell us who you are first."

I am the eldest son of Emperor Kayode, Tau thought to himself. I am the rightful heir to the throne, and if Kayode is truly dead I am your Emperor. He thought of saying these things, but instead Tau shook his head.

"It does not matter who I am," he said aloud. "I am just a traveler. What does Ghana want with this city? With these people?"

"If you will not tell us who you are. Then you will hear no more from us," Mbaneh said proudly.

Tau glowered, but the warrior and his brother glared back. Ulrich had not understood the conversation but had sensed the impasse. He stood over Masireh and casually raised his axe.

"If they don't talk, then we don't need them," Ulrich noted reasonably.

Mbaneh spat. "It doesn't matter what you know," he said, showing teeth. "You will all be crushed soon anyway. Ghana has no need for the Garamantes. They are too weak to make good slaves. We will take their marble cities and own the rich trade of the desert ourselves."

"Is that why you are attacking Abalessa?" Tau asked.

Mbaneh shook his head. "This raid is nothing, merely a declaration of our intent. But soon the Garamante army will awaken. They will come to the edge of the desert, away from the deep Sahara, they will come to where they cannot escape. We will crush them on the grasses of the Sahel."

"A clever strategy," Tau admitted. He switched to German and explained to Ulrich what he had learned.

"What do we do with them?" Ulrich asked. He went to the door, watching the street. Blood dripped off his axe's long blade.

"Nothing," Tau replied. "They are no threat to us. We can let them go."

"That way they can live until the next time we meet," Ejnar said glibly. He wiped his falchion on a dead man's trousers then returned the cleaned weapon to its belt loop. He bent and picked up one of the discarded Ghanan spears. He frowned and drew the falchion again, comparing the two weapons, trying to decide which one to keep.

"Leave. You are free to go," Tau told the captives. Masireh helped his wounded brother to his feet, and the two of them hobbled to the door. Ulrich stepped aside to let them pass.

"And tell your kin to avoid this place," Tau called to the warriors as they left. "We protect this inn now. It is not worth the price in lives it would cost to take it." Masireh did not respond, but Mbaneh turned. He met Tau's eyes with a troubled look, then turned away. They disappeared up the street.

"Now what?" Ejnar asked.

"We need an exit strategy," Ulrich grunted.

Tau knew that Ulrich was right. They would not be able to defend this inn forever. He considered the situation. They were deep in the middle of a hostile desert, surrounded by a fierce enemy and with no way out.

"Wait," Yael spoke up. "Listen, the noise is dying down."

Tau listened. The screams, the cries of pain, and the bellowing of rage was abating. The sound of a city in terror was fading away. There were no more hoof beats.

"I need to see what is going on," Tau said and headed for the stairs.

"Ejnar and I will watch the doors," Ulrich said. Ejnar scowled at being ordered about, but he did not argue. He began pacing the lobby, his purple cloak swinging wide at each turn.

Tau mounted to the second floor, and Yael followed. On this level, three Garamante families huddled together. They were chattering nervously. Thor and Loki were patiently guarding them. The dogs lay on the floor between them and the stairway, blocking their exit. A couple of the Tuareg children had crawled over to pet the beasts, and Loki panted contentedly as a child of perhaps three years old clumsily rubbed chubby hands across the dog's face.

The people turned expectantly when Tau and Yael appeared, but explanations would have to wait. Tau ascended to the third floor and found their room. He went to the window and leaned out. The alley in front of the inn was littered with corpses, Tau could see little else. The equally tall houses across the alleyway blocked his view. The overhanging gutter was a few feet over his head, and he realized that he could reach the roof if he climbed a little higher. He unbuckled his sword belt and dropped it onto the floor. He braced himself against the window frame and reached for the edge of the tile roof. His fingers found purchase on its rough surface. As he pulled, his feet left the window, and he dangled for a moment, his feet hanging over a three-story drop to hard paving stones. He pulled himself up, rolled to his feet, and stood.

Before he could get his bearings, he heard a scrabbling sound behind him and turned to find Yael climbing onto the roof as well. She held her unstrung bow in her teeth, her arrow bag still on her back. After she found her feet, she spat the bow into her hands, restrung it, and stood tall. She looked strong and confident, ready for trouble. The wind gently tossed her unbound brown hair. Tau felt a thrill but forced himself to turn away—to focus on the matter at hand.

Together they looked out over the town. To the east the tall slopes of the Ahaggar Mountains reared. There seemed to be little activity in that direction, so Tau shifted his gaze. To the north lay the Tademait Plateau, its flat surface stretching to the far horizon. Tau could see no movement that way either, so he looked south, back toward the center of town.

The dead and dying were everywhere. Streets were splashed with blood, and small figures lay in clusters, fallen where they ran or cut down where they had been cornered, dragged from houses, and robbed. Yet, the streets were strangely empty of enemy warriors. The noise of the violence was fading away, and as Tau panned his gaze up to the southern horizon, he noticed a retreating dust cloud wavering in the evening light. Even as he watched, the cloud grew smaller and smaller until, finally, it was gone.

"It is over," Tau said.

Yael said nothing. She stood unblinking, with a faraway look in her eyes as she gazed over the town.

"How are you doing?" Tau asked softly.

Her light brown eyes found his. They were wide and clear and sad. "I killed a man," she said.

Tau leaned forward to see into the street below. The warrior Yael had shot lay on his back. His body was still. A white-fletched arrow stuck straight from his chest. His eyes were staring, and his mouth was open in pain and surprise. Yael saw Tau's gaze, but she did not look down. She met Tau's eyes when his gaze returned. She seemed to be searching for something on his face, then she looked away.

Tau felt as though he had to say something. "If you had not shot that arrow, Ulrich would be dead," he pointed out.

She looked at her bow then sat carefully on the sloping roof.

"How do you feel when you kill somebody?" she asked.

Tau joined her, squatting on the roof's hard tiles. He thought about that question for a long time. Down below came the sounds of the town's survivors rousing. There were creaks as doors opened and cautious footfalls as people moved about on the street. Somewhere a woman began crying, pitiful wails rising to meet the waning light.

"It depends," Tau said finally. "Each one is different. Sometimes it is awful, and I get nightmares and see the faces of the men I have killed. Sometimes fighting is just what must be done. And sometimes…" He shrugged. "Sometimes killing is good. Sometimes killing is to bring justice to a lost friend or to take vengeance on a hated enemy. Sometimes it feels good to win and to be glad that you are alive."

Yael did not respond, and after a breath, Tau gave her a sidelong glance. She was gazing toward the next block, at where a common city pigeon was fluttering among the eves. It landed on a roof tile and gave them a long, judgmental look from black eyes buried in fluffy gray feathers. It took a couple of short, awkward strides then winged away, flapping into the alley and out of sight.

"How about you?" Tau asked. "How do you feel?"

"I feel empty," she responded. Tau sat silent, and after another long heartbeat, she went on. "But I feel like I should feel something. Who was that man? Did he have children? Did he love his mother? Did he see it coming?"

Tau had no answers for her.

They lapsed into silence. Tau's mind wandered back to the first time he had fought and killed a man. With that memory was the image of a slave ship, burning as it turned on the current, borne slowly out to sea. He remembered other times he had faced death. He remembered the terror of a cavalry charge, his shield locked into a shield wall as the horses bore down. He had drawn courage from his companions' stubborn defiance as the panic threatened to overwhelm his mind. His thoughts drifted further. He remembered a blue-eyed German girl who stood defiant against an enemy horde in the freezing snow. He remembered when she drew him into her room on a warm spring night in a half-forgotten town on the far side of the world. Whenever Tau allowed his mind to wander, it always seemed to drift back to her.

Tau allowed himself to daydream, to become lost in his own memories. He went deep enough that he almost forgot that Masireh told him that his father was dead.

Yael stood and climbed back into the window. Tau followed.

CHAPTER EIGHTEEN

The Ghanan raiders had indeed abandoned the town, but they had done terrible damage. Hundreds of Garamantes, mostly women and children, were dead in the streets. Storefronts and warehouses had been hastily looted, and the camels of the caravan had been either killed or chased away into the desert.

Tau explored the town and found the same scene repeated over and over. The stunned survivors were mourning or attempting to take stock of their losses. There was no organized response; the raid had shattered whatever civil infrastructure had existed before the attack. Individual families fended for themselves, salvaged wares, and buried their own dead. Still, many bodies were left untended, slowly rotting in the streets where they lay.

Wherever Tau went, townspeople, seeing only his black skin, shot him looks of hate or hurled curses. Was it not for the formidable presence of his armed friends, Tau wondered if he would have been mobbed by the blind rage in that city. So many were driven near to madness in those first painful days. As it was, Tau was merely threatened in the language of the desert people, with new words that Yael did not bother to translate. He covered his face with a dark hood to protect his identity.

Later they found the bodies of Tauda, Idir, and three of their four children. Picking their way through the carnage of the shattered caravan, Tau found the bodies clustered in the shadow of dead camels. Tauda, hardly recognizable for wounds and bruises, clung to her husband even in death.

Tau wept for them. The companions buried them deep in the rocky plateau, and Ulrich covered their graves with heavy rocks to prevent animals from uncovering their bodies. Young Idlis was found later that day. He was alive and unhurt. Somehow, he had escaped the carnage, but he was mute with horror. He followed the companions to sit, stunned and blank, on the place where his family was laid to rest.

The boy was reluctant to leave the grave. Even after the last stone was placed, he sat mute and impassive, insensible to all attempts to console him. Tau sat beside him for a long while. Eventually he came back to the inn, still not talking but at least taking food and water. The innkeeper, in gratitude to Tau and his companions, agreed to care for the boy.

After this, there was no clear course of action. The loss of the caravan meant that Tau and his companions were marooned in Abalessa. The city rich with grain and water, but tactically they were at a loss. The following day, Yael reported hearing rumors of a Roman fort in the desert nearby. It seemed an unlikely story, as the nearest Roman colony was on the far side of the Atlas Mountains, but they had little to occupy them, so they went to investigate.

Surprisingly, the rumors were true. On a small rise just a quarter mile to the north of the city was an abandoned castrum, a Legion fortress. Its Roman origins were undeniable. The brick walls were crumbling in places, but they averaged about fifteen feet tall, and on one corner could even be seen an engraved Imperial Eagle. The fortress was the spitting image of the fortress of Sens, Agedincum, where Tau and Ulrich had wintered with Julian's legion the year before, itself a copy of so many Roman marching fortresses they had inhabited during their time with the Petulantes.

The fortress was abandoned and crumbling, but Ulrich considered it thoughtfully, examining the defenses with a critical eye.

"This place could be restored and defended," Ulrich noted.

"The Romans even made it this far," Tau said. It was incredible. They were more than a thousand miles from the Mediterranean. He wondered how they had crossed the desert. He wondered where else the legacy of Rome might hide.

After some time, they went back to the town. They did what they could to help those in need, sharing food with those who had lost everything and lending a hand in setting things right.

On the fourth day, word came that a Garamante army was on its way. The news was brought by a messenger, riding from the capital city of Garama in the east. The messenger said that King Ameqran was bringing the might of the Garamante nation to respond to Ghanan aggression. This was exciting news. The army of Garama had not been organized in generations. They would smite the hated Ghanans once and for all.

At the same time, whispers flowed among the blue-cloaked, shrouded Tuareg. The nomads said that a new queen had arisen. Her name was Tin Hinan, and she would arrive with the new moon to lead the people of the veil to a new future. For the first time in memory, all the nomadic, elusive Tuareg would be united under a single banner.

Both rumors proved true. Two weeks after the Ghanan attack, a cloud of dust heralded the arrival of a Garamante army. Two thousand soldiers-strong, the army rolled on hundreds of two-camel chariots. Their equipment was new and clean. They bore steel-tipped spears and round shields and were resplendent in finely dyed leather armor. Tau was impressed. He had never seen chariots in such numbers before, but Ulrich was skeptical.

"These Garamante soldiers are untrained and untested," Ulrich said. "The blades of their spears are fresh-forged and unused. Their armor is unmarred. Their bodies lack the scars of battle, and their hands lack the callouses of practice with arms."

Tau stood with Ulrich, Yael, and Ejnar in an alleyway that crossed the main street of the town. They watched the Garamante army parade by. The wooden wheels of the chariots made such a cacophony of sound that they had to shout to make themselves heard. The clamor was enhanced by the cheers of the crowd. All of Abalessa had gathered to greet their saviors.

Tau craned his neck to glimpse the man whom the innkeeper pointed out as King Ameqran. Behind the vanguard came a massive chariot, this one pulled by six silk-draped camels. Tau could just see a gray-haired man, a golden crown on his head, standing on an oversized chariot, waving imperiously to the crowd.

Tau noticed that Ejnar was carrying a long chariot spear like the Garamante soldiers were wielding.

"Where did you get that?" he asked.

"I bought it," Ejnar answered glibly.

"With what money?" Tau asked, wondering if he had stolen the weapon.

"I looted some corpses after the raid." Ejnar smiled. "There is always money to be made in war."

"I hope you only looted enemy corpses," Ulrich growled.

"Where are all the Tuareg?" Yael interrupted.

Tau looked around but, oddly, he could see none of the blue-cloaked people in the mixed crowd.

Ejnar nudged Tau with an elbow. He pointed into the alley behind them, and there, making their way unnoticed through the back alleys and drainage ditches, was a steady stream of the blue-clad Berbers. They appeared to be making their way north.

"Follow them?" Ulrich suggested, and Tau nodded. They moved down the alley. A military parade was nothing new, but the nomads seemed to be up to something interesting.

The companions joined the blue flow, but none of the Tuareg protested. They smiled and nodded to the strangers. One offered Ejnar a flask of clean water, which he drew from politely. They were all speaking softly in their native tongue, and the atmosphere was one of eager anticipation.

"What is happening?" Yael asked a young woman who was carrying a baby.

"Tin Hinan is coming!" was the happy reply.

Yael tried to get more information, but the news was vague. Tin Hinan, also called she of the tents, mother of the tribe, and Queen of the Ahaggar had arrived at a meeting place outside of town. She had come to bring the Tuareg together, to lead them to safety. How she was to do this, none knew, but all seemed confident that their salvation was here.

It turned out that the Tuareg were gathering at the abandoned Roman fortress. There were hundreds of them: Men, women, and children, and they milled about, buzzing with excitement. Soon, a hush fell over the crowd, and all heads turned west. Tau clambered to the top of the crumbling ramparts to get a better view.

A small procession was coming over the plain of the Tademait. Fifty camels with fifty riders approached. The camels moved sedately, decorously embroidered saddles swaying with each step. They reached the fort and entered, picking their way through the rubble of a collapsed section of wall. All but the lead rider dismounted, and the leader's lone camel, with its blue-clad rider, rode alone to the center of the open place. The crowd parted for her.

The rider was a dark-haired woman of perhaps thirty years of age with strikingly blue eyes. She sat comfortably atop her tall camel with her legs crossed beneath her. She wore a cloak of blue cloth, and her long hair was unbound. This was Tin Hinan, the blue queen of the Tuareg, and her people waited for her to speak.

"I know what has befallen Abalessa," she announced. "I know too that many other homes have suffered a similar fate. This senseless war with Ghana threatens to destroy our people." She turned as she spoke, her camel shuffling obediently so she could address the entire throng. As her head turned, her eyes met with Tau's, and he was certain she took note of him. She was able to give the sense that she was speaking very personally to each of those gathered there.

"As senseless as this war is," she continued, "it cannot be avoided. The Ghanans have a new queen, and she is beyond reason. There will be no parley, and there will be no mercy." She spoke with such a weight of conviction that Tau found he did not doubt her words.

"So, this war must be fought," Tin Hinan said. "And we must stand with our Berber kin, the Garamantes. They have refused assistance before, but times are dire, and circumstances call for us to offer our help again." There was a murmur among the throng, but it was soon stilled by a look from her piercing blue eyes.

"All must be ready to fight," she continued. "Every able-bodied Tuareg must be willing to die to defend our people."

"I know," she said, holding up a pacifying hand. "I know that we are not warriors, but we have no choice. We can either protect all we love, or we will die, lost and forgotten in the endless sand." Her gaze swept the crowd, and Tau saw how she held sway over these people. They would fight for her. Tau would fight for her if she asked. The weight of her conviction was irresistible. Tau noticed that Ulrich was grinning.

Tin Hinan smiled, "I need a volunteer," she said. "I need someone to tell the Garamantes that we will fight alongside them. That the Tuareg stand with fellow Berbers against the invaders."

A Tuareg man stepped forward. He looked to be about eighteen years old and had an old Roman-style sword strapped about his waist. He bowed before the queen.

"What is your name?" she asked.

"I am Basi," the young man said, straightening, "and my family was murdered by the Ghanans. I am ready to fight for you, my queen." Unlike most of the Tuareg men, Basi wore no tagelmust, so his face was open to the desert. The right to wear the tagelmust was passed down by one's father as a man entered adulthood. Basi's father had died before the gift could be granted. It was a terrible shame, and the crowd was silent.

Tin Hinan reached down and touched the young man's bare head. She spoke. "Brave Basi, you will carry my message to King Ameqran of the Garamantes. You will tell him that the Tuareg are here to help, and we can offer hundreds of strong men and women to join the fight to defend the homeland." She unclasped a necklace from around her neck. It held a great blue sapphire inset in silver. She placed it around the young man's neck. "This gem will identify you as my messenger and buy you passage to speak to the king. I know you will carry our message well." The warrior stepped back and inspected the bright stone. The crowd murmured its approval.

Tin Hinan raised her gaze and Tau realized that she was staring straight at him. After a moment she beckoned with an open hand. Tau felt compelled to respond. He stepped forward.

"What are you doing?" Ejnar hissed, but Tau had no answer. He was drawn to the Tuareg queen. He walked forward, and the crowd parted for him. He arrived before Tin Hinan, and she looked down at him from the saddle of her high camel. Tau realized that her powerful gaze was cosmetically enhanced with a delicate brushing of dark makeup around her eyes. He noticed too that her legs were tucked awkwardly beneath her and appeared too small for her body. They were half-covered with a blue blanket, but he wondered if the queen might be crippled.

"Who are you?" she asked. She spoke in a powerful voice, carrying to the entire crowd.

"I am Tau," he responded in Berber. The queen said nothing. She waited, and the power of her gaze compelled him to go on. She was curious as to what brought a stranger in her midst.

"I am a traveler, and I come with my friends from the north," Tau said.

She took in the swords and the chainmail. She looked up and considered his heavily armed companions. Her eyes said she suspected that there was more to the story.

Tin Hinan switched to Soninke. "What do you want, Tau? Why are you here?" she asked. She asked the question softly. This time her words were for Tau alone.

"I want an end to this war," Tau answered honestly.

"And whose side are you on?" she asked.

"Queen Kansoleh of Ghana is my enemy," Tau said. "She sold me into slavery when I was a child."

Tin Hinan gave a long, measured look. Finally, she made up her mind.

"Tau will accompany our champion," she announced. "Outsiders carry special power in these matters."

The crowd murmured, but none dissented, and Tin Hinan nodded. "It is decided. Now, go to King Ameqran and return with his answer. In the meantime, we will muster our strength." She turned away and rode among her people. Tau knew that he was being tested.

Basi looked at Tau. His jaw was set. He looked every bit the young warrior, determined to fight his foes, to avenge his people. He clasped and re-clasped his sword hilt, and Tau wondered if he had ever used the old weapon. With a nod, he and Tau pushed their way through the buzzing crowd.

CHAPTER NINETEEN

Abalessa was reviving. Damage that had gone unrepaired for weeks was being swiftly put to rights. Markets were reopening, and merchants were once again doing business. The army had brought with it a supporting force of craftsmen to maintain the chariots and equipment, and they were an invaluable workforce for restoration. Money came into the town as quartermasters refilled the army's stores using a mix of currency. Often seen was the golden Roman solidus, Constantinian bronzes, and even some antique silver denarii. Soldiers bought meals and wine, and city stable masters and innkeepers found themselves fully employed once again.

Tau and Basi made their way toward the central square where the martial noise of grindstone and military drum emanated. They found that the Garamantes had established a command post. Shading tents covered tables spread with inventories and charts and lists of names. Messengers rushed hither and tither. Blacksmiths sharpened weapons and platoons of soldiers were dispatched for exercise or patrol. King Ameqran was easy to find. The Garamante leader was strutting about the encampment, conspicuous in an ancient, polished-bronze, muscle cuirass. Short-cropped gray hair topped a lined, proud face. A royal guard trailed dutifully behind him.

Basi led the way between the ordered tents, clutching Tin Hinan's great blue sapphire like a talisman. He moved swiftly, but soldiers moved to block his path fifty paces from the Garamante king.

"No outsiders may approach King Ameqran unbidden," said a soldier of the royal guard. He was resplendent in white-painted leather armor. A yellow camel-hair plume fell from the back of his close-fitting leather helmet. He held his two-handed spear sideways and was immediately joined by other guardsmen, barring the way.

With a scowl Basi produced the sapphire. The gem was massive and gleamed in the sunlight, and the guards paused, mesmerized by the glowing blue stone. The lead guard dropped his spear. Embarrassment was written on his face as he stooped to retrieve it.

"Tin Hinan, Queen of the Tuareg sends us as emissaries," Basi growled. "We must speak to the king."

The guards looked at one another, then the leader shrugged and led the way. Basi and Tau were presented to the king, who turned to receive the strangers imperiously. He glanced at his visitors but did not address them right away. He made them wait as he paced to a quartermaster's table to give directions for hosting officers in the nearby houses.

Finally, the king turned back to his guests. He scowled at Tau's black skin, but after seeing the sapphire, exchanged words freely with Basi. He was familiar with Tin Hinan and the Tuareg. He knew that sapphire designated an official emissary of the queen.

Tau's command of Berber was sufficient for most patient conversation, but Basi and the king spoke quickly, and Tau had some difficulty following the flow of the words. It became clear that Basi was being rebuffed. Basi's voice became more strident as he pleaded with the king. Ameqran waved a dismissive hand. The guards closed in, and the king turned to walk away.

"He doesn't want our help," Basi growled. "He says they don't need the aid of desert nomads to fight a war." His knuckles were white as they clutched the gemstone.

"Wait," Tau protested. Ameqran, with a sigh, turned back.

"You are going to need all the help you can get," Tau insisted. "The Tuareg are offering warriors to fight alongside you. There are hundreds of strong men who follow Tin Hinan. How can you turn them away?"

The corners of Ameqran's mouth turned down in disapproval as he answered. "The great army of Garama needs nothing from those simple desert dwellers. The blue people are nomads. They know nothing of defending a kingdom."

"Many Tuareg died alongside the Garamantes of Abalessa when the Ghanans attacked. More Ghanan raids in the southern desert have killed hundreds of my kin. We have as much to lose as you do,"

Basi insisted.

Ameqran gazed about his encampment. "It matters not. The Ghanans will be crushed beneath the wheels of our war chariots. None can stand against our strength." His face was proud.

"You underestimate your enemy," Tau said. He was trying to keep his voice calm, but the frustration welled. "The Ghanans are warriors. They are strong, and they are clever. Why did they not take Abalessa two weeks ago when it lay undefended? Instead they killed and pillaged and left. Why?"

The king's eyes narrowed. "You try my patience. They could not have withstood our counterattack. That is why they retreated," Ameqran said.

"They are baiting you," Tau insisted. "They raided the city to draw you out. If you leave the desert, if you go to meet them on their terms, they will destroy your army. All your cities, all your kingdom, will lay undefended. You must not play into their hands."

Ameqran was angry. His face was turning red, and his hands twitched into fists. "How do you know this?" he asked.

Mbaneh's confession had guided his thoughts, but the strategic situation was now clear. The greatest weapon of the Garamantes was the desert. Traveling through it would be costly to Ghanan armies because of their unfamiliarity with traversing the harsh sands. If Tau were the warlord of Ghana, his first priority would be to draw the Garamante army out of the desert so he could come to grips with them. He would want to fight them where they could not disappear back into the great wasteland.

Ameqran glared. Tau sought the right words to put his suspicions to voice, but the king ran out of patience.

"Guards, escort these men from my sight," he ordered. He shot Tau a final, venomous glare. "You are lucky, stranger, that I do not hang you as a spy. Now go, wait with your blue-painted friends and watch the Garamante nation destroy the impudent Ghanan rabble." He turned away.

And Tau knew that he and Basi had failed in Tin Hinan's mission.

They returned to the fort. Basi said nothing. He was angry. Frustrated. Feeling impotent and ashamed at his failure. He glared as they walked through the town. He looked as though he wanted to pick a fight, but instead he clenched his jaw. Tau could hear him grinding his teeth.

Tau felt defeated, but he knew his frustration must be nothing compared to what the young warrior must be feeling. They reached the fort and scaled the crumbling walls. More blue-clad Tuareg had joined the swelling crowds in the castrum. A town was forming.

A forest of tents sprouted in concentric circles around the place where Tin Hinan supervised her people. She had dismounted her camel and sat, legs crossed, on a high seat made of piled saddlecloths. A length of silk spread over four upright staves shaded her from the sun. She watched Tau and Basi approach, her face inscrutable.

"Tell me," she commanded.

Basi told her, and she sighed. "It is exactly as I feared," she said. She cast a critical eye at the castrum's crumbling walls. At the wave of her hand, a group of attendants approached.

"We will repair this fortress," the queen announced. "We will lay new stone and mortar and rebuild the walls. This is where we will make our stand." The attendants scuttled away, and Tin Hinan gazed into the distance.

"The Ghanan army will come again," she said. "The Garamantes will suffer, but the Tuareg will survive. Though what happens after that I cannot say."

Basi and Tau were dismissed, and Tau rejoined his companions. Together they walked back toward the town.

"There will be fighting soon," Tau said.

Ulrich nodded; his face impassive. "If the Garamante army fights Ghana, Ghana will win. The warriors of Ghana are trained fighters, and the Garamantes are not."

"And then what?" Yael asked.

"Then the Tuareg will stand alone," Tau said.

CHAPTER TWENTY

Over the coming weeks, Garamante patrols were seen returning from the frontier. Rumors were rife. Some claimed that there was no evidence of Ghanan warriors as far as the Sahel. Some claimed to see the dust clouds of an army maneuvering to the west, and some rumors claimed many patrols never returned. Tin Hinan sent out her own scouts as well, groups of camel nomads who travelled in small groups and only at night. What information they gained Tau did not learn and Tin Hinan did not share.

While the Garamante army sat in Abalessa, the Tuareg were busy. Mortar was mixed and bricks were fired. The walls of the small fortress were rebuilt, and the place was stocked for a siege. Cisterns were dug, made watertight with lime plaster, and painstakingly filled with water. Storehouses were built and began to be loaded with grain, date-fruit, and forage for the Tuareg camels.

Tau, meanwhile, learned how the city of Abalessa drew water from the desert. There was an aqueduct, but unlike the Roman aqueducts, this one ran underground. Its only visible sign was a line of close-fitted stones snaking across the desert. The aqueduct left the city of Abalessa and went east, toward the sharp-peaked Ahaggar Mountains. At the base of a cliff it led to a foggara—a horizontal mine shaft directly into the mountain's side. A cluster of houses lay outside the entrance, and Tau and Yael were greeted by a work party of Garamante engineers. Yael explained that they had come out of curiosity, but it was a handful of coin that bought entrance into the dark, torch-lit tunnel.

They were led for a great distance through the underground space.

There was a constant sound of rushing water beneath their feet where the aqueduct flowed. The ground sloped steadily upward even here. Eventually the tunnel opened into a great chamber. The ground fell away, and torchlight illuminated a wooden platform suspended over blackness. The sound of dripping water could be heard far below.

"The water used to reach up to here," the chief engineer said, stamping his feet on the wooden platform. He was an elderly Garamante with a long, dark beard. His name was Ziri. His family had overseen the aqueduct for generations.

"The water in this aquifer will not last forever." He sighed. "Long ago, even before the memory of my ancestors, the desert was green, and water filled this great rock chamber. Now there is no rain, and every year the water level falls."

There was the distant noise of metal on rock far below. A rope ladder, jerking and shuddering with unseen workers, stretched down into the blackness from the edge of the platform.

"We are digging a new tunnel, a new foggara, to join the aqueduct you saw leading from the city," he said, explaining the sound. "The old foggara will be dry in a season."

"But if the new tunnel starts below the pipe of the aqueduct, how will the water from the aquifer get to it?" Yael asked. "Water cannot flow uphill." Tau could see her puzzled expression in the torchlight.

The old man smiled. "It can by something called siphoning. If the city of Abalessa is below the height of the surface of the water in the reservoir, the water will flow. Don't you worry about that. Water behaves in interesting ways when it is confined."

"How much water is left in the chamber?" Tau asked.

Ziri hesitated. "There is enough. I am sure that we can supply Abalessa for a hundred years or more," he said, not meeting Tau's eyes.

Tau could tell he was lying, but the tour was over, and Ziri ushered the visitors out.

The crop of winter-planted wheat ripened the next week, and all the men and women of Abalessa went to harvest it. Tau joined the harvest and received a handful of coin in return for his labor. He noticed that Tin Hinan bought a great portion of the crop, filling more newly built storehouses with the fresh grain. The walls of her fortress were nearly complete, and her reserves of water were swiftly filling. She prepared to weather a siege.

Finally, word came that a Garamante patrol had definitively pinpointed the mustering place of the Ghanan army. They were gathering in the Sahel, on the banks of the Niger River, five hundred miles to the south. On the same day, a stream of fugitives flowed into the city. They were disconsolate, wounded, and desperate. They told of attacks: of black figures rushing out of the moonlit night to burn Garamante trading posts near the desert's edge; of women and children torn from their beds and carried off into the darkness; of men slaughtered and homes put to the torch.

The Garamante army made ready to confront their foe. Basi, impetuous and incensed, made a final plea for the Tuareg to be allowed to support the Garamante army, but King Ameqran refused to see him. Tin Hinan hurried the fortification of her bulwark, and Tau and his friends made ready to travel.

Five hundred Garamante chariots formed up under the noonday sun. Each wooden chariot was a marvelous work of art, painted in white, blue, and gold over dark ebony-colored wood. Each chariot was pulled by two camels and crewed by two Garamante soldiers. The soldiers were armored in white-painted leather tunics and carried long spears. In front of this force, a thousand Garamante spear-infantry sat on camels. They formed a single, well ordered square. Before all, King Ameqran stood on his war machine.

The Garamante king's chariot was many times larger than the others. It was a war wagon. Where the regular chariots had two wheels, his had four. While the others were drawn by two camels, his had six. Elite warriors in polished scale armor filled the wagon, and two drivers sat atop a high driving bench. On this bench also stood King Ameqran, the sun glinting off the ancient muscle cuirass.

Tau, Ulrich, Ejnar, and Yael sat on camels borrowed from Tin Hinan. They were a short way behind the Garamante army, and they were not the only onlookers. Scores of men and women from had come to see the soldiers off. Basi rode from the Tuareg fortress, and he reined in beside Yael. The two of them began quietly conversing in Berber.

King Ameqran began to speak. He addressed his men. Tau leaned forward, straining to hear, but he was too far away. He sighed and sat back.

"Where did they get all the wood for those chariots?" Ejnar asked.

He sat cross legged on his camel. "I haven't seen any trees with dark wood like that in the desert."

"They buy the wood," Tau said. Loki was in his saddle, saving his paws from the hot sand. Tau scratched his head. "The Garamantes are rich. Their empire stretches from edge to edge of the Sahara. They carry the trade of many Empires. Gold from Ghana, pottery from Rome, silks from the Sassanids, iron from Nok, salt from Aksum, and even treasures from an ancient place called Egypt. The Garamantes themselves produce only wheat, dates, and camels, but they prosper on the trans-Saharan trade. They can get anything they want; in any currency you could care to name."

"But you cannot buy victory," Ulrich growled.

"They look confident," Yael said. "And well-equipped. It's quite an army."

"One thousand mounted infantry and five hundred chariots adds up to a decent number of soldiers," Tau admitted. "But I wonder how many Ghanan warriors they will face."

Tau had been only a child when he had been sold into slavery, but he recalled fields packed to the horizon with black warriors.

King Ameqran finished his speech. His charioteers cracked their reins and the war wagon led the way south. The Garamante army moved out, and the companions followed.

CHAPTER TWENTY-ONE

Tau, Ulrich, Yael, Ejnar, and Basi, along with a baggage train of supplies, a caravan of craftsmen, and a herd of anxious wives and children followed the Garamante army as they travelled southward through the desert. Once again it was the camels that made these epic journeys easy. The beasts were impervious to the dry, the heat, the sun; to thirst and to hunger. They plodded on, tossing their heads in boredom and leaning on one another for companionship as the days slid by. The Garamantes were quite comfortable with long journeys. Basi said that even a child could cross five hundred miles of desert if he knew the way. Tau had to cover his face with cloth against the cloud of dust generated by the hundreds of rumbling chariot wheels.

Finally, after four weeks, they found the enemy.

The desert gave way to the rolling grasslands of the Sahel, and in the distance a gleaming blue tributary of the Niger River flowed. This was a battlefield that was perfect for an aggressive commander. It was flat and dry, with sparse, green grass growing from hard turf and no obstacles to obstruct the movement of infantry or a charge of cavalry. Against the Garamantes the Ghanan army waited, and Tau was in awe to witness the strength of his nation arrayed before him.

Tau recalled a memory of standing as a child beside his father, the Ghana Kayode, as the warriors of Ghana paraded through Koumbi Saleh. They danced and sang to salute their emperor, bare-chested, boasting long spears and broad, leather shields.

"The strength of Ghana is in its warriors," Tau's father told him, "and the strength of the warrior is in his bravery. A warrior must stand before the strongest foe and show no fear. We are descendants of Anansi. As he defied and slew the great python of the god Nyame, you must defy the tremor that grows within your own breast."

Tau's father was a tall and powerful man with an angular face and penetrating dark eyes. Tau was his first son, and Kayode was as fiercely proud of him as he was of his great and powerful army. The title Ghana means warrior-king, and Tau had known then that he must prove himself as a warrior for his father's pride to be justified.

On the battlefield the warrior strength of a proud empire rose for war. Ejnar grunted in approval, as an impressive sight it was. Thousands of Ghanan spearmen filled the plain. Their black chests were bared to the midday sun, and they held their spears high as the Garamantes came into sight. They saluted their enemy, cheering their arrival, then began beating their spears against their shields in lively anticipation of a fight.

The Ghanans were in loose order, thus were difficult to count, but that they outnumbered the Garamantes was clear. Tau estimated the odds at perhaps two or even three to one. Standing spearmen formed the majority of the Ghanan horde, but behind them hundreds of cavalry-spearmen mounted on small Arabian horses dotted the field.

Curiously, it looked like there was a large group of women and children in the middle of the army of warriors. Tau wondered why they were there.

Then the Garamantes began to deploy. The first one-thousand soldiers dismounted their camels. On foot they formed a shield wall, making a neat rectangle in a simplistic imitation of Roman order. Their camels were led away by boys to join the baggage train. Behind them, the chariots arranged themselves into two long lines.

King Ameqran was there, and he placed his war wagon behind his infantry phalanx. He stood atop the tall driving bench, arms crossed, and gazed at his enemy. The Garamante chariots waited on the wings. The Garamante infantry, lined with military precision, stood in silence.

The Ghanan warriors began working themselves into the battle joy. The war songs of the Soninke carried on the wind. Black warriors dashed into the space between their army and the enemy and taunted the quiet Garamante soldiers, dropping shield and spear to display themselves unarmed and unafraid before their enemy. Tau wondered if his half-brother was among those men. Would he lead from the front, like a proper Ghana? Far in the rear, on a tall horse, sat a woman resplendent in shimmering gold. She wore a golden crown on her head, golden bracelets on her wrists, and heavy golden chains around her neck. Tau wondered if that was his enemy Kansoleh. A boy in silks rode alongside her, then both disappeared in the shimmering heat and Tau saw them no more.

The battle frenzy came to a climax, and the black warriors of Ghana started forward in a mass.

"Have they no shield wall?" Ulrich asked, frowning.

"Ghana has never fought with a shield wall," Tau said.

"Then the Garamantes could actually win," Ulrich said. "If they hold firm."

Ulrich's people, the Saxons, had learned of shield walls from the Romans, and Ulrich knew with certainty that a steady shield wall would always defeat an undisciplined horde. At the battle of Argentoratum, Ulrich and Tau had witnessed a Roman army defeat one three times its number simply by staying in formation. Ulrich's tactical mind calculated ruthlessly as he watched the forces square off.

The Ghanan warriors rushed toward the Garamante shield wall, and Tau`s stomach churned. His pride at seeing his people arrayed for war was equally opposed by his desire for justice for Abalessa and by his hatred for his treacherous stepmother. His fear of watching the underdog Garamantes lose was balanced by his reluctance to watch his own Soninke brothers cut down. Tau clutched his camel's saddle and looked on.

Then the Ghanan army shifted. The warriors in the fore divided, and the army vomited forth the huddle of women and children that had been trapped in their midst. Yael gasped.

The women and children were Berbers. Among them were the fine colored tunics of the Garamante city folk, as well as the blue cloaks of the Tuareg and the rough camel-wool of the caravaneers. They were bruised and frightened, and Tau realized that they must have been captives abducted from Ghanan raids into the Sahara. There were perhaps a hundred of them, and they clung together, cowering from the weapons of their captors.

The hostages were prodded forward. Spear points drew blood where they found soft flesh. A loose screen of Ghanan warriors spread out in front of the terrified mass and kept them herded into a rough globus as the main body continued to advance. Some of the

Berber women, babies cradled in their arms, tried to make a break for it. They did not make it more than a dozen steps before they were cut down. The Ghanan warriors, spear blades flashing, tripped the fleeing women and stabbed sharp steel into unprotected backs.

Exactly as the Ghanans had intended, the Garamantes were provoked to anger. They lowered their shields and brandished their spears, shouting and stepping out of formation. Several of the chariots rode forward, then hesitated, indecisive. They wanted to attack but could not fight while the mass of hostages blocked their path. The Garamante phalanx began to lose cohesion. Ameqran shouted at his men to keep their lines. Everywhere Garamante soldiers edged forward. Men toward the rear craned their necks to see what was happening. Men broke formation entirely to wave and shout at hostages they recognized among the mass.

The Ghanan horde crept closer, holding their hostages out in front like a shield. Once they were within twenty paces, the Ghanan spears began to fly. The missiles sailed over the heads of the Berber captives and found targets in the Garamante ranks. Soldiers recoiled from the unexpected attack and crouched beneath their shields. Some cowered behind the ranks of bodies in front of them, seeking shelter from the rain of missiles. Some of the spears fell short, landing among the hostages, and Tau saw a Tuareg boy, hand clasped tightly in his mother's, killed by a spear that drove into the back of his neck. He pitched forward with a spray of blood.

The screen of Ghanan warriors that had been containing the hostages parted. Prodding spears provoked terror, and the fugitives fled toward the Garamante lines. The Garamantes lowered their shields to allow the women and children into their midst.

"No..." Yael breathed.

The slaughter began. The strength of a shield wall was in its cohesion, and that cohesion had dissolved. As the fugitives ran for safety within the phalanx, Ghanan spearmen followed them. They sprinted into the gaps that appeared in the Garamante lines and cut down the Garamantes with murderous efficiency. The entire mass of black warriors flowed into the broken Garamante formation. The Garamante soldiers were disorganized and confused and they died where they stood. The Ghanan warriors laughed with battle joy as they killed, dancing among their enemy. They had no need for their leather shields now, and many warriors threw them down so that they could kill faster, stabbing and slashing into a helpless foe. Blood flew in fountains, and the spear blades flashed bright in the midday sun.

Basi urged his camel forward. He brandished his long spear and joined a group of chariots that were closing in on the fighting. Tau knew that it was hopeless and shouted at Basi to stop, but the young Tuareg warrior did not look back. Within moments he was lost amid the camels, chariots, chaos, and dust.

The Garamante chariot cavalry tried to rescue the infantry, but they failed. The power of a chariot lies in its speed and momentum, and in the confusion, they lost both. Riding close to the chaos, charioteers stabbed at Ghanan warriors and were immediately overwhelmed. The Ghanan warriors flooded over them, climbing onto chariot platforms and onto camels' backs, outnumbering and overpowering the poorly organized Berbers.

King Ameqran died fighting. His war wagon had been near the front lines when the battle started, and a dozen Ghanan warriors broke through the Garamante infantry to attack the king. The king's spearmen were the hand-picked soldiers of an elite guard, and they gave their lives in defense of their master. They stood on the wagon's high platform and deflected spear blades with their heavy armor as they stabbed down again and again into the mass of bare-chested warriors. Then, a second wave of Ghanan warriors rushed forward, and the defenders were overwhelmed. Hands pulled the soldiers from the wagon, and spear blades found gaps in the armor to sink into soft, yielding flesh.

King Ameqran himself fought to the very last. Gray head bare, he was resplendent in his gleaming bronze cuirass, and he wielded his sword with the skill and speed of desperate pride. He parried one spear that came for his face, but another found his thigh and sank deep. He killed the spear's owner and stood tall, roaring his challenge at his attackers. He slashed the steel point off another spear and took a crippling wound to his right arm. He switched his sword to his left hand and laughed as he stabbed his blade into the chest of another black warrior. He was still laughing when final spear caught him in the throat. He snarled in defiance as he died, gritting his teeth even as the blood bubbled around his lips.

"Odin's blood," Ulrich cursed. He turned his camel.

Flight was the wisest choice. The surviving ranks of the Garamante square were routing. They dropped their shields and dropped their spears, and they ran toward the nearest unmounted camels or simply fled on foot the way they had come. Some of the charioteers were lucky, being farther from the chaos, and they turned away from the slaughter. But the Ghanan cavalry, quiet until now, trotted forward.

Ejnar, Yael, and Ulrich turned to flee, but Tau did not join them. He looked south, past the Ghanan army and into the green Sahel.

Ejnar hesitated, seeing Tau's gaze.

"Surely you can't be thinking of fighting," Ejnar shouted.

"We must flee or be caught in the chaos," Ulrich urged.

By this time, a flood of fleeing chariots, camels, and Garamante infantry was streaming past. Tau spotted Basi in the crowd. He was dismounted. His unsheathed sword was chipped and bloodied, but he looked unharmed. His face was set in a look of fierce anger.

"Go on," Tau said. "Go ahead and run, but this is the closest I have been to home. I must continue on to Koumbi Saleh."

Ulrich turned his camel back. "Lead on then," he said without hesitation.

Yael joined too, but Ejnar did not. He kicked his camel away to join the tide of fugitives headed north into the desert. He turned and gave a final yell.

"You're insane," Ejnar called over his shoulder, and Tau was sure that he saw fear in the ex-pirate's eyes. "But if you survive, I'll meet you in Abalessa." He and his camel were swept up in the fleeing crowd.

"Now what?" Yael shouted. The thunder of hooves was growing louder as the Ghanan cavalry swept closer.

"Now," Tau said, "we ride to Ghana."

CHAPTER TWENTY-TWO

They ran at a right angle from the chaos. A shallow ridge ran east to west and the Garamantes were flooding over it, heading north. Tau led his friends into the ridge's shadow and followed it east. The camels were not entirely hidden by the shallow crest, and Tau could see the disaster continue among the Garamante army. The Ghanan cavalry that was not slaughtering Berber spearmen was hounding the fleeing chariots and chasing scattered camels. The slaughter was only beginning. The greatest font of death came not during a battle, but after, as panicked men and women were easier targets than those who stood their ground.

The companions were only a quarter mile from the flowing chaos when they were spotted. Abandoning their hounding of desperate groups of fleeing chariots, two Ghanan horsemen broke from the greater mass to give chase. Tau's camel was already running, and while a running camel is an impressive sight, no camel can out-sprint a galloping horse. Tau twisted in his saddle to consider the enemy.

Both pursuing warriors were young, perhaps in their late teens or early twenties. They bore simple iron torques, but none of the golden necklaces that marked a veteran warrior. Despite this, their long spears were blooded to mid-shaft, and they grinned with the battle joy. Their fast horses were gaining fast.

Tau considered trying to turn his camel to fight them, but he had little faith in his ability to manage the big animal in combat or to fight from the tall, swaying perch. He shifted in his seat, careful not to disturb Loki who crouched in the front of the saddle. Tau gave the dog a scratch behind the ears, and the animal looked up with a quizzical expression. Tau checked that his sword belt was snug around his waist, then he dove from the saddle.

He had been aiming for a soft hillock of sand, but instead landed on a patch of hard, dry earth. Camels are quite tall, and they travel a bit faster than a healthy person can run, so Tau hit the rocky ground harder than he had expected. The breath was driven from his lungs. Still, he knew his pursuers were close, so he pushed himself to his feet, gasping for air. He felt a nudge at his hand and looked down to find Loki, quite calm, blinking at him.

"Dammit, Loki! You were supposed to stay with the camel," Tau wheezed.

The dog made no response, and Tau shook his head. "Just like your master, always ready to dive in," he said.

Tau drew his swords. His enemies were a hundred paces away, and they leered at what must have looked like an easy target. Their spears were leveled, and they leaned forward in the saddle as they charged.

Tau mentally planned his moves. Both men were right-handed, so right before they struck, Tau would dodge to his right. This would place the body and horse of the nearer enemy between him and the other warrior, reducing his immediate opponents to one. Then, Tau would slash his swords into the man's unprotected left side. Meanwhile, the other warrior would need to curb his horse and wheel to attack, losing momentum. Tau could deal with him after finishing off the first one. He gripped his swords and braced himself.

Loki, unconscious of Tau's plan, growled and charged. The dog bared his teeth and let out a soul-chilling howl as he ran. The sound was the embodiment of savagery, and it filled all the space between earth and sky, drowning out the thunder of hooves and the deafening rumble of chariot wheels.

The Ghanan horses, hearing the call of a hunter among prey, panicked. The nearest reared from the charging mastiff, dropping its rider into a thorn bush. The other horse bolted, carrying its surprised rider back westward, away from the terrible predator.

Tau laughed. The fallen Ghanan warrior was stunned. He blinked at the sky and groaned, so Loki left him alone. The spooked horse scampered away, and Loki loped back, tongue lolling lazily from his big mouth. Tau sheathed his swords.

"Who's a fierce warrior?" Tau asked the dog. He rubbed the dog's floppy face with both hands. "You are. You're the fierce warrior." He patted his head. "Good boy."

Tau turned to find that Ulrich had caught and curbed his camel a short distance away. With Loki at his heels, Tau ran for safety. He mounted his camel and looked back. The dry ground was littered with bodies. Another band of Ghanan horsemen spotted the companions and began trotting their way.

"Time to go," Tau said, and turned away. Thus ended the Battle of the Sahel, last stand of King Ameqran and the first great battlefield defeat of the Ghanan-Garamante war.

They were not pursued for long. The horsemen must have decided that there were easier pickings among the fleeing Garamantes, and they turned back after little more than a mile of desultory chase. The running chaos faded into the distance as the companions turned their camels south. The sandy ground gave way to firmer footing, and grasses sprouted thicker from the dark earth.

As evening fell, they found themselves on a rolling plain of scrub wattle, hanza, and tall grass. To the west, a red twilight suffused the cloudless sky, and Tau scanned the horizon carefully for pursuers. Seeing none, he curbed his mount and kneeled his camel to climb from the saddle. A mild breeze rustled the green leaves of a patch of desert date trees. Ulrich and Yael, following his lead, dismounted as well.

Mechanically Tau rustled through his camel's saddlebags, bringing out a hunk of smoked jerky and a flask of stale water. He sipped the water and gnawed at the dry meat as he unsaddled and brushed his camel, who munched on desert dates fallen from the nearby branches. He checked the camel's hump to find it was firm and healthy. The camel's tongue was moist, but their reserve of spare drinking water was running low. They would have to find a fresh water source within the next couple of days.

Tau sat on the ground and rested his back against a desert date tree. The bark was rough, but he was glad to be out of the saddle. The first stars were emerging overhead, though the fading glow of the sun still lingered on the horizon. The moon was a silver crescent, nearly at the zenith. Thor sucked marrow from a bone Ulrich brought out of his pack, and Loki sat patiently as Ulrich inspected him for fleas. Yael sat in a patch of sunlight and began writing intensely in her journal.

Tau leaned back and closed his eyes.

He had not meant to fall asleep, but weariness had overtaken him. It was full darkness when he awoke. Somebody had tossed a camelhair blanket over him, for which he was grateful as the night wind carried a dry chill. Loki's heavy head rested on his lower legs, and the dog snored gently. Yael lay a few paces away. Wrapped in blankets, she appeared to be sleeping. Ulrich was awake. He sat cross-legged on the ground with his back to Tau. His gentle hand was on Thor's side as he kept watch in the night.

Tau tried to disengage himself from the sleeping Loki without rousing him, but he failed. The dog woke to gaze at Tau with large baleful eyes. Tau petted him and rose, wrapping himself in the blanket as he moved to join his friend.

Ulrich acknowledged Tau with a nod and turned back to the starlit darkness. He looked content. His body was relaxed, and he wore a smile as he scratched the big mastiff's head behind the ears. Ulrich seemed the same as he had on a hundred similar nights, keeping watch, calm and stoic. Vigilant and patient, a great reserve of strength rested within him, and Tau had long drawn from it.

Tau looked into the night. Through the sparse branches of the dry wattle, he could see the glow of the milky galaxy that covered a great swath of the celestial sphere. A star fell. Tau's eyes flicked toward it, but it was already gone, left only as a splash of fading white light, an afterimage at the fringe of vision's memory.

"Something on your mind, friend?" Ulrich asked. His voice was heavy with the harsh intonations of his native German, but his words were kind.

Tau sighed, and despite himself, gave voice to his somber thoughts.

"I was wondering what the point of all this is," he admitted. Even as the words came out, he felt ashamed of them.

Ulrich said nothing. Loki jealously pushed his big head between Ulrich and Thor, and Ulrich unlimbered his other hand to pet both dogs equally. Tau sat down.

"We've travelled thousands of miles," Tau continued. "We froze in the mountains; we burned in the desert. We fought pirates and raiders, even made friends that we were forced to bury. We have come so far, and for what? The Garamantes have lost. Our enemies say that my father is dead, and it seems that my stepmother has won. I don't even know what I would do once I got to Ghana."

Tau looked over at the sleeping Yael.

"And I've led her so far from home," he said.

He felt a sadness creep into his heart. The dry soil crumbled in his hands as he clenched his fists. He stared at the ground for a long time. A sudden gust of wind shivered the dry branches of the wattle.

"There was a time very like this in Germany," Ulrich said. "After the Alemanni crushed two Saxon armies. After they killed the prisoners for sport. Our people were defeated, and the enemy had won. They only let us live out of pity and shame. But you would not let us give up then. You said that as long as we live, we can keep fighting."

Tau remembered that moment: On a cold Saxon hill, next to two fresh graves, the graves of men who had died fighting for what they believed in.

"I used to believe in good and evil," Ulrich continued. "As a child I imagined that my father was good, and that my uncle was evil. I believed that my quest was good, and that I was opposed by evil men. That belief gave me courage for a long time. That conviction possessed me to storm the slave ship at Brunswick. It drove me in the fight to rescue the hostages at Kassel. When we met the Alemanni, they were Germans, my kin, but I joined the Romans against them. But when we defeated Chnodomar, I realized that these fights are not about good and evil at all. They are about strength, and the strong will always prey on the weak."

Ulrich closed his eyes, leaning back to allow the night wind to wash over him. "Right now, the Ghanans are strong, and the Garamantes are weak. The Ghanans will bully them, and if nobody helps them, the Ghanans will win, and the Garamantes will be slaves. Their defenseless cities will be destroyed, and good people like Idir and Tauda and young Idlis… even their memories will be erased."

Ulrich opened his eyes and met Tau's gaze. "But we are here, so we will fight. And we will win because we must. In doing so you might accomplish something I never could. You could win back the kingdom that is rightfully yours."

Tau smiled. "Thank you, friend, but how will we do it?"

Ulrich gave a savage grin. "I already know how," he said. "I have a plan."

"What is your plan?" Tau asked.

"We will use something that I learned from the Romans," Ulrich answered with a distant look.

Tau wanted to probe further, but Ulrich yawned and stretched, standing to move to his bedroll. He curled himself into his blankets, and Tau was alone, gazing into the darkness.

CHAPTER TWENTY-THREE

One week of travel later, they reached the jungle of western Africa. It began as a line of green on the southern horizon. From a distance, the green was so dense it looked black. The thick canopy cast perpetual shadow on the land beneath it. It stood like a great fortress, malevolent and unforgiving, blocking the way south. It had been raining all day, and lightning flashed beyond that terminus. Each bolt flared brightly before its light was absorbed by the stygian wall.

Tau was glad for the landmark, but he realized that they had come too far south. He had hoped to encounter another trunk of the Niger River and follow it home. He knew its water flowed east to west along the Sahel and should act as a guide directly to Koumbi Saleh. However, beyond the first tributary and a broad floodplain of stream-crisscrossing marsh, the mighty river failed to manifest. So, they sat on their camels, soaked in rain, and watched a storm blaze over the thick rainforest, the domain of the leopard and forest hippo.

"I don't think we can travel through a jungle on these camels," Yael noted.

"We don't have to," Tau said. "We just need to go west."

They were well supplied. Two days before, they had encountered a herd of antelope in the grassy savanna. Ulrich had speared an elderly male when Yael and Tau cut off the animal's retreat. Clean streams had refilled their water casks and their camels' humps. This land was rich, the weather had turned warm, and their present journey was a pleasant change from the dry Sahara. They had seen no further settlements or people as they crossed the grassy fields, empty under the boiling rainclouds.

Tau led over a rise and a beaten cow path appeared before them, paralleling the run of the jungle. Tau turned his mount westward along its cleared surface, leaving the thick grasses and muddy earth of the wet savanna. Tau swatted at a massive fly that had settled on his left hand.

"Get down!" Ulrich yelled.

Tau ducked as a spear whistled past his head.

Adrenaline surged through Tau's veins. He swore. He kicked his camel into a run and twisted, scanning for the threat. The tall grass whipped by, but he could not be sure what movement was caused by the wind and rain and what could have been an enemy.

Ulrich surged past Tau and drove his camel into the grass. Ulrich's axe swung down to splash blood into the rain-filled sky. A second man fled from him and sprinted onto the path in front of Tau. It was a tall black warrior with the gold of Ghana around his neck. He screamed curses in Soninke as he fled.

Ulrich did not hesitate. He whistled calmly to Thor.

"Corpora," he commanded.

The dog leapt from the saddle. In moments he had caught up with the fleeing man. With a brutal wrench on a flying leg, Thor pulled the man down. His teeth found the warrior's throat, cutting the warrior's screaming short in a welter of blood. Tau reined in his camel. He gave an involuntary shudder as Thor loped, red jaws dripping, back to his master.

A hunting horn blared. Tau turned to see a group of horsemen crest a hill to the east. The horn sounded again, and the horsemen flew toward the companions at a gallop.

"That's a Ghanan hunting party," Tau said. It was part of the initiation of every young warrior to demonstrate his skill against the beasts of the wild. "We are intruders in their territory."

Ulrich brandished his bloody war axe and snarled. Yael unlimbered her bow and strung it.

"Do we fight them?" she asked. Her eyes were clear and calm. There was no fear in her voice.

"No," Tau said. "There are too many." He counted at least twenty warriors in the band. He wondered, too, how many more spearmen might lurk in the tall grass.

"We have to make for the jungle," Tau said. "We may have to abandon our camels, but horsemen cannot follow us in there."

Tau urged his camel to a run, and the others followed. He put an arm around Loki to steady the dog as the camel bounced, throwing mud from its heavy hooves.

By the time they reached the shade of the tree canopy, the war band was drawing close. Scattered pairs of hunters had risen from the grass in response to the hunting call, but none were near enough to intercept the fleeing camels.

"Grab what supplies you can," Tau said. "Abandon the camels."

Tau leapt down and unstrapped the saddle bags. He let the big wooden water cask drop to the ground and threw a leather pack over his shoulders. It was heavy with blankets, tools, spare flasks of water and smoked meat. Ulrich strapped his axe to his back and took both his and Yael's supplies in his burly arms.

"I will take the packs. Just ready your bow," Ulrich told her.

He strode to Tau and took the bag from him as well, draping it loosely about his shoulders. This freed Tau's arms to unlimber his swords from their scabbards.

"Come on. It's time to go," Ulrich said.

Tau slapped his camel on the rump, and it lumbered north. The other camels followed, and a pair of the charging warriors peeled off from the pack to head off the beasts. The war band was almost upon them as they fled into the jungle. But as Tau had predicted, the undergrowth was too thick, and the trees were too closely packed for the horses to follow.

That same vegetation made the companions' passage slow. In a few steps Tau slipped on wet roots, became entangled in vines, and sank ankle-deep in mud. Ulrich was trying to force his way through the undergrowth, but even his brute strength was having little success. Yael stood between the two men, bow drawn and ready, and the dogs waited at her heels. The horsemen began to dismount. Already their forms were shrouded by the overhanging leaves.

"Here," Tau said to Yael, handing her one of his swords. "Take this and clear the way for Ulrich. I can watch our rear."

She pushed her way past Ulrich to chop at the vines that blocked their path. Their passage became easier, and they moved deeper into the jungle. The Ghanans were speaking to each other, and several sank stakes to tie off their horses. Tau paced backward and brandished his remaining sword. A swarm of gnats burst from a bush to fill his nostrils and cloud his vison. He swatted them away.

It was growing dark beneath the eves of the dense canopy. Raindrops drummed on the leaves above and peals of thunder sounded. The ground was wet underfoot. Water ran in rivulets down the tree trunks, but the leaves blocked the droplets from falling on their heads. Two Ghanan warriors, just dark shapes in the murk, advanced into the trees. Tau took another step backward.

The warriors were following the path Yael and Ulrich were slowly blazing into the depths of the rainforest. Fortunately for the companions, the density of the jungle meant that the Ghanan warriors would have difficulty flanking their prey. Tau stopped backing and waited for the enemy.

The two warriors approached cautiously. They bore leather shields and long hunting spears but were young and nervous and had none of the golden ornaments of proven warriors. The rightmost warrior, face pockmarked with acne, swallowed and shifted his grip on his sword. The leftmost, fear plain on his face, edged behind his companion. Tau almost felt sorry for them.

They came within a spear's thrust of Tau, but then they hesitated. They glanced at one another, each waiting for the other to make the first move. Tau did not give them time to gain their courage. He leapt forward. With his left hand he grabbed the shaft of the nearest spear. He pulled hard, and the young warrior holding the weapon stumbled forward. Tau's sword flashed across his face, slashing into his eyes and blinding him instantly.

The other warrior shouted and attacked with a lunge of his spear. His thrust was clumsy, slow, and too well telegraphed. An expert knows how to make a blow a surprise, to anticipate his opponent, and drive his blade forward without warning. This man was no expert. He cocked his spear back to his shoulder before stabbing it forward, making it a simple act for Tau to dodge out of the way. Tau's sword point flashed up into his outstretched armpit, and the young warrior howled in pain. He dropped his weapon, screamed in terror, and turned to flee. Tau let him go.

Tau looked down at the blinded spearman, who kneeled on the ground before him. The young man was clutching his face, which was streaming with blood. Both of his eyes were destroyed. In that brief moment Tau had dealt him a terrible wound. He would never become a warrior. He would be an invalid, a shame to his family and an embarrassment to his people. Tau stepped forward. The young man was whimpering and shaking in pain and fear.

"I am sorry," Tau said in Soninke.

Tau placed the point of his sword just above the warrior's hunched neck. He found the point where the spine entered the skull, where the vertebrae were spread far apart, where a blade would not be blocked by bone.

"Go to our ancestors," Tau told him softly. "I will meet you there."

Tau thrust his sword down, severing the young warrior's spinal cord and killing him instantly. The young man collapsed, boneless, to the ground.

Tau was filled with a sudden anger.

"You cowards," Tau yelled. He knew the warriors in the field could hear him. He could hear them muttering to each other. "You send your young and unproven because you are too afraid to fight a proper warrior."

One of the warriors swore. "Come on out, you horse turd," he called.

"Who are you?" another yelled.

In his anger, Tau answered honestly. "I am Tau, first son of warrior-king Kayode and true heir to the Ghana throne of Wagadu, Lord of Awkar, Chief of the Soninke."

"That is a lie," the warrior called back. "These are Garamante camels, and you are a Garamante spy. Come out, and we will kill you and dance on your corpse."

Tau spat. "Come and retrieve your companion. He fought honorably and deserves the proper rites of burial."

No answer came. Tau's felt Yael's hand on his shoulder.

"Come on," she said gently.

Tau turned to find that she and Ulrich had pushed into a soggy creek bed, the course of which allowed easier passage into the jungle. Tau wiped his sword clean of the swiftly clotting blood and followed.

CHAPTER TWENTY-FOUR

Everything in the jungle was wet. The ground was wet, the foliage was wet, and even the air felt sodden. The heat was oppressive and blazing a trail through all of this—the damp, the thick undergrowth, the swarms of insects, and the cloying mud—was exhausting. Deeper in, the lack of sunlight did not allow as much scrub vegetation to cover the ground, but the mud, vines, and entangling roots still slowed their passage. After an hour of slow travel, Tau estimated that they had travelled less than a mile. There was no sign of pursuit, so he called to his companions to rest.

The dogs, muddy and miserable, stood uncomfortably. They were already scratching and biting at ticks and burrs that infested this place. A massive log lay astride the path, and Tau sat on it, only for the rotten wood to immediately crumble under his weight. A swarm of termites poured out. He stepped back and looked for a better place to rest but found nothing. The world seemed entirely composed of wet leaves, muddy ground, and tangled vines.

Yael had the idea of laying all the blankets on the ground and resting on that. With this semblance of drier ground, they sat and began going through their packs. They were desperately overloaded. They had gear enough for a trans-desert journey by camel, with food and supplies for a month, and it was far too much to carry on straining backs. They began sorting through it and tossing out things they did not urgently need. The wooden tent-poles and camel-leather tarpaulins were the first to go, along with flasks of spare water and saddle blankets for the camels. They shifted as best as they could, rearranged the saddlebags into makeshift rucksacks, and pitched camp.

There was no dry firewood to be found, so several of the tent poles were broken for a campfire. The wood burned only feebly in the damp air. Ulrich set to making a jury-rigged drying rack for their wet clothes. Tau's feet had already begun to swell in his damp leather boots, and he tugged them off gratefully.

"We can't travel much farther like this," Yael said.

There was fatigue in her voice. Tau was tired too. The single hour of pushing through the rainforest had been more wearing than entire days of travel in the Sahara.

"You're right," Tau said. "We have to go back."

"Go back?" Yael asked.

Tau looked around. The perpetual twilight of the jungle made it impossible to tell what time it was. He could see his companions and about twenty feet in every direction, but the rest of the jungle faded into blackness. He assumed it was evening, because if it had been nighttime it surely would have been even darker still. The rain-drumming and thunder-rumble of the storm had ceased, only to be replaced by a deafening buzz of insects. The noise was such that they had to speak loudly to be heard over its din.

"I can't tell which way we're going in here," Tau said. "Without the north star or the sun or the moon to guide us, we're lost. We need to get back to the savanna."

"I agree. I would rather go back and fight an army of warriors than try to go another mile in this morass," Ulrich grumbled. He was using his fingernails to pull burrs from Thor's fur. The dog looked miserable.

Tau nodded. "Let's rest for now. We are safe enough here. Let us spend the night, get our strength back, and retrace our steps in the morning. Perhaps by then the warriors will be gone."

They ate their smoked meat, drank from their flasks, shifted their clothes that dried over a small fire, and settled in for the night.

Tau woke with a start. The forest was pitch black. He could not see his hands in front of his face. The deafening noise of insect life pervaded the air, but he was certain he had heard something else. Something dangerous. He rolled to his feet and listened intently. There was nothing. He stooped and groped in his bag for flint and tinder.

He heard the noise again. It was a thump. Like a heavy footfall. It was only a few feet away. Terror gripped Tau, and he struck the flint with a desperate panic.

In the flicker of the spark, Tau saw a man's face. Captured in that brief instant was a visage of terror staring into his from only feet away. Wide eyes shone from a black face with a grimace of yellow teeth. The kindling failed to light, and blackness retook the jungle. Tau howled as a searing pain struck him in the leg.

Tau reached down to find a spear embedded in his right thigh. The blade was twisting and gouging as the unseen attacker tried to twist it free. Tau clutched the shaft, pinning it in place. He struggled to maintain his balance, but the pain was sapping his strength.

Ulrich struck sparks onto kindling, and a blaze of embers lit the scene. Visible in the firelight, the enemy stood: a warrior of Ghana, bedecked in gold with a broad leather shield on his back. Both hands were on a long spear that he struggled to free from Tau's flesh. His face was set in a rictus of anger, and his eyes blazed in the budding flame.

Also framed in that small light was Yael. She stood tall with bow drawn and arrow nocked. She released, and the missile leapt from her string and lanced into the Ghanan warrior's chest. The sharpened steel point punched through the man's ribcage, shattering bone and puncturing lung before coming to rest in his aorta. Blood rushed into the man's lungs, and he coughed, spraying a red mist as he fell backward. His hands released the spear shaft. The warrior was choking as his own heart pulsed blood into his throat. His eyes clouded with terror and he scrabbled at the wet ground. He pushed himself back to rest upright, sitting against a tree, gasping for the air that would not come as he died.

Ulrich added bits of dry wood to the fire he had started, and the light from the flames grew. Unable to stand anymore, Tau fell to one knee, still clutching at the spear. The blade was lodged deep in the muscle, and the steel glistened in the firelight. A trickle of blood escaped the wound to run down his leg onto his bare foot.

"Don't move that spear," Yael said.

She dropped her bow and knelt at Tau's side.

"Let me look at it. It could be blocking the flow of blood." She palpated along his leg.

"Lie down. You are moving too much," she ordered.

Tau moved slowly. He felt as though he were in a dream, his mind drowning in thick molasses. The pain, which had been so excruciating a moment ago, was beginning to ebb. He recognized the edge of shock, and he shook his head, trying to focus. His pulse raced, and he was breathing in short, quick gasps. He felt as though his heart were going to beat out of his chest.

Tau laid down at Yael's insistence. She cut through his pants with a knife and exposed Tau's leg from groin to ankle. She had Ulrich steady the spear while she felt for pulses, first in the groin, then behind the knee, and finally at the ankle.

"You're in luck," she said. "Your artery is intact. The blade must have missed it." She palpated the thigh carefully, looking for the swelling in the muscle that could indicate a broken blood vessel.

"No bones broken, either," she noted. She looked into Tau's face. "We can pull the spear out, but we must do it very carefully." Her deep brown eyes were calm, and her hands were steady.

"Slow your breathing," she instructed. "Focus on every breath. Count to four as you breathe in. Count to four as you breathe out. It will help your heart to relax."

Tau closed his eyes and tried to focus on his breathing. Counting helped clear his mind, but the pain, which had been dulled by shock, began to return.

"Steady the shaft Ulrich," she said, "and I will hold the leg in place. On the count of three pull straight up. Keep the pressure steady, and do not twist or wiggle the blade."

When Ulrich pulled the spear out, Tau felt a horrible, excruciating pain, like his leg was being pulled apart. Mercifully, his consciousness faded into blackness.

When Tau awoke, Yael was bandaging his leg. She sacrificed a yellow linen dress to make bandages. Their blankets were wet from the clean water Ulrich poured over the leg to flush out contagion. Soon the thigh was tightly wrapped, and Yael's hands held pressure on the wound. She saw Tau was awake, and she smiled.

Tau blinked to clear the fog from his mind.

"How do you learn so much medicine again?" Tau asked. "Just from helping around the inn?"

"And I read all the books in the library," Yael said. "That includes Galen."

Tau stared at her, and she grinned nervously and continued. "I've also seen the dissection of two pigs. Last year a philosopher came to Saldae and performed surgery in the arena. I learned that the blood is created in the liver," she pointed at his abdomen, "mixes with air in the lungs, and then is pumped to the body by the heart. The blood carries the life essence into the extremities where it diffuses into feet and hands. If the stream is broken, the vital essence leaves the legs, and they die. That is why you must preserve the arterial flow."

Tau felt comforted by her confidence.

"Your leg will be safe unless the miasma enters it and causes a pollution," she added.

"Then what happens?" Tau asked.

"Then contagion can enter the body. If the leg becomes red, warm, swollen, or oozes pus, you must immediately open the wound, pour wine to clean the contagion, and drink a cup of colostrum, the first milk from a mother's breast."

"And if that fails?" Tau asked. He remembered the Roman camp after the siege of Sens, of the men under the surgeon's blades, of gangrenous amputated limbs thrown in stinking piles.

She shook her head. "Let's hope it does not come to that."

CHAPTER TWENTY-FIVE

They retraced their steps through the fetid jungle. Their clumsily blazed path guided them out, and by the time they reached the grassy plain, dawn was breaking. Tau noticed, with relief, that the young warrior's body no longer lay across the trail head.

Bereft of their mounts, their ability to cover ground was a mere fraction of what it had been. For Tau, walking was pain. Dull throbs of agony pulsed from his wounded thigh. Placing weight on the limb turned the dull pain into a sharp lance. Ulrich threw his arm around Tau's shoulders and half-carried him as they hobbled along the beaten path.

Tau's mind was muddled by pain. The short distance they crossed left him exhausted. All he wanted was to lie down. He wanted to sleep and wished, that when he awoke, the pain would be gone.

"We are too slow and too vulnerable in the open," Ulrich said.

"You're right. If we come across another hunting party, we will be defenseless," answered Yael.

"We need a plan," Ulrich grunted.

They stood on the edge of the rolling fields of the savanna. Tall grass bent in the gentle wind, and the yellow sun rose into a dusting of high clouds. To the west, the full moon set in opalescent brilliance. The hum of insect life pervaded the air. To the north, Tau could just see the moving figures of a herd of antelope, their saber-like horns bobbing as they jogged along a shallow ridgeline. The sunlight hurt his head, and he shut his eyes tight against the pain. Another wave of agony rolled from his leg, and he clenched his teeth to keep from whimpering aloud.

Tau felt something wet and soft on his ankle. He looked down to find that Loki was licking him gently. The dog's wide brown eyes were filled with sympathy.

"Could we wear disguises?" Ulrich asked.

"We can't, not convincingly, but he can." Yael pointed at Tau. "If we can make him look like a Ghanan lord, we could pass as his slaves," she suggested.

Ulrich shrugged and growled his assent. Tau opened his mouth to speak, but only a groan came out. He tried to focus his mind on something other than the pain. He failed.

Yael had kept the clothes from the Ghanan warrior that ambushed them in the jungle. She had washed the blood from the buffalo leather vest. The man's loose trousers were made from an unfamiliar type of yellow cloth that was mercifully soft. Yael believed it was palm fibers. Over vest and trousers went a loose garment, intricately fashioned from yellow, black, and red strips of silk, the colors making a repeating pattern of rectangular and triangular designs.

"This is a kente," Tau muttered, recognizing the item.

"It was in the warrior's pack," said Yael, gently.

"The colors all have meanings. Yellow is for wealth, black for a mature spirit, and red represents sacrifice," Tau remembered.

Tau rubbed the cloth between his fingers and tried to recall the pattern his father had worn. He thought it had much blue to its design. His mother had worn a deep and brilliant purple.

They dressed Tau in the kente and over it hung three necklaces of heavy gold, intricately carved with geometric patterns. The mass of these was impressive, and Tau suspected that each could have bought a warhorse in Rome or paid rent on a large house for a year.

No Ghanan warrior would go abroad without spear and shield, so Yael fashioned slings and strapped both to Tau's back. The spear proved too long to move easily, so Ulrich chopped several feet from it with his axe. The leather shield was chased with leopard skin, decorating it in the yellow and black patterns, but was mercifully light. Tau was grateful to be shorn of his heavy chainmail.

Yael used a camelhair blanket as a robe and unstrung her bow, using it as a walking staff. Ulrich, meanwhile, was more difficult to disguise.

"His armor," Tau said. "Isn't that a bit obvious?"

Ulrich's heavy armor was made of interlocking horizontal segments of case-hardened steel. Lorica segmentata is what the Romans called the cuirass. The hot-forging process left the dark metal stained and blued into liquid patterns that flowed across its surface. No two segments were identical. The steel ran from shoulder to shoulder and neck to waist. His muscled arms were bare while leather strips bearing steel medallions hung down to protect his groin and upper legs.

Yael considered him. "He looks like a Roman," she noted.

"A Roman with an axe," Tau whispered.

Ulrich hefted his axe and narrowed his eyes.

"Odin himself, along with Jesus and Jupiter as battle-brothers, could not force me to remove this armor," he growled.

Yael looked at Tau anxiously.

"We'll have to chance it," Tau said.

Yael looked away. "We have to keep moving," she said.

They headed west. The cow path merged with others and soon turned into a well-traveled road. Merchants, their horses loaded with grain and wares, ambled in both directions. Tau's disguise worked. With Tau in the garb of a Ghanan noble, none questioned their passage. Speaking to travelers revealed that this road was the main trade route between Ghana in the west and the smaller empire of Gao in the east.

The weather was fair. Yael bought fresh fruit and meat from travelling vendors. The pain in Tau's leg was getting worse. When they camped for the night Yael removed and washed the dressing before rebandaging the wound, but Tau slept fitfully. The wound itself had begun to scab over, but the skin around the wound began to feel warm and tight. Chills and sweating racked Tau's dreams, and when he woke in the morning, he found that a purulent yellow pus was seeping from the wound, soaking his loose cloth trousers.

Of the rest of that journey Tau remembered very little. The fever cooked his brain, and his vision narrowed to a black tunnel. His breath caught in gasps of pain and sweat ran from him in rivers. He recalled Yael bringing flask after flask of water, but he still felt thirsty. She probed and drained the wound, but the pain only grew. They walked on and on, but for how long he was not sure. He hallucinated then, seeing Ima standing before him, but no matter how far he walked he could never catch her.

Perhaps it was the next night that Tau awoke lying on the ground. Ulrich had covered him with leather blankets. He shivered. He felt cold but sweat dripped off him. His wound was unbandaged, and the pus was copious and tinged with blood. The leg felt hot to the touch. Loki leaned against Tau, comforting him with his warmth. Thor licked at the open wound. Tau tried to push the dog away, but he was weak, and the dog was insistent. Thor continued his licking, urgently cleaning the wound as Tau lay in a delirious stupor.

Ulrich and Yael were close in counsel nearby. They sat around a small fire that flickered against the evening sky. The sunset painted the world a dozen shades of brilliant ochre. Tau gazed into the sky, and his mind felt far away.

"The merchant said we are still one hundred miles from Koumbi Saleh," Yael said.

"We don't know if that is accurate," Ulrich responded.

"It is the best we have to go on," Yael answered.

"Tau will never make it that far," said Ulrich.

"We have to do something," Yael said.

"We haven't seen a real town since Abalessa. Nothing that would have a healer with medicines that you don't have," pointed out Ulrich.

"Koumbi Saleh is still our best bet then," Yael said.

"We need a horse," said Ulrich.

"Yes," Yael agreed.

"They have horses," Ulrich said. He indicated a Ghanan hunting party that camped nearby.

"That is true," said Yael.

"But they will not sell them to us," said Ulrich.

"What are you suggesting?" Yael asked.

"We could kill them and take their horses," said Ulrich.

"There are eighteen of them. All warriors. Spearmen and archers," Yael noted.

"Do you have a better idea?" asked Ulrich.

"We have gold. Are we sure that they will not sell? We could try and barter with them," said Yael.

"We are not Ghanans. They think that we are slaves. If they see gold, they will just kill us and take it," said Ulrich.

"What did you have in mind?" asked Yael.

"We wait until midnight. We attack them while they are sleeping.

If you go on the hill, you can rain arrows on them while I keep their attention." Ulrich sounded increasingly enthusiastic.

"I don't like this plan," said Yael.

"What don't you like about it?" asked Ulrich.

"They are not stupid. They are a Ghanan war party. They will set sentries," said Yael.

"So, we should try and barter instead? Walk up to them with gold in our hands?" Ulrich asked skeptically.

"If they draw weapons, we're just back to where we started," said Yael.

"Then we kill them all?" Ulrich asked.

"If we have to," said Yael.

"Alright. We will try it your way. But you go up on the hill and ready your bow. I will go to their leader. If they do not cooperate, you know what to do."

Ulrich and Yael moved off until the sound of their footsteps faded into the soft crackle of flame from the campfire. A small bird perched in the thorny tree above Tau. It cooed into the gathering dusk, its high notes sounding lonely on the windswept plain.

The noise of laughter reached Tau ears. The laughter was from men. Many men. It was mocking and mixed into the laughter were insults. The words were in Soninke, but Tau could not decipher them. His fever-addled brain mixed the syllables until they were unrecognizable.

Next came a harsher sound. A battle cry, laden with rage, howled beneath the heavens. Even in Tau's delirious state, he could recognize Ulrich's voice. The barbarian summoned his Germanic gods. He called for his ancestors to watch the slaughter of his enemies. The laughter stopped. Tau noticed that Thor and Loki were no longer at the campfire.

"Corpora," Ulrich commanded, and the snarling of the mastiffs could be heard.

The sounds of battle rose into the air. Tau heard blades clashing, wood splintering, and men screaming. The thrum of Yael's bow sounded again and again. Ghanan warriors howled in pain and anger, and the Soninke beseeched their gods and called to their mothers. Above it all came Ulrich's barbaric cries as he gave himself over to the joy of battle. His axe thumped as it tore into flesh and rasped as it ground against bone. The clink and snap of steel sounded as blades glanced and broke on Ulrich's hardened armor.

Soon, the noise faded, and Ulrich and Yael returned to the small fire. The stomp and snort of three horses followed. Thor's muzzle was wet with blood. Ulrich and Yael's hands picked Tau up and lay him across a horse. Fresh scratches and dents marred Ulrich's dark armor, and Yael's forearm was bleeding where the bowstring had chafed her skin. Steady hands fastened Tau securely to the horse with leather straps.

"Let's go," Ulrich said.

CHAPTER TWENTY-SIX

Tau was jostled by the galloping horse but was past caring. He remembered the stars wheeling overhead. He remembered the sun rising. He was still strapped to the saddle when Yael forced the nozzle of a flask into his mouth and begged him to drink. He remembered the sun setting: The celestial sphere turned, and the sun rose again. The horse was sweating, and its sides were heaving with effort, but still they rode on and on.

Finally, the walls of a sand-colored city loomed against a clear sky and then the walls swallowed him whole. An elderly woman touched his arm, touched his face. He was lying on a bed. His leg was unwrapped. A blade, bright shining in yellow candlelight, was drawn dripping from a jar of distilled spirits. A lancing pain erupted from his leg, and he tried to draw away. Yael's soothing voice was in his ear. Ulrich's steady hand was on his shoulder. A thick liquid, sickly sweet, was forced down his throat. The pain slowly faded. Tau fell blissfully asleep.

When Tau awoke, the fever had broken. His head throbbed, and his mouth tasted like cotton. He looked around.

He lay in a hanging cot that was suspended from the floor by sturdy bronze poles. The cot stood in a small room with sandstone walls and a white tile floor. Nearby, a wooden table was neatly laid with surgical tools and small pots of colored fluids and powders. An alembic bubbled pleasantly, distilling a clear liquid. Sunlight entered the room through a square window that was set high off the floor. The window's shutter was thrown open, and the outside sounds of a bustling marketplace flowed in.

Tau sat up to find that the pain in his leg was a mere fraction of what it had been. He was wearing a clean white linen shift, and he drew it up to find that the wound had been drained. A vertical incision marked the bottom edge of the jagged wound left by the spear's tapered head. A clear yellow fluid seeped from the incision, but there was no pus. The swelling had reduced. The redness was gone. The leg was no longer hot to the touch.

Tau found that he was both ravenously hungry and painfully thirsty. He swung himself out of the cot and steadied himself against the bronze poles as he found his feet. He felt weak, but he could stand. A single wooden door led out of the room, and he went to it, pulling it open by its copper handle. This led to a narrow hallway pierced by high windows. Three other doors opened from this passageway. Tau hesitated. The hallway was quiet.

The sound of footsteps came from the next room, then the door opened. A small woman stood in the threshold. She looked to be fifty or sixty years old with coarsely wrinkled, black skin, but her eyes were bright and young. She wore a kente that was decorated in broad patches of blue, green, and purple. A silver band bound her graying hair.

"You're awake," she noted. She spoke in Soninke.

"Where am I?" Tau asked.

"Koumbi Saleh," she said. "And in my home. I am a healer. My name is Newma."

Tau hesitated. He had more questions, but he did not know where to begin.

"I imagine you are very hungry and very thirsty," she said.

Tau nodded.

"Come this way." She beckoned.

Newma led the way down the hall. She walked very slowly, so that Tau could keep up. He felt extremely weak, and he put a hand against the wall for support. They turned the corner at the hallway's end and entered a broad entryway. Two large wooden tables filled the room and were set with low benches. A double-door led out to a stone-paved street, which could be seen through square windows.

"Go ahead and take a seat," Newma said, indicating the benches, then she turned toward an interior door that opened off the side.

"Hallasoh," Newma called. A girl appeared. Her dark hair hung to her waist, and she wore a neat dress of yellow. "Bring our guest some food, if you please. A loaf of the dark bread and a bowl of the soup and a cup of the diluted wine. Thank you." The girl bowed in acknowledgement and turned away.

Newma turned back to Tau. "Hallasoh is my granddaughter," she explained, "and a good girl, to spend so much time helping an old healer."

The food was brought, and Tau consumed ravenously. The soup was thin, made with reeds and chicken bone, but it felt like ambrosia to his starving body. The bread softened in the soup, and Tau washed the meal down with the thin wine.

"Let me see that leg," Newma ordered when he had finished.

She came around the table and helped Tau straighten his injured leg to rest it on the bench. She inspected it closely, palpating the clean tissue about the wound with both hands.

"It had become badly infected," she said. "I was forced to reopen the wound to release the contagion and allow the miasma to depart your body. Your sanguine humor was also grossly out of true, although we were able to relieve much of that imbalance with the same procedure. It is best now to leave the wound open to allow the good air to penetrate the wound and complete the flushing of the harmful miasma. The skin will close again within the week."

"Thank you," Tau said.

"Your gratitude is unnecessary." She stood. "Your friends paid me well. Perhaps too well, but they insisted."

"Where are my friends now?" he asked.

"I believe that they are out spying on the town," she said placidly.

Tau froze. Spying? Had he heard her correctly? He stared wide-eyed at the healer, but Newma's face was impassive. She held up a placating hand.

"Before you speak, allow me to tell you that they claim your name is Mbaneh and they claim they are your slaves. Strange slaves, to carry foreign currency and know nothing of our customs or etiquette." Her eyes held Tau's gaze. "I am no fool, but it is not my duty to investigate suspicious travelers. My duty is to life and to health. You may tell me your purpose, or you may not, as you choose."

Tau nodded, feeling a wash of relief. "Thank you," he said. "For now, let me say that while I was born in Koumbi Saleh, I have been away for some time and return now as a traveler."

Newma held Tau's gaze but said nothing. Just then Tau heard a familiar growl, and Thor appeared in the doorway. The dog sniffed the air intently as he approached. He brushed aside Tau's welcoming hand and inspected the injured leg with a professional eye. He sniffed the wound gravely, appeared satisfied with what he found, and nuzzled Tau's hand to receive a scratch behind the ears. Ulrich and Yael, laden with packs and with Loki at their heels, entered next.

"You are awake!" Ulrich exclaimed. His face was bright with pleasure. In two steps he crossed the room and lifted Tau bodily from the bench in a fierce embrace. His eyes were wet, and he brushed at the unexpected tears with his free hand as he steadied Tau with the other.

"How are you feeling?" Yael asked.

"Weak," Tau admitted, "but the pain is gone, and the fever seems to be broken."

Newma spoke. "The happiest part of my day is seeing a healthy patient, but I must go check on my other patients. If there is anything else you need, call out to Hallasoh."

"Thank you," Tau said.

She bowed and walked from the room, her steps as quick and sure as one half her age. Tau turned back to his friends.

"We have gathered much information about Ghana and the war," Yael said in a low voice, "but there is still much more to learn. Can you walk?"

Tau could, although he insisted on donning the kente, pulling on his sturdy boots, and strapping his familiar swords about his waist before leaving the house of healing. They exited to the street. The house was on a busy thoroughfare, and they could hear the bustle of a marketplace away to the left, while to the right, the center of Koumbi Saleh lay quiescent under the noonday sun.

Tau gazed out over the city. His city. The city of his youth and of his people. Koumbi Saleh was beautiful. Within the embrace of a circular wall spread an elegant expanse of sand-colored buildings that sparkled as if lit by tiny pieces of glass. Narrow streets ran between tall houses. Sprouting from the clustered homes were tall towers, yellow stone shining like gold in the bright sun. There stood the green-painted temple of Asase Yaa, the black-draped tower of Bida, and the great double-spired golden temple of Nyame.

A quarter mile away lay the royal palace, its domed roof rising above all the others and its grounds bordered by the sacred grove. Tau remembered running through that grove as a child, climbing its trees, and being scolded by the palace priests. He could still see the airy chambers of the palace, laden with sedans and busy with servants, and hear his mother's voice, singing through the hallways while Tau played with the other palace children.

Tau felt a curious sense of disconnection. Of unreality. The towers were shorter than his young mind remembered them; the colors less vivid. His child's eye had believed the spires towering into the very heavens. The palace he remembered as a veritable world, a microcosm of its own, and the town an endless paradise of mystery and wonder. Reality, he realized, could never match the expectations of youth.

"So," he said, forcing his thoughts to the present, "what have you discovered?"

"Koumbi Saleh is a tinderbox," Yael said. "The people are unhappy. The marketplaces buzz with discontent, and the guards are nervous. Violence is liable to erupt at any moment."

"Why?" Tau asked.

Just then, they got their answer.

CHAPTER TWENTY-SEVEN

A commotion arose from the marketplace. Angry shouting disrupted the normal buzzing hum of trade, and a troop of guards hurried by at a jog. Tau, Yael, and Ulrich followed the noise.

All regular activity in the plaza had ceased. A mob was gathering, and merchants hastily packed their wares. The pain in Tau's thigh was stabbing whenever he placed weight on it, so he unstrapped his left-hand sword and leaned on the scabbarded weapon as a crutch. He hurried to follow Ulrich and Yael as they sought a vantage over the crowd.

A ring of guards protected unseen activity about a set of stairs at the west end of the plaza. The Ghanan guards were in leather vests and brandished shields and spears. They fended off the crowd that pressed in from all sides.

From behind the warriors, a tall pole was being hoisted. A rope was tied to the top of the pole, and from it dangled a tattered set of yellowed rags. At first, Tau thought the pole just held a ragged collection of clothes. He stared, uncomprehending, until he realized that he was looking at a corpse.

Dangling within the rags was the body of a young man; his face was emaciated, and his limp arms and legs were wasted. A swollen tongue protruded from chapped lips. Empty eye sockets stared from a broken face, frozen in a rictus of pain. Clotted blood filled the spaces where his fingers and toes had once been. The pole was set upright and the body swayed there, a grotesque puppet, dangling before an open sky of the clearest blue. The building beneath the corpse bore a decorative façade, and the chiseled stone beneath the amputated toes seemed to flow like a swimming shore as the corpse danced languid in the open air.

"That man's name was Tana," said a voice. "He was a priest at the temple of Asase Yaa." Newma had silently joined the three companions. Pain showed behind her dark eyes.

An official of the royal house came forward. He climbed onto a stage between the corpse and the ring of guards. He was short and thin, perhaps in his early twenties, and wore a linen tunic. He was bedecked in golden jewelry and had a gem-encrusted short-sword strapped a little too high about his waist. He held his chin high and cleared his throat imperiously.

"This man," the official declared, "dared to challenge our God-Queen Kansoleh, and for his treason, he has received an appropriate punishment. Let him stand as a lesson to any who would defy the true lords of Ghana." He bore a self-satisfied smirk, and Tau felt an overwhelming desire to hit him.

"God-Queen?" Newma spat. "Kansoleh goes too far."

A woman walked through the crowd. She was very pretty, with long black hair bound away from a gentle face. She wore a green dress, and four small children followed close behind her. The crowd parted for her and she stopped two paces short of the circle of guards.

"And how, exactly, did my husband challenge the queen?" the woman asked. Her voice was deep and strong. It carried well even over the muttering crowd—a crowd that quivered with energy. Tau glanced around. Faces were fixed in states of tension. Pupils dilated, pulses raced, people's weight shifted restlessly from foot to foot, and fists balled. The people were desperately close to riot and Tau felt afraid.

The official did not answer. He cowered behind his guards, and the woman turned her back on him. She held her head high and addressed the crowd. "You knew my husband," she said, pointing to the pole. "Tana was a good man. He cared for the poor, and he dedicated his life to the rites of Asase Yaa."

Her children clutched at her dress, fear and incomprehension written bold on their young faces.

The woman continued. "Now who will bring Asase Yaa's blessing to your harvest? Who will lead us in prayer for the rain, and when the water rises, who will pacify the spirits of the Niger?" Murmurs of agreement rose to greet her words. "My Tana died for this message, and in respect for his memory, I will speak it again. He merely said that Kansoleh is no god, and Asase Yaa did not bear her in her womb. This truth is self-evident, and it was the duty of Tana to speak the truth. Insisting these lies more loudly will not make them true." She turned to glare at the official, but he seemed cowed by the moral weight of her presence. His free hand fiddled with the jeweled scabbard of his sword.

She turned to walk away, and the official, finding his courage, leapt down from the stage and dashed after her. He yanked his sword free and slashed at her back, but the woman saw the blow coming. She turned and contemptuously slapped the weapon away. The sword fell to the ground, and the official stumbled. Before he could recover, the woman struck him with an open hand, the sound of the slap loud in the sudden silence. The ring of guardsmen rushed forward, and the woman backed away, gathering her children about her as the spearmen closed in.

"Seize her!" the official cried, brandishing his recovered weapon.

Then the first rock flew from the crowd. It was a loose piece of masonry, sharp and well thrown. It struck the official in the right eye. He screamed and clasped his free hand to his face. A trickle of blood and clear fluid escaped his clenched fingers.

More rocks were thrown. They rained down on the guards, who turned on the angry crowd with leveled spears. The townspeople panicked. Some, near the middle of the crowd, pushed forward, thinking to overwhelm the guards, but those facing the advancing spears tried to back away. Unable to flee and unable to fight, unarmed men and women were cut down by those vengeful blades. At the edges of the crowd, more sensible people fled down side streets. The bloody spears drove forward. They tore into terrified men and women who threw up their hands only to be pierced again and again by the implacable blades.

A rallying horn blared. The noise of marching sandals heralded the approach of more guards down the central causeway.

Newma's grabbed Tau's elbow. "This way," she said.

The direct route home was chaos, so Newma led the way through a serpentine maze of back alleys and twisting stone walls. Soon they stood at a dead end. The walls of tall buildings stood on three sides of a narrow alleyway. The massacre continued, and the screams of fleeing and dying townspeople drew closer.

"Lift that stone," Newma said, pointing at one of the street's paving stones. Ulrich bent to pry at the heavy slab.

"Watch the street," Newma warned, and Tau and Yael kept watch.

The paving stones were wide and flat. They were fitted closely together and mortared with a thick gray conglomerate. The stone Newma indicated was about three feet wide and two feet long, and alone of all the stones on the street had been skillfully cut from its binding mortar. Ulrich heaved it up on its edge to reveal a narrow tunnel. Without a backward glance, Newma dropped in. Yael was next. Thor and Loki were more hesitant, but the sound of heavy footsteps pounding up the street encouraged Ulrich to nudge Thor into the tunnel with a gentle boot, and Loki followed. The drop from the street was farther than Tau expected, and his thigh throbbed with pain when he landed. He edged forward to allow Ulrich to clamber down, and they were thrown into total blackness when Ulrich replaced the paving stone.

"Follow my voice," Newma commanded. As they edged forward, she began to explain.

"Incidents like this are becoming more and more common. The people are angry and Kansoleh, already unpopular, grasps for control with both fists. First, she reinstated the sacrifice of Bida, which may have some link to the old traditions, but greatly distresses those families forced to give up their virgin daughters. Next, she claims cannibalism is a part of the worship of Nyame. It is not, or at least has not been since primitive times. Then she declares this foolish war on the Garamantes, which deprives our merchants of the desert trade. Our entire economy depends on healthy trade, and without it the city stagnates. The merchant houses cannot pay their debts, and everybody suffers. In the wake of it all, she has the gall to insist that she is a god come to earth." Newma chuckled, "I can assure you that Kansoleh is human. I should know—I was her mother's midwife."

A spark flashed in the darkness. Newma stood with a lit oil lamp in her hands. In the light Tau could see that they had emerged into a darkened corridor with wooden walls. A low stone ceiling was an arms-length above their heads.

"We are beneath your house?" Yael asked.

"Quite right," Newma answered. She opened a wooden door to reveal an underground dormitory with two cots, a small table, a lamp, and a box stuffed with blankets, tunics, and leather sandals. More doors led off this corridor, presumably to similar rooms, and additional tunnels branched off in four directions, providing several escape routes from this small hideout.

"What is this place?" Ulrich asked suspiciously.

"I disapprove of the slave trade," Newma said flatly. "When slaves wish to escape their masters, I find ways to help them."

"Why are you telling us this?" Tau asked. "How do you know you can trust us?"

"Because," she answered, her eyes fixing him in the dim lamplight, "I recognize Emperor Kayode's son when I see him."

CHAPTER TWENTY-EIGHT

Tau opened his mouth to protest, but Newma held up a hand.

"Before anything else, I must explain what is going to happen next," she said. "When word gets to Kansoleh, she will send the royal guard from the palace to seek the instigators of the riot. Since those instigators are likely already dead, they will seek scapegoats. The guards will pound down the doors of all houses within a convenient radius of the square. Any who fail to bribe them will be dragged out of their homes and will be killed in the street. The death will ripple outward, and anybody caught outside their homes will die. The violence will continue well into the night. By tomorrow morning, there will be a dozen new poles mounted in the square, and some minor official in Kansoleh's service will make a speech about how King Kabu or Goddess Kansoleh rescued us from a rebellion. Then things will be quiet for a week or two until the next riot."

"You three will stay hidden until it is safe to emerge," Newma ordered. She shifted her gaze to Thor and Loki, sitting patiently at their master's heels. "Can those animals stay quiet?" she asked.

"Silent," Ulrich promised.

Newma looked unconvinced. "It is more than your own skin that you risk. If you are discovered here, both I and my granddaughter will be killed, and slaves seeking freedom will have one less place to hide." She glanced at Ulrich's axe. "If you have any doubts, you should kill the beasts now."

"They will be quiet if I tell them to be quiet," he said firmly.

Newma shrugged.

"Come and help me lift one more stone, Ulrich. I feel old and tired today." She turned away.

"Tana was a friend," she said as she left, and her voice was sad.

"So, Newma knows who you are," Yael commented once the healer was gone.

Tau rested on a cot, massaging his thigh against the pain. Yael sat on the opposite cot, and Ulrich squatted on the floor, performing maintenance on his equipment. He methodically greased the joints of his segmented armor, forcing minute amounts of reduced animal fat into each intricate hinge and swivel. His busy industry reminded Tau to inspect his own weapons, and he unclasped his sword belt as he answered.

"I do not remember meeting Newma as a child," Tau said. To his chagrin there was a spot of rust on one of his blades. He rubbed at it experimentally to find with relief that it was only superficial. He had no vinegar or sand, so he attacked it with a rough wool cloth.

Yael sighed and drew up her pack. She carried two yew bowstaves, both in good order and kept unstrung to maintain the elastic recoil of the flexible wood. The bowstrings, made of finely woven camel sinew, rested curled in a small leather pouch. She kept them soaked with lanolin to keep out the damp. She checked each one then moved on to the arrows. She had two dozen of these, long and elegant in imitation of Roman fashion, with delicate bird's feathers as fletching and tipped with various bronze and iron heads she had managed to purchase on their travels. They were packed into a bulky quiver reinforced with wooden paneling and covered with a linen, drawstring bag. She removed and inspected each one before returning it to its case.

"She must have known your father then," she commented absently.

"Everybody knew my father. He loved this city," Tau answered. "It was his joy to walk the streets and address each of the shopkeepers by name. He told me that it was important for the people to know their leader."

Yael stopped her inspection to look up.

"I'm sorry about your father," she said.

Tau had not realized how much he had been driven by the desire to see his father again. He had heard the rumors that he was dead; warriors and travelers, Ghanans and Garamantes had all carried the news of how Kabu and Kansoleh had dethroned Kayode to rule the kingdom, but it had not felt truly real until now. The truth of his father's death was carried in Newma's face when she mentioned his name.

Tau gripped his sword's hilt.

"It is because of Kansoleh that my father is dead. Because of her, I was sold into slavery. Because of her, my childhood was spent on an oar beneath the cold sky rather than at my father's side. She killed Kayode, and now she and her son are killing my home. Koumbi Saleh is suffering, so for this city; for the Garamantes; for Tauda, Idir, and Idlis; for Abalessa and the Tuareg; and for me." His fist tightened on the pommel. "I will stop her."

"Yes, you will," came Ulrich's gruff voice. "And we will help you." Thor stirred in response to his master's energy, and Ulrich calmed him with a steady hand.

They stayed in Newma's dark hideout the rest of that long day. There was banging at the doors above when soldiers came to inspect the place in the evening, but they left soon after. New noises came in the night, the stomping of feet and the sounds of voices betrayed constant comings and goings. Hallasoh came into the cellar, bringing fresh bread and water, and assured them that all was well. In the morning, Newma invited the companions to join her upstairs.

She looked haggard. She had not slept. The infirmaries were filled with victims of the night's violence.

"It should be safe to go out," Newma told them. "Kansoleh has likely sated her blood lust by now."

"Let me help you with the wounded," Yael offered. "I have some experience with healing."

"I could use the help," Newma admitted. "I have some fractures that need setting, and I could use a steady hand."

"We can help too," Tau offered.

Newma gave him a skeptical look. "Do you have any experience with healing? No? You cannot help me. I have no use for unskilled brutes in my infirmary today. Why don't you help by getting out of the way?"

So, Tau and Ulrich stepped out the door.

The city was quiet. The populace was cowed by the violence that had so suddenly vomited itself upon them. Thor gave a warning growl, and they ducked into an alley to avoid a troop of soldiers that hurried by. The spearmen paid them no heed, looking grim as they patrolled the sullen town. Once they were gone, Tau and Ulrich moved on. Tau leaned on his scabbarded sword for support.

Doors and shutters were closed and barred. The plazas were deserted. They passed an alleyway that was splashed with blood. A rise in the road allowed a high place from which to view the royal palace, and Tau paused.

He gazed down on his childhood home. Shadowed figures moved among the sacred grove. Gold-bedecked guardians shifted restlessly at their posts. Tau stared for a long time, filled with a curious sense of detachment.

Ulrich gave his arm a nudge.

"Look there," he said. "To the east."

Tau lifted his gaze. Marring the clear horizon was a low cloud. As they watched, the cloud drifted closer. It was dust kicked up from thousands of feet, sign of an army on the move. The Ghanan army was returning home.

A flight of stone stairs rose to an outdoor landing nearby. Tau knocked on the house door, but no one stirred within, so he and Ulrich ascended to get a better view. From here, the dark shapes of men could be seen as a mass, moving purposefully across the rolling plain. The day was growing warm. Tau took a long pull from a clean water flask. He and Ulrich watched the army approach in silence.

Soon, the massive gilt doors of the palace swung open, and a royal procession appeared. A covered litter, carried by a dozen men, moved slowly through the palace grounds.

"Let's get closer. I wish to see our enemy," Tau said to Ulrich.

CHAPTER TWENTY-NINE

The Ghanan army was tired, hot, and dirty, but they were allowed no rest. The warriors stood on the parade ground while a stage and throne were laboriously assembled. Groomsmen tended horses. Sheltered awnings were erected for tribal war chiefs while servants brought them food and wine, but the warriors were forced to wait, swaying and exhausted, beneath the midday sun.

Horse drawn carts entered the city behind the army, bearing the plunder of war. Captured Garamante chariots rolled alongside wagons loaded with women, terrified children, and piles of the loot the battlefield had delivered. A crowd of townspeople began to gather, and Ulrich and Tau joined them. The people of Koumbi Saleh clustered and muttered, curiosity mixed with a still-sullen resentment.

Finally, Kabu and Kansoleh emerged from the royal litter. Tau recognized his half-brother. Kabu was now a tall, well-built teenager, but he still retained the fat, indulgent cheeks and petulant mouth of the small child Tau remembered. Kansoleh, Tau's stepmother, looked thinner and older than he remembered her. Her high cheekbones stood prominently above a proud sneer.

They climbed to the stage. At Kansoleh's direction Kabu sat on the single throne. He wore a silk robe of shimmering yellow cloth and a golden circlet on his cropped black hair. Kansoleh stood before him and held her hands up for silence. The muttering of the throng faded away.

Both Kabu and Kansoleh began to speak at once, interrupting each other. Each then fell silent and shot the other a look of annoyance. The crowd shifted uncomfortably.

Kabu began again.

"Warriors of my great nation," he said. He did not stand, and his weak voice did not carry well. It was a strain to make out his small words.

"We have won a great victory against the desert filth," he squeaked.

"We?" Tau heard a nearby warrior say. "Where was he at the Battle of the Sahel? I did not see him wielding a spear."

Already Kabu was losing his audience. Grumbling began to drown him out.

"Old Emperor Kayode would have been fighting on the front lines. He was a proper warrior," another warrior muttered.

Kabu's words were lost in the rising noise. He stopped talking and glared impotently at his army. He looked to his mother for support. She stepped forward.

"The next man who interrupts will be put to death," she called.

Her words had no effect. The hubbub grew in volume. Clearly these warriors had little fear of her.

"Put to death by who?" One warrior commented. "By your warriors? By us?"

"She doesn't know who's fighting for her!" called another.

An angry voice broke through the commotion.

"You are killing this city," the voice shouted. Tau turned to find the words came from a portly man in the green and blue of the merchant class. He had a belly like a hippo and held a tin speaking trumpet to his lips. He had climbed on top of a wooden cart.

"The Garamantes are vital to our livelihood," he roared, his face red with anger. "The wealth of Ghana relies on the desert trade, and you have crippled it. Who will carry our gold across the sands now? Will it be you? Or your spoiled whelp?"

Thor and Loki drew closer in as the mass of people shifted with restless energy.

Kansoleh must have realized she had lost control. She ignored the crowd and leaned off the stage to beckon to one of the war chiefs who stood nearby.

"Let's get out of here," Tau said. He and Ulrich began pushing through the crowd.

The violence came quickly. The tired warriors were still proud men, and they were loyal to their commanders. On the orders of the war chiefs the army advanced on the angered mob with leveled spears. Tau heard the screams, but he did not turn to watch. They broke from the mob and made their way back to Newma's home.

There was nothing more to learn in Koumbi Saleh. Tau had seen what he had come to see and was disheartened. It was time to leave. Yael detached herself from her medical work, and they gathered their supplies. They met in a corner of the entryway, increasingly crowded with the groaning wounded which overflowed from the packed infirmaries.

"There is nothing left for us here," Tau said, his soul oppressed. He felt as though the gloom of this city had infiltrated his heart.

"Where do we go?" Yael asked.

"Back to Abalessa," Tau decided.

"We would need camels or horses to try to cross the desert but can't afford any. We gave the last of our coin to Newma," Yael said. Bloodstains marred the front of her dress. She looked tired and jaded.

"And I won't ask Newma for the money back," Tau said. He looked around the busy room. "She needs it more than we do."

"The Ghanan army has horses," Ulrich said. "They can part with a few of them." His voice was hard. He hefted his axe and the honed edge of its blade gleamed in the slanting sunlight from the open window. Tau nodded.

They left to walk, wordless, through the paved streets. Sandstone towers loomed over the vacant markets. Anxious citizens hurried to and fro, arms laden with possessions. From somewhere behind them came the sound of shattering glass. A pillar of smoke wafted onto the street, casting a pall over the sun. A scream pierced the evening. Tau did not look back.

At the mustering grounds, slaves busily piled stolen wares into massive heaps. Hundreds of horses were loosely herded into a paddock, watched by a group of boys. Three guards stood before the captains' tent, but otherwise the scene was empty of enemy. The army was gone. There was blood on the grass where the mob had been. The stage held an empty throne.

Yael went to the horses. She picked three of the least tired ones and led them to the paddock gate. Two of the boys, nervous, moved to intercept her but a growl from Thor brought them up short. One ran into the town, and the other toward the guards' tent. Tau made no attempt to stop them.

Tau tried to help Yael and Ulrich with saddling and loading the horses, but he was hampered by his injured leg. He brought the horses a final bucket of water from a wooden trough instead.

The guards from the war-captains' tent took notice of them at last. They ran across the field.

Tau gazed at the warriors with no enmity, only fatigue.

"We are not your enemy," Tau called. "Let us pass."

"You're not an enemy?" The nearest snarled derisively. "You look like horse thieves."

"I suppose we are." Tau sighed. "But just let us go. Hasn't enough blood been shed today?"

"Release the horses, and we shall kill you quickly," sneered one of the guards.

Ulrich stepped forward. His axe was unlimbered and ready in his massive grip. Yael, busy with the horses, ignored the standoff.

"They are just soldiers, doing their duty," Tau observed.

"They are the enemy, and they are in the way," Ulrich responded.

Tau had no response, and Ulrich went to his grisly work. The Ghanan spears glanced impotently from his heavy steel armor. Ulrich's axe made a butcher's sound as he chopped into the men.

Tau gazed at his city—at Koumbi Saleh. Smoke rose as the riots spread. His mind wandered. Was a man guilty for following orders? He pondered that question. The world was replete with obedient men—the warriors of Ghana, the soldiers of Rome. As a soldier, one was not privy to the reasons or politics behind an order. A soldier's loyalty was to their honor, to their commander, and to their people.

Tau realized that he and Ulrich were blessed. They had strength but also the freedom to fight as they wished. Had the warriors of Ghana been given such a choice? They fought because it was expected of them, because they were proud to be warriors, because to do otherwise would bring shame to their families. In another life Tau may have been another such warrior, personal morality drowned, destiny swallowed in the greater tides of war.

Soon Ulrich's work was done. Wet blood dripped from his axe, and three fresh corpses littered the ground. The companions mounted their horses and rode north, and Tau tried to forget the screams.

CHAPTER THIRTY

The fresh air and open fields of the savanna began to restore Tau's spirits. Yael rode easily, guiding her horse next to his. The dogs, freed from the cramped city, loped behind while Ulrich scanned the horizon, keeping watch for any pursuit. Acacia trees rose from the tall grass. The calls of strange birds filled the air, and a moderate breeze kept the day pleasantly cool.

"I do not know if I can guide us all the way to Abalessa," Yael noted. She had a hand-drawn map spread before her in the saddle. "Not in one go. Not without the endurance of camels or a train of supplies. But Newma told me about a nearer Garamante town, one closer to the edge of the desert." Reaching into her saddle bag she withdrew a star chart inked on very thin silk. She overlaid this chart upon the first map, studying it intently.

Ulrich rode next to her, blank expression on his face as he stared at the charts and figures. He gave up and turned to Tau.

"You look disconsolate, friend," he said.

Tau shook his head. "That was not the Koumbi Saleh I remember. That was not my father's Ghana."

"We'll tear it down so that you can restore it," Ulrich said.

"How?" Tau asked.

"I have a plan," Ulrich answered enigmatically.

They rode across the savanna for two days, making comfortable progress across the rolling plains. A clean stream filled their canteens and marked the transition to the drier Sahel. They rested for a day, sleeping through the daylight hours to transition to nighttime travelling. Yael felled a wandering antelope with her bow, and they filled saddlebags with smoked cuts of sweet, gamey meat. After two more nights of travelling they stood on the edge of the great Sahara Desert.

"How far to this city?" Tau asked. "What is it called?"

"The map says it is called Araouane," Yael said.

"Araouane, then," Tau responded.

"One hundred Roman miles," Yael responded.

Tau gazed into the vast emptiness. The dusty plain stretched from horizon to horizon. The sun's glow was just fading in the west, scattering a blue hue across the edge of the world like the shore of a celestial ocean. The stars began to emerge, filling the blackness with a million-million tiny points of winking, glittering, waiting light.

Vertigo gripped Tau with sudden violence. He was struck with the sensation that the world had inverted. Instead of standing on the edge of a desert, he was clinging, upside-down, to a tenuous earth. He was suspended above a bottomless well of night. He looked up, or what felt like down, into the abyss, terrified that gravity would release, and he would plunge, falling forever, into that star-strewn blackness, consumed, forgotten by all but the sky itself.

A painful swallow pushed against the lump that rose in his throat. A ghost of wind, whispering with a soft hiss of sand, breathed from the desert's open mouth.

"One hundred miles is a five-day journey," Ulrich said. "We have only barely water enough."

"If we lose our way or if there is no water at Araouane, it will be a one-way trip," Yael replied. "Certain death."

Their voices sounded small, far from where Tau balanced, on the precipice between earth and sky, between grassy plain and empty desert.

Unbidden, Tau's horse took a step forward, and then another. It whinnied impatiently as it moved down the slope toward the rocky Ténéré, "the loneliness."

Ulrich and Yael exchanged a shrug. They brought their horses to a walk and followed. They passed from the green earth and into desolation.

Travelling during the night was tiring, but the daytime was the hardest part. The horses suffered under the harsh desert sun. The animals alternated between lying down from exhaustion and standing to avoid the heat of the ground. Yael did her best to comfort them with damp cloths on their parched faces and rationing the limited water as best she was able. Four nights of wearing journey dragged by.

On fifth night, by Yael's calculations, Araouane was only ten miles away. They saddled the horses and stowed their makeshift tent. They had made good time, but this would be the hardest leg of the journey, as the Ténéré gave way to a great erg. The dune sea stood before them, blinding sand blowing in the strong desert wind. They had just run out of water.

The horses hated the soft sand. Their hooves sank deep into the shifting, treacherous grains. The companions dismounted to save the horses' strength and led the mounts on foot. They kept to the crests, braving the wind to avoid the blinding sand that flowed through the troughs. Yael held her chart before her, sharp eyes fixed on the guiding stars.

After some time, Tau noticed the horizon was changing. In the east, the stars were disappearing. One by one the stars winked out. He stared for a long while, perplexed as the blackness quickly grew. The wind died, and the night fell utterly silent. The only noise was the shuffling of foot and hoof across the flowing sand. A dark shadow stretched up to consume the lower arm of the milky galaxy. With horror, Tau realized what was coming.

"Sandstorm," he whispered.

Ulrich swore. There was little they could do. They wrapped protective cloths around the horses' faces and over the dogs' mouths and eyes. There was nowhere to hide. They crouched in place, hunkering down against the expected blow.

With a roar the storm struck, shrieking and bellowing in a cataclysm of perfect fury. The blowing sand slammed into their bodies as they clung together, leaning into its terrible force. The horses whined as the abrasive sand tore at their hides. Tau cringed from the pain. The sand found every uncovered nook and crevice in his clothing and scoured his skin. Tau's face, the back of his neck, and his unprotected wrists and hands were flayed by the hot, dry torrent. He clenched his eyes shut and focused on his breathing, taking slow deep breaths through the doubled cloth wrapped tightly over his nose and mouth.

The storm seemed to go on for hours. Time was meaningless in that blind, confused world of pain and noise, waiting, waiting for the storm to pass. Tau felt Loki's comforting weight as the dog whimpered, leaning against his side.

After an eternity, the force of the blast lessened, then, as suddenly as it had come, it was gone. They arose, blinking, into a darkened, altered world.

A haze of dust hung in the still air. Visibility was low. The dunes had shifted, creating an alien landscape. The stars were lost in the haze, and the moon had dipped below the horizon and faded from sight.

Tau brushed sand from his clothes with raw, chapped hands and followed Yael as she inspected the horses. Two were still lying nearby, weary but alive, but the third was nowhere to be seen. After a search, Yael found it halfway down the slope. It was dead, and partially buried by a shift of sand. The cloth meant to protect its face was gone, and the animal's nose and mouth were filled with sand. The poor beast, suffocating as the grains filled its airway, must have panicked and bolted, only gaining a few paces before it collapsed. Tau and Ulrich rescued what supplies they could.

Eventually, the dust cleared enough for Yael to make out the stars, and they moved on. On and on, through the shifting sand, leading tired mounts they trudged, heads heavy, boots encumbered. They were chafed and parched, burdened and oppressed, but they marched on. Tau's wounded thigh ached with every painful step. Thirst clawed at his mind.

Yael, leading the way, saw the town of Araouane first. Cresting a rise, she breathed with relief, and Tau hurried to join her.

A ridge of rock opened into a dusty plateau, sheltering a small stone village perched above the sandy wasteland. Tau gazed at the town that would be their salvation, relief washing over him. A small grove of hanza trees lined the worn rock path into the village, their stunted forms hazy in the wan, pre-morning light. Tau, Yael, and Ulrich moved, dazed, across the frozen space to pass into Araouane's paved streets.

There were no lights. Silence greeted their passage. A dozen stone houses stood in a loose assemblage. No life stirred the still, heavy air. The town seemed abandoned. A well marked the center of the town. Tau shuffled toward it.

There was a wooden bucket and a frayed rope at the well. There was no pulley or winch. Tau held the bucket in his hands, his heart heavy with apprehension. Carefully, he lowered the bucket into the well, saving the old, threadbare rope from the rough-carved stone of the well's rim. No splash met the bucket's arrival at the bottom of the well. Instead, there was a hollow thud as the bucket thumped onto dry sand. He brought the bucket up, dry and empty. Tau felt sick. He passed a swollen tongue over parched lips.

"Let us look through these houses," Ulrich croaked. "Perhaps we will find something useful."

One of the horses, too tired to stand any longer, lowered itself to the ground with a long sigh. It never stood again.

Tau checked the nearest house to find it empty. Two living rooms were joined by a doorway hung with dry, yellow, palm fronds. The sandstone walls were decorated with drawings of dromedaries, oceans, and snow-capped mountains. Bedframes, stark and bare, inhabited desolate rooms. Out back was a small pen where animals had likely been kept, but nowhere was there any sign of life. Whoever had abandoned this place had taken everything of value.

The next place Tau wandered into was as empty as the first. It had been a storehouse. All that was left was a dozen sacks of white, glistening salt.

"Over here," came Ulrich's voice, echoing as it passed between the hollow, windless spaces.

Tau exited the storehouse. The horse on the ground had stopped breathing. Its companion was wavering where it stood, gaunt, starved, and half conscious.

Ulrich had found a storefront. A large table dominated the center of the small room and narrow shelves filled the walls. Most of the shelves were bare, but a few held bulging leather flasks. Dark liquid dripped from Ulrich's mouth. He passed Tau a flask, wiping his mouth as he did.

The flask was full of wine—sweet, cloying wine made from the sap of the date tree. It had been concentrated for transport, intended to be mixed with water before it was consumed. It was not meant to be drunk without dilution. It was strong and thick. Tau's throat spasmed against its bitter taste and sharp tang of alcohol. His chapped lips burned on the caustic liquid, and his empty stomach turned. He took a long, deep drink. Yael entered the shop, and he passed the flask to her without a word. Her face turned with distaste at its sickly smell, then with a shrug, she drained the container.

The last horse died that morning. Yael tried to persuade it to drink the wine, which was the only potable liquid they could find, but it turned its head away from the sweet, heavy drink. After a few hours, it stood, staggered heavily, and then fell. The sun rose. Its harsh rays burned inexorably into a desolate world.

    They slept. Sleep came upon Tau unexpectedly, and he dozed sitting against the empty shop wall—still thirsty, still hungry, and holding a full flask of the concentrated wine in his nerveless hand. He did not dream.

CHAPTER THIRTY-ONE

That night Tau was the first to wake. His head throbbed, and his tongue was thick. He choked down bites of dry, smoked antelope as Yael and Ulrich awoke, groggy and dazed.

Yael took a swig of the sweet wine, swishing it about her mouth to flush away the sourness of sleep.

"Come with me," she said. "I want to show you something."

She left the shop and crossed the street. The night was cold. A constant, bitter wind blew across the rocky plateau, whistling between the houses. Tau shivered. She led the way into another small building, built similarly of tan stone and with a small, low doorway. Yael lit an oil lamp against the dark within.

They were in a small, square room that was filled with scrolls and parchment. Honeycomb shelving lined the walls, each compartment filled with a scroll, and tables were scattered with empty ink pots and reed pens. One of the shelves had fallen down, and parchment, faded and yellow, littered the floor.

Yael knew what she was looking for. She went to a shelf against the wall and selected a scroll, unrolling it on the nearest table. She weighted down its corners with clay weights, forcing the curled paper flat. Tau took the lamp and leaned closer.

The parchment bore a network of tracery. A spider's web of inked lines unraveled across its surface. Words in Berber were written in an elegant, flowing hand.

"It's a map," Tau said.

"A chart," Yael corrected. "See these figures? They refer to which stars to follow in which seasons. These numbers indicate the steepness of slopes, and here you can see reference markers to known landmarks with distances for each of the various caravan routes."

"This must be where we are," Tau said, pointing to a spot marked with a familiar name. "Araouane."

"Yes," Yael responded. "Araouane lies on a caravan route to the salt mines at Taoudenni." She tapped another spot on the map. "And here is Abalessa."

Her finger hovered very far away.

"How far is that?" Tau asked.

Yael sighed. "Almost five hundred miles."

A long silence hung over the room. They would never make it that far.

After some time, the silence was broken by a strange noise from the street. They left the building to find Thor and Loki tearing into the dead horse. Ulrich was sitting complacently nearby, looking tired.

Tau realized that the dogs were drinking the animal's blood.

"Of course!" he said. He rushed to find an empty flask. Returning, he held the vessel to the ragged gash the dogs had ripped in the beast's side. They stepped aside to allow Tau access, clotting blood and strips of viscera hanging from their reddened jaws.

Tau did what he could to get the seeping blood into the flask, but it was coagulated and thick. By using his hand, he was able to half-fill the leather container. He lifted it and hesitated. He held the flask to his lips for a long moment. Ulrich and Yael watched apprehensively. Finally, he tipped his head back and drank.

The blood was thick and salty. It tasted harshly metallic and went down only with effort. He took another experimental sip, and quite suddenly, vomited.

He did not wretch for long. His stomach was already close to empty anyway. He wiped his mouth, and Yael offered the flask of thick, too-sweet wine. Tau took a grateful swig to clear the taste of vomit from his mouth.

"I was afraid of that," Ulrich said. "The blood is too salty. The horse was dehydrated when it died. The dogs might be able to handle it, but we cannot." He shook his head and took a drink from his wine flask. Swaying slightly, he climbed to his feet.

Together, the three returned to the library and studied the chart that Yael had found. With a fresh look at the map, Tau noticed something else.

"What is this?" he asked, placing a finger on a small blue circle. The blue circle was not far from the black dot of Araouane.

Yael, also noticing the small marking for the first time, focused on it. "It says 'Eff Adrar,' which roughly translates to 'mountain shelter.'"

"How far is that?" Tau asked.

Yael consulted the scale on the edge of the chart, estimating the distance with her fingers. "It's about twenty miles away."

Tau stared at that blue circle. He tried to convince himself that there would be salvation there. He scanned the map, finding another blue circle, although this one was much farther away.

"And what does this say?" he asked.

"That says 'Air Oasis,'" she said.

Tau breathed out slowly. Oasis. Water. Blue must indicate water. It had to.

"We should try and make it to Eff Adrar," he said.

Yael shrugged. "There's no guarantee that place will be any better than this one," she said.

"Yes, but..." he stared at the map again. "The dot is blue."

Ulrich chuckled. His breath was sour with wine. "Might as well try. What the hell else is there to do?" he asked. He took another deep swig.

Yael gazed at him. "How much wine do we have?"

"I took inventory this morning," he said. "There are six flasks of this size." He held up his half-full leather container. "Each approximately equivalent to, or a bit more than, a Roman sextarius. That gives us a total of between one, and one and a half congii of concentrated wine."

Tau did the math in his head. "That is enough liquid for about two days travel on light rations," he concluded.

"Or a bit more," Ulrich replied, nodding.

Tau thought about that. The problem with the wine was that it was concentrated. It had been intentionally fortified for storage and transport. The Romans and Garamantes always diluted their wine, often at ratios as high as four or five to one. Mixing the wine with water both sanitized dirty water and protected one from becoming too drunk. Two days of drinking nothing but thick, concentrated wine would be awful. They would be drunk and thirsty and stumbling on their feet. But it might keep them alive.

The night was almost half over. They took some time to rest and repack bags, lightening the load where possible. When he was done, Ulrich returned to obsessively cleaning and inspecting his weapons and armor. The dogs, bloated on blood and fresh meat, rested heavily at the house's threshold.

Once Tau finished stowing his gear, there was little more for him to do. In his thirst, he had drunk heavily of his daily wine ration, and his head swam. He stepped into the empty street. The wind had died, and the stars blazed across a moonless sky. A low stone wall marked the edge of the town, and Tau rested on it, gazing up at the brilliant stars and allowing his mind to wander.

He strayed far from this place, remembering a wintery German field and the feeling of peace that came as a battle joined. He dreamed of a full, warm meal in his belly, friends at his side, and a woman with yellow hair.

Tau felt a soft hand on his shoulder and turned. Yael was there. He shifted to make space, and she sat beside him on the wall. The moon had risen over the horizon, and it illuminated Yael's calm face with its opalescent glow.

"I never tire of looking at the stars," she said. The smooth skin of her hand brushed against Tau's, and he did not pull away. His heart beat faster.

"Ursa Major," she said, pointing. "One of my favorites."

She pointed out what constellations were visible and told the story of each one. There were images of lost heroes emblazoned the field of stars. Tales held immortal on the celestial sphere. Eventually she fell silent. Her face was turned toward Tau, and he turned to meet it.

The moonlight washed away all color. The brown of her eyes was replaced by a deep black. Her tan skin was milky white. Her dark hair fell in curly waves, framing the elegant curves of her face.

She kissed him, and his head swam. Her soft, full lips locked onto his. There was a feverish desperation in her open eyes. Passion, but mixed with melancholy. She pulled away slowly, before kissing him again. This time tilting her head and closing her eyes. Her hand found his neck, and she held him there for a long moment, breathing slowly and deeply.

No words would come. He could taste her scent on his lips. She pulled back and smiled.

"We could die tomorrow," she said.

She flashed a playful grin and hopped down from the wall, turning away as she did. Her voice came floating through the darkness.
"Good night, Tau," she said.

CHAPTER THIRTY-TWO

They slept through the heat of the next day and made ready to travel as night fell. Tau's pack was heavy on chafed shoulders. A pounding headache and growing nausea answered a small meal of dry meat, choked down with the wretched wine. They moved out into the still landscape.

The full moon rose early in the east, and they walked directly into its ghostly glare. The dunes were left behind as they trekked across a flat plateau of windswept rock. Tau fell into a dreaming half-stupor, moving unconsciously, silently, as the stars wheeled, and the wind howled across the desolate plain. His body seemed to move of its own, step after step after step, and his mind was merely a passenger, riding, trapped within an exhausted vessel.

A flash of motion drew his awareness. Across their path fled a lizard. Low and long, it scuttled over the rocks and disappeared into the blackness. It was the first sign of life Tau had seen in five days. Yael guided them still, walking ever eastward. They walked on and on, the miles dragging beneath worn leather shoes. The armor in Ulrich's pack jangled as he heaved himself across high, tumbled rocks. Tau's swords slapped on his thighs as he followed. Ahead, mountains rose into the sky, their jagged peaks slashing black shadows into the celestial carpet.

On and on they walked, and Tau's wounded thigh ached. His head pounded, and his calloused feet blistered and tore. He drank again and again of the detestable wine, hating the waves of drunkenness that rose behind his eyes. His balance became increasingly unsteady, and the world rose and dipped, canted and swam.

Finally, the mountain's foot approached. A wall of rock rose stark from the flat ground. The landscape was different here; it seemed as though the world had been lifted, shaken, and then dropped, smashed and discarded. Cracks became deep fissures into the earth, and shafts of rock lifted dizzily into the air. Yael led ever upward, ascending a steep slope to reach a narrow defile. The sky began to brighten in the east as the sun neared the unseen horizon.

In a quarter mile, the defile opened, and the rich smell of vegetation rose into the air. A clearing appeared, and scraggly thorn bushes surrounded a stone structure. It was a well. An old one, hardly more than a hole in the earth with some crude stones placed about it to prevent washout. They rushed toward it, stumbling over their feet in their thirst. Tau had emptied his final flask hours before. His tongue was thick in a parched mouth.

Yael stood rigid at the circle of stone. Her face was flat and expressionless. The sun, rising through a cleft in the rocky mountains, burned Tau's face as it struck into the defile. The light was harsh, and he squinted against its glare. He looked down into the well.

The well was empty. Reflected sunlight poured into the hole. The dusty bottom was not far below.

Tau's thirst, whetted by anticipation, was suddenly painful. Ulrich sat heavily on the stones, staring at nothing. Yael's face was unreadable. The dogs, worried expressions on their faces, paced and watched their master. Loki walked toward Tau and licked his hand. The dog's tongue was moist. Tau scratched him behind the ears absently. A curious calm had descended upon Tau, and he stood still, exhausted legs on the point of collapse. He closed his eyes and allowed the cool wind to blow through his short-cropped hair.

A snort and stomp from the ridgetop made him turn. Framed by the rising sun, a Tuareg woman, dressed in the deep blue of her people, sat atop a camel, curiosity on her tanned, elderly face.

CHAPTER THIRTY-THREE

A family of Tuareg emerged from the rocky pass. Kwella, the youngest, a girl of eight, was excited to meet new people. Tadla was her mother. Idirfan was her brother. Old Siman was her grandfather, and grandmother Damya, matriarch of the clan, was the old woman on the camel. Dazed, the companions could find no response. Seeing that the strangers were close to death from thirst, Damya interrupted her granddaughter to lead the way to the hidden oasis.

Behind a sheltering rock, through a narrow cleft, and past a maze of jumbled stones was a clear pool of fresh water. Tau fell to his knees at the water's edge. He cupped his hands and brought the cool liquid to his face. With the first mouthful he bathed his swollen tongue. He wiped his chapped and tender lips. He drank deeply, and his stomach swelled with the life-saving water. The young girl, Kwella, brought the strangers a basket of fresh dates, a cheerful smile on her face as she rambled in Berber. The fruit was sweet and, after Tau had lived so long on only dried meat, infinitely welcome.

The Tuareg family went to work cultivating the date palms that grew in the oasis. Tending the grove was the whole reason for their visit to this isolated place. They left the three strangers on spread blankets beneath the leaves. Tau quickly fell into a deep, inescapable sleep.

When Tau awoke, the sun had sunk behind the western mountains. He had slept through the entire day. He sat up to find himself in the lee of a broad acacia tree. Strange, artificial towers of piled stone formed hollow circles around the bases of the trees in the grove. As Tau blinked in the evening sun, Yael came into view. A blue linen tunic clung tightly to her lithe form. She looked refreshed and healthy. She led a young camel to a stone trough near the water's edge. She poured a bucket of water into the trough, and the camel drank noisily. Yael turned and noticed Tau sitting up. She smiled.

"Do you see these stones?" she asked excitedly. "The Tuareg placed them. It's amazing. The stones keep the grove alive despite there never being any rainfall."

She indicated the delicately stacked rings around the base of each tree. Within the stone rings, short grass grew about the roots of the tall, healthy trees. The empty ground in the spaces separating stone circles was dry and bare.

"Dew rises from the surface of the oasis during the day and then falls back to the ground at night where it condenses on the circles of stones. As liquid water it drips from the stones to wet the earth and thus feed the trees." Yael's eyes were alive with wonder.

Yael stooped and dug in her pack. She brought out her journal and turned to the latest page. She showed Tau how she had sketched the grove, trees ringing the oasis pool, small towers of stones sheltering the spreading roots.

"I hadn't realized you were such a good artist," Tau said. The scene was drawn with a piece of charcoal, delicate strokes capturing the complex shades of shadow and light that dappled the sheltered place.

She blushed. "Well I wouldn't say I'm an artist. More a lover of nature. I don't draw people. Just plants and animals and landscapes."

"Can I see more?" Tau asked.

She pulled away, covering the book with her hands. "I don't know. Maybe later. I'd be embarrassed," she said. She looked away, and her unruly hair fell across her shoulders in curly waves.

"Let's go see how Ulrich is doing," she said, returning the book to her pack.

The pool of clear water sat quiescent, nestled within this hidden depression in the steep mountains. The fading sunlight was climbing the slopes of the hills as the sun sank into red iridescence. A graded path led around the oasis. They followed it.

They found Ulrich sitting near the cooling embers of a small fire. He was pitting dates with a small knife. Each fruit he placed into a small bowl for Siman, the old grandfather, who perched on pile of saddlecloths. Siman took a date from the bowl and gummed it toothlessly. His eyes winked into a smile hidden beneath his tagelmust as Tau and Yael appeared.

Thor and Loki sat nearby. Their eyes were fixed on a wooden bucket at Ulrich's side. Out of curiosity, Tau walked to the bucket to find that it held generous portions of dried meat, softening as they soaked in the clear water. Loki gazed at Tau with mournful brown eyes. Tau scratched him behind the ears. The dog whined and licked away saliva, dripping from his downturned mouth.

Ulrich chuckled. "Don't let them fool you. They've been fed this hour. They're just greedy." He whistled to Thor who paced to him and laid down, a grave look on his long face. Ulrich put down his knife and rubbed the dog with both hands. Thor immediately broke into a toothy smile, tongue lolling as he rolled in the dirt for a belly rub.

The dog's mood matched its owner's. Ulrich looked clean and refreshed. His chin, recently overgrown with beard, was neatly shaved. His hair was loosely bound behind his head and clean brown locks fell to his shoulders. His leather tunic was patched with fresh stitching.

Tau felt gritty, sandy, and was suddenly aware of his own stench. Yael watched him sniff an armpit and chuckled.

"Damya says we must not bathe in the oasis lest we taint it with our filthy bodies," she said with a smile. She pointed back down the trail. "There is a basin just down the path and a bucket if you want to wash up."

Tau found the wooden basin within a sheltering circle of trees. A large bucket sat nearby, and Tau walked to the pond's edge and filled the bucket with cool, clear water. A small fish, curious, swam close, then darted away. Tau lifted the bucket to his lips, taking a long refreshing drink, feeling the coolness slide down his throat. He filled the bucket again and then shed his clothes, shaking sand from his boots as he went to the basin. He held the bucket high and poured it over himself. The water felt wonderful, sweeping away fatigue and the grit of weeks of grueling travel. He filled the bucket again and repeated the process, slower this time. He rubbed chafed shoulders where the hard leather straps of his heavy pack had dug into them. After some time, he dressed again, this time forgoing his hardy travelling gear for the soft yellow kente. He returned to the clearing.

The Tuareg family had returned, and they were striking camp.

Their twelve camels were picketed nearby while the family filled baskets with the seeds of the acacia tree, filled jugs with dates, and filled leather-lined wooden casks with clear water from the oasis. Saddlecloths were cleaned, and camel harness and tack were inspected with meticulous eyes.

Damya, the family matriarch, noticed Tau approach. She sat on the back of her high camel, saddled with the deep blue cloth of the Tuareg. Her face was impassive.

She addressed Tau, and she spoke in a deep singsong Soninke. "Our family is of an old and proud Tuareg lineage. We give our bodies and souls to the high desert and honor our ancestors by caring for the hidden oases—gifts left by the old gods. We know nothing of the politics of our city dwelling Garamantes, still less of this war of your people's black empire, but your companion Yael has told us of your quest, and we find our destiny must intertwine with your own. You will ride back to Abalessa with us. Queen Tin Hinan will decide your fate as she will decide the fate of all our people."

Tau glanced at Yael and found that she was smiling reassuringly. Ulrich gave a stoic nod. Tau bowed to Damya. The dogs wolfed down their softened meat, and the next stage of the journey began.

To reach Abalessa from the oasis was a five-hundred-mile journey across open desert. The camels covered twenty miles each night, and the moon spun through a full phase during the journey, a journey broken only by a single day's stop in another hidden oasis to refill water casks. Compared to their last, grueling, passage the week before, this trip felt like a restful dream. The days seemed to flow into the gentle stream of time as they settled into the dreamlike rhythm of the high desert.

Sand flowed from the erg and danced on the wind. The hard rocks of the Ténéré sheltered insects and tiny animals that scampered through the night. The stars and galaxies wheeled above as the camels traveled on, sailing through the night like great placid ships, swaying with the gentle, constant, easterly wind.

Until they finally arrived back at Abalessa.

CHAPTER THIRTY-FOUR

The sun was kissing the eastern horizon when they ascended to the great plateau. Abalessa's winding streets and high stone towers sprawled before them, but something was wrong. Dirty smoke rose from the desert city. The fig orchards were scorched and barren. Standing water drowned the fields of grain. Sodden, rotting stalks drooped where the verdant wheat had once stood. New banners showed from rooftops. Somehow, Ghana had taken the city.

As soon as the party crested the ridge they were spotted by the enemy. Ghanan warriors, garrisoned at Abalessa's outskirts, sprinted to their mounts. Spear points glinted in the morning sunlight. A hunting horn sounded somewhere deep within the bowels of the captured city.

Damya put her camel to a run, leading the party north. Soon the old Roman fortress was in their path. To Tau's relief he saw that the Tuareg still held the bastion. Banners of blue cloth were draped over the battlements, and blue-cloaked figures patrolled the wall's top. Meanwhile, a squadron of Arabian horses ridden by bare-chested Ghanan warriors was angling to cut Tau's party off from safety. Their paths were closing rapidly. Tau realized with dread that the enemy would catch them long before they reached the safety of the fortress.

The new fortress doors of green wood opened, and a group of a Tuareg cavalry burst forth. A tall, white horse led them, quickly outpacing its camel consorts as it pounded toward the enemy. The rider bellowed a challenge as he charged. The rider was Ejnar.

Ejnar wore a shining chainmail tunic and brandished a Roman spatha. Tau was familiar with the long, sleek sword, having wielded one for a campaign with the Roman auxilia. He wondered how Ejnar had found such a modern weapon so far from Rome. Ejnar wore a cloak of purple silk and tall boots of camel leather. His bare, tanned arms were resplendent in golden bracelets, and a golden torque hung about his neck. A silver circlet, studded with gemstones, bound his golden hair. Recognizing Tau, he waved, then turned back to his quarry.

He aimed his horse at the nearest enemy, a big Ghanan warrior who rode a dun Arabian mare. The warrior snarled and leveled his long spear. The distance closed fast as they hurtled toward each other. The warrior's spear point, sharpened to a glowing edge, reached for Ejnar's chest. At the last moment Ejnar spoke to his horse. The white stallion danced to the left, and the Ghanan weapon missed him by inches.

With an upward slash Ejnar's sword shattered the enemy's spear and he galloped past, leaving the warrior holding a splintered stump of wood. In an instant Ejnar was upon the next warrior in line, his hooting laugh carrying clear across the plain.

This second warrior was a younger, less experienced fighter. A shocked look flattened his face, and he froze with fear as Ejnar bore down upon him. With a contemptuous glance, Ejnar twisted in his saddle and booted the young warrior clean off his horse. The man landed with a thump in the dust beyond. The other Ghanan warriors, disconcerted by the defeat of their leaders, wrenched their horses away. Ejnar, laughing at their confusion, turned his back on the enemy, galloping instead toward Tau's party.

Behind Ejnar, the steady Tuareg camel squadron advanced on the disorganized enemy, and the enemy fled. The disheartened Ghanan patrol turned their mounts and galloped back toward the town. The young man that Ejnar had dismounted, having lost his horse, sprinted after them. The Tuareg did not pursue. They wheeled away, turning to escort Damya's group into the fortress.

Ejnar, his swift-running horse effortlessly closing the distance, reined in. He matched his mount's speed to Tau's camel, putting his horse to a high-stepping canter and sheathed his sword. With impressive grace he leapt to stand on the saddle. He balanced there as the animal bounced along.

Tau ignored his showing off. "You seem to be doing well for yourself," he said.

"It's like I said. There is always money to be made in war," Ejnar replied cheerfully. He turned to Yael. "Milady," he said, bowing elaborately, mischievous grin on his handsome face. Yael blushed but said nothing. Her eyes traced his masculine frame. Handsome clothes accentuated his long legs and broad chest. His flowing cloak billowed in the running wind.

The Tuareg camel squadron closed up, and Tau recognized Basi leading them. A fresh scar marred the left side of his face. He looked troubled.

"How goes the war, Basi?" Tau called.

"Poorly," he answered. "It is best you speak to Tin Hinan."

Basi was disinclined to talk more. His brow was furrowed in a dark study. They rode on toward the fortress. Ejnar rode alongside Yael, and the two of them spoke privately. Tau saw that her face began turning a deeper red. He forced himself to look away. The big wooden doors of the fortress opened. Loki, perched on the front of Tau's saddle, perked up expectantly.

They rode into the courtyard, and Tin Hinan herself came to greet them. She rode on a blue-bedecked camel, the blue sapphire again at her neck and her legs curled beneath her. Tau noticed again that he had never seen her walk. She beckoned them into the shade of a leather awning. Damya rode close, and she and the queen held a private conference, then Damya led her family away. Tau, Ulrich, and Yael dismounted. Tin Hinan waited as they recovered their packs and stood before her, tired, sore, and expectant.

"Yael of Rome, Tau of Ghana, and Ulrich of Germania, I see the desert has brought you back to us. I trust you have learned much of our enemies," Tin Hinan said.

Tau opened his mouth to respond, but Tin Hinan held up a hand.

"Whatever you have discovered in Koumbi Saleh can wait," she said. "We have an urgent problem. One month ago, the Ghanan army rose out of the night. On the heels of the defeated Garamantes and a flood of fugitives, the enemy came. They bore a mass of captured camels, chariots, and Garamante slaves. They tore into the undefended city once again, but unlike the raid before, this time they came to conquer. After capturing the city, they launched an assault on this fortress. Again and again they were repulsed. Ejnar and Basi led the defense as my councilors of war."

"But why is the city flooded?" Yael asked. "Why are the groves burned and the fields of wheat drowned."

"It was Ejnar who proposed sabotaging the aqueduct," Tin Hinan answered. "But eventually we all agreed. This fortress can be supplied by caravans to the hidden oases, but Abalessa is dependent on water from the aquifer. By cutting the aqueduct, we hoped to drive the Ghanans away with thirst. While Ejnar torched the fig groves, Basi and Ziri led a team of engineers to cut Abalessa from its lifeline."

Tin Hinan shook her head and a shadow fell across her face. "But instead of blocking the flow, the water was accidentally released. It poured forth in a great wave. The flood soaked the town and the fields. A hundred years' worth of precious water was lost in moments, soaked forever into dry desert sand. Deprived of food and water, we had thought that the enemy might finally retreat, but the Ghanans are more desperate than we supposed. They do not have the supplies to attempt the journey back to the Niger. They have nowhere to go. They are trapped in the town, and there they starve. The surviving citizens of Abalessa starve as well, held hostage by their desperate captors."

"How many hostages do they have?" Ulrich asked.

"There are more than three thousand civilians trapped in Abalessa," Tin Hinan answered. "Many are close to death from thirst. Our time runs short. We must defeat the Ghanans to save the people of Abalessa."

"What are the odds?" Ulrich asked.

"Three hundred and forty-seven Tuareg men and women are prepared to fight for us. We estimate that the enemy number approximately one thousand spear-warriors," Tin Hinan answered.

Tau whistled. Even the Roman Legion would hesitate to fight at such a disadvantage.

"Those poor people," Yael said. "Could we bring the city food and water? Must there be a battle?"

"Any supplies we have offered have been either consumed or hoarded by the Ghanan warriors. The captives continue to suffer," Tin Hinan said.

"What if we surrendered? What if we offered to help? Surely the Ghanans would feed the hostages if they had a clear line of supply," Yael suggested.

Tin Hinan shook her head, and her eyes were flinty hard. "I sympathize with your compassion, but I will not surrender my people. I will allow all of Abalessa, Ghanans and Garamantes alike, to perish of thirst and hunger before I allow the Tuareg to become slaves to Ghana. To save the people of Abalessa we must fight, and we must win."

Ulrich looked thoughtful. "Victory is never impossible. In war anything can happen, but your people are untrained. They are not warriors," he said.

"My men and women may not be trained warriors like the Ghanans, but all my people can ride a camel and use a camel spear." Tin Hinan responded. "We will fight. We know what is at stake."

Tau was distracted by the whinny of a horse. He turned to see Ejnar, still atop his tall stallion, trotting away. Tau wondered how much that horse had cost. Where did he get such an animal anyway? It was clearly of a different breed than the small Arabians that the Ghanans and Gaetuli used. This was a big European warhorse like the ones the Romans loaded with heavy steel armor. It must be a monumental effort to maintain such an expensive animal this deep into the great desert. Tin Hinan followed Tau's gaze.

"He thinks too highly of himself," Tin Hinan explained of Ejnar. "But he is very useful. He has led many successful raids against the Ghanans."

Ejnar rode to a yellow tent and dismounted his horse. He handed the reins to a waiting Tuareg boy and ducked through the tent flaps. Tau turned back to Tin Hinan.

"How many camels do we have at our disposal?" Tau asked, returning to the task at hand.

"Two hundred and eighty camels reside within the fortress now and another five hundred are scattered among the oases within a week's ride." Tin Hinan answered.

"If things are as dire as you say, we do not have a week. We will have to make do with what we have on hand," Tau said.

"Do you have a plan?" Tin Hinan asked.

"I do," Tau said, glancing at Ulrich. Ulrich gave a mischievous smile.

"Then tell me what it is," she said.

So, Tau told the Tuareg queen how three hundred and forty-seven desert nomads would defeat one thousand Ghanan warriors and rescue three thousand starving Garamante captives. Ulrich grinned savagely, for he knew the plan would work. Victory would come tomorrow.

CHAPTER THIRTY-FIVE

That night, every able-bodied Tuareg man and woman stood in the cleared central space of Tin Hinan's fortress. Yael and Ulrich beside him, Tau addressed his small legion.

"I need fifty volunteers," he announced. "Those fifty will form a shield wall and stand against the full force of a Ghanan charge. Your only chance of survival will be to hold firm against the tide of your enemies." Tau looked over the crowd. "This will be the most difficult and dangerous task of the upcoming battle."

Basi was the first to step forward. He walked confidently across the open space to stand before Tau. His eyes challenged his brethren, shaming them with his pride, and more began to step across the gap. Some needed no encouragement. There were many Garamante fugitives from Abalessa, and the fire of revenge blazed in their eyes as they joined the line. Soon a small crowd stood before him.

Tau inspected the volunteers. He dismissed a few who were too small, a few who were too young, a couple of older men who had fear in their eyes, and a big burly man who had only one arm. He was left with fifty men and women who waited expectantly for his commands. The rest he sent to speak with Tin Hinan and Ejnar.

The first order of business for Tau's company was to prepare their equipment. There were plenty of camel-spears already in the fortress. These weapons were long, thin shafts of wood tipped with sharpened iron and designed for use from the back of a running camel. They were sensible weapons for their intended purpose. Their lightweight design and small heads made them manageable from the high beasts, and each rider carried several extra spears slung on the camel's side for when the fragile weapons inevitably broke. However, the long weapons would be awkward in the tight confines of a shield wall. Some ancient Roman gladius, likely keepsakes or souvenirs, were scattered about the company, and they looked serviceable enough, but the rest of the force lacked weapons that would be appropriate for what Tau had in mind.

After some consideration Tau had each man or woman take a camel-spear and cut it down to a third of its former length. He had no confidence that the fragile weapons would survive any prolonged engagement, but if this fight went on for too long, they would all be dead anyway. The shortened spears would have to suffice.

Tau had already inquired around and found that there were no shields anywhere in the fortress. Shields were always the first thing abandoned in a rout, and not one of the Garamante infantry shields had returned from the Battle of the Sahel. But Tau's plan required a shield wall, so they would have to improvise. Wood was scarce in the Sahara, but Yael had gone to Tin Hinan, and the fortress was scoured. Crates were broken, barrels were sacrificed, and the contents of a fleet of wooden water casks was drained into leather bladders to provide as many planks of wood as could be scavenged.

Many craftsmen were present among the Tuareg. Blacksmiths made iron tools and forged bronze rings for tack and harness. Refugee Garamante engineers were experts in lead and concrete for the maintenance of aqueducts, and even a family of chariot-makers had survived the cataclysm. Tau put them all to work. Based on the shape and size of most of the planks, a rectangular shield design with slight convexity was chosen, incorporating the natural curve most of the wood carried from its prior life as the sides of barrels. Wood deemed too soft, rotten, or warped was discarded, and the hammers and saws began their tasks.

Soon, the first jury-rigged shield was in Tau's hands. It had no boss; the curved iron handle was held on with simple rivets. Rough wood edged the rimless square, which Tau knew would soon begin to splinter in combat. Compared to the laminated Roman scutum, this was a primitive and heavy tool, but the wood was hard and thick, and Tau believed that it would serve their purpose.

Shortly, fifty such shields were ready, and the volunteers began to train. They practiced forming a shield wall. Each volunteer had an assigned place in the line, and Tau made sure that they knew their neighbors by name. Volunteers that were already friends were arranged together. Tau went down the line and spoke to each one. If a man or woman did not know his or her neighbor, Tau made them introduce themselves. They embraced in Tuareg fashion, and Tau made each talk about themselves. They spoke of their childhoods, about their families, and about their dreams and ambitions. The socialization was forced, but these people had to become a fighting unit capable of tackling an overwhelming horde. The closer they bonded, the better they would fight.

Finally, Tau addressed the group as a whole. "A shield wall is only as strong as its weakest soldier," he called.

Tau instructed them in holding their shields, grasping the handle firmly, bracing it with arm and body, holding it high enough to protect faces, crouching slightly to protect ankles.

"Your own shield does not protect you. It is the shield wall, as a unit, that protects you."

Tau showed how the shields must connect, each man protecting the right side of the neighbor on his left, in turn being protected by his own neighbor on his right.

"Every shield must touch every other shield to make an unbroken bastion of wood. You defend the man or woman who stands on your left. That life depends on your left arm and on your courage. Your life, in turn, is in the hands of the man or woman who stands on your right."

They were a small shield wall, only fifty men across and two deep. They practiced again and again, lifting their shields and crouching behind them as the second row strained to hold their own heavy shields higher still. Ulrich paced the line, straightening shields and correcting men's stances. Tau could see that the volunteers were becoming restless. Murmuring talk rose into the air, and people shifted uncomfortably from foot to foot. He frowned.

"It is not just your own life that will be at stake tomorrow," he announced. "You fight for your homes and your people. You fight for your brothers and sisters. You fight because thousands of men, women, and children will die if you fail."

The volunteers slowly improved. Eventually Tau noticed that the sky was lightening in the east. They had been up all night. Tau yawned.

Yael looked troubled. She had been biting her lip and frowning, staring at nothing in particular.

"Is something on your mind?" Tau asked.

"Where is my place in the battle line?" Yael asked.

Tau made no response. He did not want Yael to be in the shield wall, in the midst of the greatest danger.

Yael saw his hesitation. "There are twenty women in that line," she said, indignantly. "I can fight, and you need every good fighter you can get. You cannot turn me away if I wish to join."

Her unruly hair tossed in the freshening desert wind. Tau's eyes traced the delicate curve of her chin.

Tin Hinan appeared on her camel, silhouetted in the light of the rising sun.

"Yael wishes to fight," the queen confirmed. Her voice was mild, but her face was implacable.

Tau realized that he could not refuse Yael if Tin Hinan supported her. All of his volunteers owed allegiance to Tin Hinan alone. All authority came from her. His heart thumped. The queen's eyes bored into him.

"Behind me," Tau said finally, feeling the words dragged out of him. "You will stand behind me."

CHAPTER THIRTY-SIX

Ulrich wanted to attack at first light, but Tau talked him out of it. The volunteers were tired. They settled on initiating battle in the evening. That would give the men and women the day to rest. Tau found that Tin Hinan had prepared rooms for them on the second floor of a rebuilt Roman house. The place was clean and profited from the steady easterly breeze that brought a coolness through the open windows. Tau pulled off his heavy chainmail and collapsed onto a mat of woven palm fibers.

Tau awoke that evening feeling more refreshed than he had in weeks. He was suffused with purpose. Before him was a tangible enemy and a clear plan of battle. He sat up to find Ulrich busily inspecting his armor, checking for spots of rust and squeezing fresh grease into the joints. Ulrich must have been up for some time because Tau found his own chainmail had also been scrubbed and freshly rubbed with oil. Ulrich gave him a confident nod and Tau grinned back.

Tau dressed in the soft yellow Kente and went about his waking routine. The Garamantes had borrowed the Roman custom of brushing with toothpaste made of burned eggshells, and Tau scrubbed his teeth with a frayed twig and washed his face with a dampened cloth in a basin of cool water. A row of latrines was in an alley behind the houses, and Tau stepped across the street to relieve himself.

The fortress was alive with all the vigor of a small town, packed close within four high walls. The plaza was noisy with children at play. Tau noticed that young Idlis was there, kicking a ball with two other boys. They ran and laughed under the feet of the busy adults.

Men and women mended clothes and tended the small herd of camels. A small marketplace boasted stalls selling pots, tools, cloth, and fresh food.

On his way back to the house, Tau noticed Tin Hinan on the northern ramparts. Her back was to him, but she was instantly recognizable from her blue silk dress and straight-backed carriage. The queen sat on a litter which itself was raised on a wooden crate so that she could see over the wall's crenellations. She was framed by two guards who stood on either side of her elevated cushion. Tau ascended a stone stairway to join her.

Tin Hinan glanced up as Tau reached the top of the wall, then she looked back over the desert before her. She faced north, away from Abalessa. Her blue eyes, subtly enhanced with a touch of dark ash, were striking. Her dark hair was bound with cord and hung down her back. A necklace of silver medallions had replaced the great sapphire around her neck. Tau followed her gaze into the open wastes and saw a line of camels approach across the plateau. They were making their unhurried way toward the fortress, and Tau could see that they were heavily laden with supplies. Round casks of water hung from the camels' flanks. Mounds of forage were packed in nets. Bags and cases covered the colorful saddles. Tau realized that the approach of the camels was cleverly hidden from the enemy by the bulk of the fortress itself.

Tin Hinan spoke. "The Ghanans have failed to encircle this fortress, so we have no trouble maintaining our supply lines."

A tiny lizard raced across the wall's top. It paused and considered Tau, black eyes winking, then it disappeared off the edge of the precipice, feet gripping the rough stone as it fled down the wall's outer face.

Tin Hinan looked up. "It is time to strike. Ready yourself. A meal is being prepared for you and your volunteers. After the meal we will begin."

Tau bowed and returned to the house. He found Ulrich and Yael within the entryway. Ulrich was giving Yael some last-minute shield training. He instructed her on the proper lift and balance of the shield, how to lean into a blow to absorb the force with your body rather than your arm, how to turn the shield so it would deflect a blade rather than splintering. They paused when they saw Tau.

"We fight soon," Tau said.

Ulrich hefted his axe, and his eager grin spoke more than any words. Yael gripped her makeshift shield and nodded. They prepared their gear. Ulrich looked formidable in his segmented Roman armor, brandishing his massive battle axe. Yael donned a reinforced leather tunic and carried one of the shortened camel-spears. Her bow, together with her arrow bag, was strapped across her back. Tau donned his coat of auxilia chainmail, fading yellow emblem of the Petulantes still visible on its front. He strapped his twin Frisian longswords about his waist, and the three hefted their heavy wooden shields. The dogs would remain in the care of Tin Hinan's servants. They were war mastiffs, but there was no place for them in Tau's plan of battle. The companions went out into the street.

Tables and benches were being set up in the square, and the volunteers began to appear, spears and shields in hand. Spirits were high. Soon, a meal of boiled millet dough, a dish known as ugali, and a thick millet soup were laid out. Tau counted heads as he pulled apart the sweet dough. All the volunteers were present and accounted for. They chatted amicably as they ate. Tau wondered if they truly knew what they were in for.

Ejnar stalked into the yard wearing a flowing purple cape over a tunic of white silk. He strode confidently toward Tau, half smile on his handsome face. Tau moved over on the bench, making space for him to sit. The former pirate jangled with silver medallions and gold chain. Tau offered him a piece of the dough, but Ejnar refused with a wave of his hand. Tau noticed that Yael would not meet Ejnar's eyes.

"This is a fine plan, Tau, and you can be sure that my cavalry will do its part to bring us victory," Ejnar said. He smiled but his friendly tone sounded forced. He fidgeted with a silver coin that was tied into the hem of his tunic. Ulrich was glaring at him.

Ejnar coughed and spoke again. "I understand that you reached Koumbi Saleh. You will have to tell me about your adventure when this is over."

"And you must tell us of your exploits here," Tau replied with equanimity.

"I want you to know that I was not just running away at the Sahel," Ejnar said, suddenly defensive.

Tau gazed at the agitated pirate, not knowing what to say.

"All that I care about is that you fight today," Ulrich said.

Ejnar stiffened. "I will," he answered.

Across the courtyard Tin Hinan appeared, seated atop her high camel. Her eyes caught Tau's. She nodded meaningfully, and he stood. The hubbub died away.

All eyes were on Tau, and he felt the weight of that gaze. He looked about the silent crowd.

"It is time," Tau said softly.

"It is time," Basi bellowed, and the people cheered.

CHAPTER THIRTY-SEVEN

The southern gate swung open, and Tau's volunteers emerged onto the plain. The evening sun was low, but the desert still shimmered with its heat.

They walked in step. The line was twenty-five men and women across and two deep. On the right side stood Ulrich while Tau, with Yael close behind, held the left. Basi strode in the center and set the pace, unhurried, toward the gates of Abalessa. Tin Hinan watched from her bastion.

The enemy response was immediate. Like an anthill disturbed, a flood of Ghanan warriors erupted from Abalessa's streets and alleyways. The vast host swarmed onto the plain. Some were on small Arabian horses, some were on camels, but the vast majority came on foot. They closed fast, but Basi did not hesitate. He marched on, walking directly into the teeth of the foe.

Tau felt the edge of fear creep into his mind. His volunteers were so few, just a handful of untested men and women, and they stood against a horde. He took a breath and pushed the fear away.

Basi stopped. They had reached the chosen place of battle, and he planted his shield on the rocky ground. He drew his ancient gladius and held it high. The world held its breath. He slammed his sword into his shield.

Thump.

Again.

Thump.

Again.

Thump.

The rest of the shield wall followed suit and the hollow drumroll rolled across the empty plain, filling air and sky with a giant's heartbeat.

Thump.

Thump.

Thump.

The sound of weapon on shield. An even beat.

The noise checked the enemy. They hesitated a hundred paces away. Perhaps they scented a trap. Hundreds and hundreds of Ghanan warriors crowded into a loose mob that covered the dusty plain between the city and the fortress.

A leader emerged from the Ghanan crowd. The warlord shouted an order to his men, who lowered their weapons. Then, the warlord walked alone. He approached the Tuareg line with lowered spear and shield.

Tau recognized the man. His name was Masireh. They had met in the besieged inn during the first raid on Abalessa. In the heat of battle, Ulrich had removed Masireh's brother Mbaneh's arm with his axe.

Tau stepped forward, and Masireh's face twisted with recognition. He sneered, raising his spear. Tau made a show of dropping his shield. He sheathed his sword and walked forward to meet the warlord with hands outstretched.

Masireh looked as though he had passed through hell. His once-youthful face was thin and drawn. A poorly-healing scar marred his mouth and nose. His chest was bare above traditional Ghanan trousers, and he now bore the golden torques and armlets of a veteran.

The warlord stopped just out of reach.

"I remember you." He spat and pointed at Tau with his spear.

"Yes," Tau replied. "And I remember you, Masireh."

The warrior glared at Tau. His anger was a tangible thing, clawing its way through glutinous air. The two stood alone, between a massive host and a tiny shield wall. The only sound was the voice of the wind on the sandy plain.

"Mbaneh died of the fever," Masireh said accusingly. His eyes were slits of pure hatred.

"I am sorry to hear of your brother's death," Tau said. "He was a warrior. We were kin in that. In another life, we may have been brothers as well."

Masireh ignored the sympathy. "What are you doing here?" he demanded. He waved his spear, indicating the shield wall of volunteers.

"We are here to drive you out of Abalessa and free the townspeople held hostage," Tau replied.

Masireh raised an eyebrow. The scar tissue ran across his face, pulling the corner of his mouth into a leer.

"With this? You have no more than fifty men in your pathetic little line," he said.

"And women." Tau corrected him gently. "Men and women."

Masireh's expression did not change. "I have over one thousand hardened warriors under my command. Warriors that survived the journey across the burning desert. Your resistance is foolish. It is a waste of time, both yours and mine," he said.

"If you wish to surrender, I will happily accept," Tau said.

Masireh frowned in confusion, then shook his head. He looked at his men, then back at the tiny shield wall and his eyes dawned with understanding.

"I understand now. You are a fool," Masireh concluded. There was no rancor in his voice now, only exhaustion.

"We will defeat you quickly," the warlord said. He sighed and turned to walk away.

"How hungry are your men?" Tau asked. Masireh whipped around, and the anger returned to his face. "How thirsty?" Tau persisted. "And the captives of the city, how do they fare?"

"That is not my fault," Masireh snarled. "That blue bitch, Tin Hinan, and her pet bandit who rides the white horse, it was they who torched the groves and destroyed the water supply and flooded the city. The deaths of all the people of Abalessa shall be on their hands."

"And what of the lives of your warriors?" Tau asked. "You are too deep into the desert and too low on supplies to attempt the return journey. Your men are living on borrowed time."

He glared at Tau but did not respond.

"It does not have to be this way," Tau said. "If you stand down, if you surrender, the Tuareg can bring food and water from their hidden oases. Nobody has to die."

Masireh's face softened. He considered. He gazed past Tau and looked at the impregnable walls of Tin Hinan's fortress. The blue fabric of her palanquin could just be seen, peeking over the crenellations of the southern rampart.

"Or you and I can fight, one on one, in the traditions of our ancestors," Tau offered, drawing his swords.

But the Ghanan warlord was looking past him. His eyes scanned the tiny shield wall, still and quiet under the noonday sun, until he saw Ulrich. Tau followed his gaze to find that Masireh was staring at the big Saxon, who stood leaning on his axe, dark in his blackened armor.

"No," Masireh said softly, then more loudly, "No. We will crush your pathetic rabble, storm the fortress, and with the stores and camels hidden there we will ride victorious back to the gates of Koumbi Saleh." His decision was made. He turned away, and Tau's heart sank.

"And my brother will be avenged," Masireh growled.

CHAPTER THIRTY-EIGHT

Masireh walked back to his army. With a heavy heart, Tau watched him go. After a moment, Tau sheathed his swords and returned to his own line, boots crunching across the dry, rocky earth.

"What did he say?" Basi asked.

Tau replied in a voice loud enough for all to hear. "He says that they are hungry. That they are thirsty, and that they want to go home," he called.

"It sounds like they are weak," Basi called back. "Let us show them the strength of the desert."

The Berbers cheered, and Tau glanced at his shield brothers and sisters. Despite the odds, morale was high. Neighbors chatted in small voices, and Tau wondered at their confidence. Few of these men and women had been in any kind of fight before. Tau hoped that they would hold fast once the fighting began. Tau looked back at Yael. She was checking the tautness of her bowstring but caught his glance and gave a reassuring nod.

Basi began to thump his shield again, and his people followed suit. The thumping was faster this time, less restrained, and joined by shouts and taunts. Across the field, Masireh held up his spear, and the enemy host started forward.

The Ghanan horde spread wide, outflanking Tau's small line. Bare-chested black warriors brandished gleaming spears and leathern shields, and they jostled with each other as they moved. Within a few steps, they were running. They howled as they came, each singing the war song of his family, reciting the words taught by their warrior fathers, sung by their heroes, and passed down from their ancestors.

The few horses and camels among them were swamped in the advance. A black tide of enraged warriors filled the world.

"Tau, I'm scared," Yael whispered.

"We will win," Tau reassured her.

The shield-beating stopped, and Basi shouted an order.

"Testudo," he called, and the formation changed.

Knowing that they would be surrounded when the enemy attacked, they had trained for this. The rear rank turned, the wings closed in, and, suddenly, instead of a line, they were a circular huddle of shields, facing outwards in all directions. The shortened camel-spears poked from the defensive shell.

Their spot had also been chosen carefully. They stood on the highest of a series of small rises on the flat plain. The rise did not lift them more than a couple of feet, but that was enough. The enemy would fight from lower ground, making it easier to defend.

The enemy was fifty paces away. The earth trembled with the rumble of their passage, and the air was torn with their howls.

"Hold men," Tau shouted. "Hold your ground."

And the Ghanan horde slammed into the small circle of shields.

Basi stood at the center of the line, and it was he and his shield brethren who took the greatest force of the blow. At a full run, the foremost warriors threw themselves upon the testudo. The weight of their bodies struck with staggering force. Basi did not try to use his weapons. He simply leaned into his shield, bent his knees, and weathered the blow. The men and women beside him did the same. They reeled, but they did not fall. In another instant, the tide of warriors lapped about the formation, and the testudo was surrounded.

Tau's view of the battlefield shrank to a few claustrophobic feet. Directly before him, a tall Ghanan warrior, handsome with a clean-shaven face and a heavily muscled torso, probed at the junctions between the shields with his spear. He patiently tackled the problem, but the Berber shields were too tightly packed together for his broad spear blade to push through.

He tried another tactic. He pushed the point of his spear into a tiny gap between Tau's shield and that of the man next to him. It wedged there, and the warrior leaned on it, attempting to pry the shields apart using the spear's shaft for leverage. He was strong, and Tau felt his shield begin to be pulled away. In desperation he clutched the handle with both hands.

The man next to Tau, a Tuareg nomad who wore the blue tagelmust of his clan, slid his shortened camel-spear forward. The point approached the Ghanan warrior's chest, and the warrior casually stepped back to avoid it, but the crowd of his kin was pushing too close. He was unable to draw away. The black warrior's eyes widened as the spear drove home, and he cried out in pain. The spear slid between ribs, letting out a wash of blood as it found the man's heart. The handsome warrior died, a look of surprise and horror on his face as he fell forward. The thin spear snapped, point stuck fast in the dead warrior's chest, and the Tuareg nomad threw away the useless haft.

"Hold," Basi grunted. "Hold them off." And the air was filled with the noise of grunting, sweating, shoving men.

The shield wall held. The enemy's numbers could not be brought to bear in this tight, confined brawl. The vast majority of the Ghanan warriors were not part of the fight. They were waiting in the great crowd, unable to do more than shout encouragement or push at the men in front of them. The volunteers' shields were only faced by a relative handful of warriors, and the defenders' defense was staunch. The next warrior who faced Tau was timid, and he did little more than jab at Tau's shield with his spear. His lips were chapped, and he looked thin and hungry. He was impeded, too, by the corpse of his comrade. He tried to stand on the dead man's back, but it was a soft and mobile purchase, and he continually fought for balance as he jabbed again and again with his spear.

To Tau's immediate left, a Ghanan warrior swung his spear like a club. He, too, looked thirsty and thin, but he was throwing a desperate energy into the attack. The blows rained down on Yael's shield, held just above Tau's own. She had dropped her spear to support the shield with both hands. She weathered the storm, and her eyes looked into Tau's from inches away.

"It won't be long now," Tau said.

"I know," she said.

Ulrich, on the opposite side of the formation, was enjoying himself. Three bodies were piled at his feet already, and his axe swung for another warrior, heavy blade dripping blood. He roared at his foe, inviting them to come to their deaths. Ulrich hated shield walls, barbarian that he was, and was itching to hurtle into the fray.

Ulrich's axe found its fourth victim and sought a fifth.

But despite all Tau's hopes, Berber men and women began to die. It was a slow process. Hunting Ghanan spears eventually found gaps in the shields, or men became tired and weakened their guard. The circle of shields began to shrink. Berber bodies collapsed in the dust. Tau was forced to shuffle backward when the Tuareg man beside him died, struck in the head with a flying spear. The man fell forward with a spray of blood from a shattered skull.

They huddled for what felt like an age. The enemy hacked and stabbed, and Tau's volunteers waited and waited. Few of the Berbers were brave enough to try to fight back with the thin spears, and those who did found that the light weapons quickly broke. Slowly, slowly, people died. The shield wall shrank again.

Tau wanted to turn his head to count their losses, but two Ghanan warriors were jabbing at him. It took all his attention to block their spear points as they came forward again and again. The evening heat grew oppressive, and sweat trickled down Tau's back, running beneath his heavy chainmail. Sweat dripped down his brow, stung his eyes, and he grimaced as he blinked the drops away.

Finally, a new sound began to fill the battlefield. It came gradually, only slowly breaking in upon Tau's consciousness. The earth rumbled, but not with the light patter of feet. This sound was the heavy thumping of running camels. The Ghanan warriors must have heard it too, for they stepped away to glance around, seeking the source of the noise.

Tau straightened and looked west, for he knew what was coming.

CHAPTER THIRTY-NINE

Two hundred and eighty camels thundered across the plain, skilled Tuareg riders on their backs. Ejnar led the charge. His white horse formed the point of a wedge of vengeful nomads.

Tau's shield wall had been a diversion. While the fifty volunteers marched toward the city, Ejnar had led Tin Hinan's cavalry out the northern gate. They followed the low paths along the edge of the plateau, their passage hidden by the lay of the land. Now they charged out of the setting sun and bore down upon the enemy rear.

The enemy rear is the best place to attack, for the rear is where the weakest hide. Even in the best armies, the strongest and bravest force their way to the front, while the cowards straggle in the rear. Attacking an enemy's rear breeds panic when those weak men flee. Once a rout starts, even the bravest warriors cannot stop the disaster.

The enemy saw the threat but could do nothing about it. The best warriors were tight within the packed crowd, frustrated and impotent as they struggled against the still-holding shields. The weak and hungry men at the rear, frightened by the mass of Tuareg cavalry, were already beginning to edge away. Ghanan shields were falling to the ground, and men began to scatter.

Ejnar spurred his horse ahead. His fast stallion left the Tuareg camel squadron behind. He would challenge the enemy alone. He would prove his bravery. His face was set in a rictus of anger, a rage that hid his shame for abandoning his friends at the Battle of the Sahel.

Ejnar struck the enemy ranks. The momentum of the galloping horse carried him deep into the crowd. Warriors who failed to dodge aside were knocked down by the horse's flailing hooves. Ejnar's sword was red with blood as he cut again and again, slashing the sharpened steel to the left and to the right. For a moment, Tau thought that Ejnar might carve a bloody path straight through to the safety of the shields, but then the stallion began to slow. Too many enemies were packed too tightly. Horse and rider came within fifty paces of the shield wall before they could no longer force their way through the dense press of men.

The horse tossed its head and snapped at the Ghanan warriors who impeded its path. Its eyes were wide with fear. Ejnar was snarling, cutting down men left and right. Then the horse backed away from a gleaming spearpoint that was thrust toward its face. It reared up, kicking with its front hooves, but the spear drove deep into its chest, cutting through breast and sternum and finally into the stallion's heart. A gush of blood soaked the nearest warriors, and the horse screamed. Ejnar clung desperately to the horse's mane as the animal fell. Tau saw Ejnar's eyes widen in pure terror as the animal collapsed on top of him, trapping him beneath its dead weight.

Yael leapt into action. At the center of the huddle of shields was a moderate boulder, and she climbed to its top. She balanced there, just high enough to see over the crowd, but that was all she needed. Her strung bow was already in her hand, her arrow bag was open. She brushed the unruly hair from her face and nocked an arrow, taking careful aim as she drew.

Ejnar struggled. His fallen mount trapped both of his legs, and he pushed at the dead beast, trying desperately to free himself. The warrior who had killed the horse stood over him, blood dripping from his broad chest and long spear; he raised his weapon high for the killing stroke.

The warrior never saw the arrow that killed him. Yael's broad-headed missile passed cleanly through the man's neck and flew out the other side. The warrior fell forward, lifeless, landing heavily across Ejnar. His spear clattered uselessly to the rocky ground.

Yael did not savor her victory. She slid another missile from her bag, nocked it on the string, drew, and released. In fluid motion another arrow was in the air, and then another. The bow twanged as the arrows leapt into the evening sky. She had eighteen arrows in her bag, and she flew through them as she struck down the men who clustered about the fallen pirate. After the first eight men fell, the others became more wary, edging back from Ejnar who was hidden by a pile of dead and wounded men.

A spear flew from the crowd. It flew directly at Yael, unprotected and exposed above the ring of shields. Tau yelled, but Yael did not move. The spear missed her face by a fraction of an inch and slid along her forearm, drawing blood in a long shallow cut. She did not flinch. She stood still, arrow nocked and ready. Her unblinking eyes were vigilant for any movement about the downed horse. She was ready to strike down any who dared to attack her lover.

Finally, the squadron of Tuareg camel cavalry struck the enemy rear. Their long spears were held low from their tall mounts. They struck with such force that the Ghanan army trembled. The thin camel spears showed their true worth. Long and quick, they outranged the Ghanan spears. The iron points drove past leathern shields and into warriors' heads, chests, and backs. When a spear broke, as they often did, the Tuareg rider dropped it and produced another that had been strapped and ready on the camel's flanks.

The rearmost Ghanan warriors tried to back away, but they only entangled the efforts of the braver warriors who pushed against them trying to counterattack. The men nearest the shield wall recognized the cavalry as the greater threat but could do nothing about it. They shouted and argued, hesitating in their indecision.

From the fringes of the battle, Tau could see Ghanan warriors fleeing in ones and twos. Like a leaking dam, trickles of men flowed away from the verges. They dropped their shields and fled toward Abalessa, seeking the safety of the city's buildings and alleyways.

The Tuareg cavalry was winning. They carved through the mob. They soon overtook Ejnar's position, driving away the men clustered there, and Yael relaxed her bow.

Tau let out a long breath that he had not realized he had been holding. The nearest warriors were edging away, and Tau realized that they were going to win.

But from across the battlefield came a shout that drowned out all others. Tau turned to see Masireh above the crowd, tall on one of the scattered Ghanan horses. His face was dark with fury, and he waved his spear as he rallied his men. Warriors stopped fleeing. They turned back to the fight. Men gathered about him and hefted their spears. Men on the verges heard his call and snatched up their fallen shields.

"Fight!" Masireh screamed, his voice cutting across the chaos. "They are few, and we are many. Kill them." He pointed his spear at the camels, now being checked by the steadily increasing resistance.

"Kill them all," he ordered, and the routing Ghanans rallied.

A spear point broke on Tau's shield. All across the huddle of shields the enemy was attacking with a renewed vigor. The Tuareg woman on Tau's left fell. She had lowered her guard to watch the cavalry attack, and a Ghanan spear took her in the stomach. Her face turned toward Tau. Her eyes were wide in disbelief and pain. Tau stepped back, locking his shield with the next man in line as she collapsed to the ground. The enemy pressed close.

"Yael, shoot that bastard," Ulrich growled.

Yael shifted her aim. Masireh was far away, and he was moving, pushing his way through the crowd on his horse. It would be a difficult shot. She took a breath, and as she exhaled, she drew the string back to her chin and released.

The arrow arced upward as it left the string. Curving high through the air, it seemed to hang in the sky for a long moment before it fell. It struck true. Masireh had been howling at his men, ordering them to regain his victory, and the arrow slid into his open mouth. It smashed through the back of his throat and severed his spinal cord at the base of his skull. The Ghanan warlord fell, boneless and limp, to be swallowed in the milling crowd.

The Ghanan army broke. It was chaos. Masireh's death started a panic, and the panic infected the whole of the army. Nothing would stem this tide. Like a shattered dam, the leaderless and demoralized horde scattered. Warriors poured toward Abalessa in a chaotic flood.

Tau and his volunteers huddled as the men rushed past all around. In a few more moments, it was over. The tiny, shattered shield wall rose and counted the dead. Only twenty of Tau's people were left.

But they had won.

CHAPTER FORTY

Tin Hinan entered the city of Abalessa. She found desolation. The flood had swamped the city with a smear of glutinous mud. The streets smelled of spilled sewage and decay. Throngs of the tired and hungry came to meet her. They were filthy with effluent and desperate with thirst. Tin Hinan remained stoic, her camel touring the city while her followers distributed food and water.

There was no resistance from the remaining Ghanan warriors. Some took horses and fled into the desert, but most surrendered, asking only for food for their empty bellies and water for their parched lips. Tin Hinan was merciful. They were fed. Their weapons were taken, and they were kept under heavy guard by watchful Tuareg sentries.

It took a full week to return the city to some semblance of normalcy. The greatest task was to restore the flow of water. To do that, a new foggara had to be connected to the partially crippled reservoir.

Tau was present the day that the new pipe was laid. The Garamante engineers sweated to tunnel the new watercourse even deeper than the last.

"I lied before," Ziri admitted. "I lied when I said that the water in the aquifer would last us a hundred years," The engineer's face was drawn and pained.

"All across the Sahara, the reservoirs are running dry," he said. "Our people have depended upon these hidden aquifers for eight centuries. They water our fields, they fill our cups, and they bring life to our streets. All the great Garamante cities are sustained by reservoirs like this."

Ziri's arms were crossed over his chest. He spoke abstractly, as though to nobody in particular. He looked like a phantom, grave and tall, as he stood illuminated in the pale lamplight of the tunnel.

"Some refuse to believe that we are running dry. They deny it. They say that the engineers' calculations are wrong. They say that the gods will save us. They say that if our fathers and our fathers' fathers and their fathers' fathers for thirty generations lived off the foggara, then how can the foggara fail us now?"

Ziri shook his head. "But our cities have expanded. Our demand for water has grown every year. We use our water as though the supply is endless, but every drop that leaves the reservoirs is gone forever. The water must have been deposited by the gods because no stream, no rain, no spring refills the aquifers now."

"What happens when the aquifers run out?" Yael asked.

Ziri turned to look at her. His face was cold and hard. "Then the Garamantes die."

"How much is left in this pool?" Tau asked.

"After the damage we did? Maybe a couple of years. More if we ration ourselves, which we likely will not," Ziri said.

A final stone was laid, a dam of wooden blocks was knocked away, and the water began to flow. It trickled down a concrete course that would pour into the thirsty town. Ziri turned and walked away into the darkness.

The next week a caravan headed south. It carried the defeated Ghanan warriors back to the green Sahel. Some of the people of Abalessa were angered by Tin Hinan's mercy. They demanded blood, calling for vengeance for dead sons and daughters, mothers and fathers, sisters and brothers, but Tin Hinan refused to massacre the men.

"One day we will make peace with the nation of Ghana. This war will be set aside, and what will happen then? Will the trade flow? Will the caravans ply the desert sands, or will the death begin anew? Killing these men would only beget more violence. Must we murder each other in a hundred years of blood feud? No. The less blood spilled, the better. The Ghanan invaders must go home."

The camels plodded south, and their demoralized passengers were released into the Sahel. The Ghanan warriors were humiliated, but they would survive, and word of Tin Hinan's mercy would spread throughout Ghana.

The Garamantes could grumble, but Tin Hinan was the Queen of the Tuareg, the savior of Abalessa, and her power remained unchallenged.

Soon after, work on a new campaign began in earnest.

The war between Ghana and the Garamantes had been raging for nearly a full year. It had devastated nearly all the southern Garamante towns and many of the Tuareg settlements. The Battle of the Sahel had destroyed the greatest army the Garamantes could bring to bear. The war had broken the back of the Sahara trade and crippled Abalessa, one of the greatest of the desert metropolises. Tin Hinan declared that it was time to put an end to the conflict. She called a council of war.

The council met in her fortress, which looked ever more like a military encampment now that Abalessa was again open for business and the civilians were resettled. It was a staging ground for the convoys headed north and east, reconnecting the scattered Tuareg oases and the great Garamante cities. It was a hub of organized military and economic activity.

Upon the central yard was erected a great tent, flaps drawn back to allow bright sunlight to fill the interior. Within sat Tin Hinan, perched on a blue cushion mounted upon a blue dais. About her were other cushions, arranged in a circle of which she formed the head. Basi was there, seated at her right hand, and when the companions arrived, Yael was invited to sit at her left. Tau sat alongside Yael, and Ulrich joined, his two dogs crouching passively behind. Ejnar was to his left, and the rest of the circle was filled with Tuareg and Garamantes alike, some of whom Tau recognized and some that he did not.

Ziri, the engineer was there, looking tired as he lowered himself onto his cushion. Two Tuareg men, impassive in their shrouding tagelmust sat quietly to the engineer's right. The matriarch Damya, sardonic smile on her ageless face, sat beside them and, finally, a handsome Garamante soldier, resplendent in an ancient Roman muscle cuirass, filled out the final seat. Tau looked at this newcomer curiously. The bronze of his polished armor gleamed in the diffused light, and a vintage gladius hung from his hip. His face looked vaguely familiar.

"I have called you here today," Tin Hinan announced, "to discuss how to end this war."

Tin Hinan allowed her words to hang in the air, turning over and over in the desert wind. None spoke for a long moment.

It was Damya who broke the silence, stirring from her cushion to address Tin Hinan.

"My Queen, Ghana will not settle for peace. I have now sent four families to parley, and all have failed. Their bodies are now strung up, food for crows in the streets of Koumbi Saleh," the matriarch's voice was flat. Her words were met by a mutter of discontent from the council.

Tin Hinan nodded to Damya, then turned to Tau. "Tau, you know more of our enemy than anyone else. What would it take to end this war?"

Tau thought carefully before he responded. "I believe that Damya is right. They will not agree to any peace under any terms. Kansoleh and Kabu of Ghana need this war to continue."

The Garamante soldier spoke up, and anger colored his voice. "If the Ghanans want the war to continue, then they are fools. This conflict is as bad for Ghana as it is for Garama. The trade suffers. The gold no longer flows. The great caravans of the Sahara sit idle while the Ghanans destroy their own profits."

Tin Hinan's eyes were mild. "Tau, I do not think you have met Amestan, son of Ameqran, recently King of Garama."

Tau looked at the man, and in the soldier's face was his father's fierce pride. Tau remembered his final sight of the gray-haired King Ameqran, battling fierce odds as the Ghanan army overwhelmed him, fighting to the very last from his eight-wheeled chariot. King Amestan looked every bit his father's son.

"Tau is the first son of the Emperor Kayode and thus the rightful heir to the throne of Ghana," Tin Hinan introduced him.

Hushed whispers rose. King Amestan's eyes narrowed.

"Then, Prince, perhaps you can tell us why the Ghanans are such fools," he challenged.

"Foolishness has nothing to do with it," Tau answered levelly. "Kabu and Kansoleh are proud rulers of a proud nation. They cannot be seen to give up on this war, no matter how unprofitable it may be."

"It is more than pride. They are afraid," Yael added. All eyes turned to her.

She continued, "I have learned much about Ghana. Both from

what I have seen and what I have read. When I went to Koumbi Saleh, I walked the streets and spoke to their people. I have read their history, and I have seen their altars. The people of Ghana revere the warrior tradition. The position of Ghana is not just as a king; he is also a warrior—the Ghana is the first warrior of a warrior nation. All warriors of Ghana follow their fathers, and that father-to-son relationship is valued above all others. Thus, when Kansoleh deposed Kayode, and Kabu usurped his older brother Tau, they upset that tradition. They disturbed the natural order, and the people are discontented. This war allows Kansoleh to focus all eyes elsewhere. She is using the war to unify her people and to keep them under control. If she and her son show weakness, they will lose the throne and likely their own lives."

"It sounds like the people of Ghana need a return to tradition," Tin Hinan said, glancing at Tau. "If Tau defeats Kabu, perhaps the Ghanan nation will follow him."

Ziri spoke, his tired voice gruff and flat. "Well, whatever the reason, if they won't agree to peace, that means we have to fight."

"We all know what is at stake. The only way to end this war is to meet the Ghanans on the field of battle and deliver a decisive defeat to their army and morale. Now, how do we do it?" Tin Hinan asked.

"I know how," Ulrich said. He scratched Thor behind the ears, and the dog panted happily.

In the silence Ulrich explained how they would win.

CHAPTER FORTY-ONE

Tin Hinan allowed three months to prepare. Three months, she estimated, was how long the nation of Ghana would stay quiet. They had lost much. Tin Hinan had discovered that the Ghanan losses in battle had paled in comparison to their losses to attrition. Unused to desert travel, for each Ghanan warrior that had attacked Abalessa, two had entered the Sahara and never left. Even before Tin Hinan's counterattack, desiccated corpses littered the harsh sands. It would take time for Ghana to recover its strength.

They had only three months, and yet so much to accomplish. Tin Hinan offered the full support of her people. Volunteers from across the Tuareg tribes gathered until the fortress was swollen to bursting with skilled camel cavalry. Meanwhile, the scattered embers of the Garamante nation were drawing back together. Nothing like the great army of Garama, lost forever at the Battle of the Sahel, could be expected, but strength remained nonetheless. Chariots appeared once again, and with them proud Garamante soldiers from the far garrisons, some even hefting archaic, but serviceable, shields and spears.

The council's first task was to establish a military chain of command. Tin Hinan appointed Ulrich and Tau officially as her advisors of war, although unofficially Tau knew that it was Yael that the queen trusted most. The camel cavalry of the Tuareg nomads would remain under Tin Hinan's command with Basi appointed as chief warlord and Ejnar as his lieutenant. The Garamante infantry and chariots gathered under King Amestan's banner.

Although nearly as proud as his father, King Amestan was willing to compromise. The king agreed to allow Ulrich and Tau to propose strategies of battle, but under the condition that Garamante soldiers remained firmly under Garamante officers and Garamante command. His heart was filled with a desire to see his father avenged and Ghana humbled. He would do whatever it took to achieve those ends. He would work with the outsiders and cooperate with the Tuareg. Once he was convinced that Tau and Ulrich's methods were the most efficient and effective ways of gaining victory, he drove his men as hard as any Roman drillmaster.

And drill is what they did. Tau and Ulrich taught the desert dwellers the Roman way of war. It was not fancy; it was not flashy. It did not value individual strength or skill. It did not reward heroism or gallantry. They taught as they had been taught by the Petulantes, by their own centurions and legates.

Shield drill was the core skill for the Garamante infantry to train. Day after day after day. They taught the men to lock their shields in the Roman manner, to never slash but always to stab, to never expose a shield brother, and to never break formation. Keeping station was more important than killing the enemy. Holding fast won battles.

They trained to march in line. They trained to change directions while marching and to snap into close order. One hundred men formed each fighting unit, and each unit had its own officer. The Garamante centuries learned how to stand on their own, but also how to link up to form an unbroken line of battle. Back and forth they marched on the parade ground, and when the old Roman fortress became too small for their growing strength, back and forth they marched on the great plain outside Abalessa.

Their numbers swelled quickly. By the end of three weeks, there were five hundred Tuareg volunteers and nearly a thousand Garamantes filling the marching ranks. Equipment ran short. The Tuareg, their hereditary battle experience focused on skirmishes from camel-back, had next to nothing in terms of heavy weapons and armor, and the Garamantes, the vast majority of their stores lost at the Battle of the Sahel, were little better off.

But King Amestan promised arms and equipment. Despite the setbacks of the past year, the Garamante empire was rich. Amestan claimed that the craftsmen of Garama, the far-off capital city, were the greatest craftsmen in all the world. Soon, wagons loaded with spears and shields began to appear, rushed across the desert by sweating camels. There was no time to fashion body armor, but tall shields of imported wood replaced the hastily constructed barrel-shields, and sturdy stabbing spears filled right arms throughout the infantry lines.

Ulrich and Amestan focused on the infantry while Tin Hinan tasked Ejnar and Basi with management of the cavalry. The Tuareg were naturally skilled at managing their tall camels, but much still needed to be taught in terms of maintaining cohesion, responding to orders, and working in concert with slow, vulnerable infantry. Wings were organized. With each led by a veteran, blue-cloaked Tuareg tribesman, they honed their craft to a razor's edge.

Finally, there were the Garamante chariots. While impressive to look at, Tau had no faith in the awkward, cumbersome contraptions. The Romans had discarded the chariot as a weapon of battle centuries ago, and Tau had a tendency to defer to that empire's opinions about warfare. Instead, he and Yael prepared something special for the chariots.

During his time with the legions, Tau had learned a thing or two about artillery. Meanwhile, Yael was a gifted natural philosopher. She sketched some plans, and together they approached the engineer Ziri with an idea.

In addition to the larger siege weapons—catapults, trebuchet, and ballista—the Romans also fielded a smaller piece of artillery affectionately called a scorpion. The scorpion was essentially a scaled-down ballista, but rather than the metal torsion springs of the larger weapon, the scorpion used the elastic rebound of a thick wooden bow, mounted horizontally, to shoot its missiles. A scorpion could shoot a massive arrow farther than even the best archer. Because of their weight, they were usually mounted on cumbersome wooden frames or used as fixed defenses atop fortress ramparts. Tau had the idea that they could mount scorpions on the sturdy sides of the Garamante chariots.

Ziri quickly grasped how such a weapon could work, and he agreed with the plan. The Garamante engineer added that he thought he could mount them in such a way that they would rotate on wooden mounts. Within days, his team had two prototypes built. They looked crude, held together with lashings of iron wire rather than elegant Roman rivets, but they threw a heavy bolt both far and accurately, and Ziri's wooden pintle-mount design worked well. They were mobile artillery pieces, and they would be a perfect complement to Tau and Ulrich's plan of battle.

Thus, they established three essential components of a field army: infantry, cavalry, and artillery. They lacked skirmishers and archers, and the camels in place of horses were a bit unconventional, but Tau felt confident that this force would be immediately familiar to Julian, Severus, or any of the Roman generals.

"The essence of good generalship is proper use of combined arms tactics," Ulrich said. He stood with Tau, Yael, Ejnar, and Tin Hinan above the parade ground, watching Basi and Amestan exercise the troops.

Ulrich continued. "The infantry is our first concern. Because infantry takes and holds the battleground, infantry wins or loses battles. The task of the infantry is to break the other side's infantry. But, if deployed alone, infantry can be broken by ranged units or flanked by cavalry. That is why we deploy our own cavalry. Cavalry defends the infantry from skirmishers, protects the flanks, and exploits weakness in the enemy. Meanwhile artillery weakens the enemy formations so that your own infantry maintains the advantage."

Yael's face was troubled. "But is three months enough time to prepare? We face a warrior culture from a warrior nation. We pit a mere season of training against a lifetime."

"We will win," Ulrich said.

Ejnar spoke up, "Our scouts report that the enemy is massing in great numbers. For each soldier we field, we will face three or even four warriors." Ejnar grinned, reveling in a challenge.

"We will win," Ulrich repeated.

Tin Hinan's brow was furrowed. She looked to Tau for confirmation.

"The Ghanans are better fighters than our men," Tau admitted. "Each Ghanan warrior is a master with spear and shield. Each is an adept horseman, and their physical strength and agility are unmatched. Yes, one Ghanan can beat two Garamantes or Tuareg in solo combat, and yes, they will outnumber us, but Ulrich is right: We will win."

Tau had Tin Hinan's full attention, and he continued. "Strength, fighting skill, or even numbers will not be the deciding factor. It is martial philosophies that are in competition. The Ghanans, my people, are great warriors, but what you are training is not warriors. You are training soldiers. And soldiers fight, not as individuals, but as a unit. The weight of hundreds of men becomes a single weapon, and even the bravest fighters cannot defeat properly packed shields. Soldiers, well led, will always beat warriors. The Roman Empire taught us this."

Tin Hinan shifted her gaze back to the field. "The Romans may be far from here, yet still their shadow lays across our world."

Hundreds of men drilled on a dusty plain. The courage of two cultures built its strength, and the current of time drew inexorably on. Soon, the time to train was over. It was time to fight.

CHAPTER FORTY-TWO

On a cool evening beneath a full moon, the combined Berber army began its trek across the desert sands. The Tuareg, with their nomadic culture and long memories, retained the skirmisher energy of earlier days, but the city-dwelling Garamantes had not fought a pitched battle in one-hundred and fifty years—not since their famous defeat to the Roman Emperor Septimius Severus in the Roman year 203. Thus, they went to battle solemnly, with every man and woman heavy with the gravity of war. Their shields clanked against the caravan camels' sides, and the wooden axles of the Garamante chariots squealed. It was nine hundred miles to Koumbi Saleh.

The days flowed by in that dreamlike way that Tau had come to associate with the vast desert. The distant horizon was occasionally dotted with a sharp-peaked mountain or marred with a dark sandstorm. Most of the time it was flat and empty. The days were a drifting peace on the rhythmically swaying camels as they sailed across the sandy sea.

Yael visited Tau on one cool morning. It had been a dusty night of travelling, with a strong wind from the west that had forced the caravaneers to pull cloth across faces against the flying sand. Tau had just finished pitching his tent when Yael invited herself in.

Yael was wearing a tan-colored tunic that clung close to her slim body. Her light brown eyes caught the slanting rays of early morning light that broke into the tent. Tau entered behind her and sat on the folded camelhair saddlecloth which also passed as his bedroll. Yael sat on a cushion with her journal in her hands. Tau passed his flask of clean water. She took a polite sip and handed it back.

"Did you know that this desert was once underwater?" she asked. He noticed that her eyes were touched with red, as though she had been crying.

"No," Tau answered. "How do you know that?"

"Tin Hinan showed me. In the desert there are skeletons of ancient fish, like no species we have ever seen, buried beneath the surface." She turned her journal, showing a sketching of a fossil fish with tall dorsal spinal bones and long sharp teeth. "There are also intricate seashells, preserved like rock in the dry hamada." She turned the page to reveal another detailed drawing.

Tau frowned. "The desert was underwater? How is that possible?" he asked. He gazed out the tent's open flap.

They were in the Adrar des Ifoghas, an area of wide valleys, steep plateaus, and sharp mountains. The ground was hard and dry. Everywhere was dusty sand and pale dirt, broken only by clusters of jagged boulders. It was a forbidding and inhospitable place.

"Perhaps there was a sea here, and it dried up. Or maybe the ocean was once much higher and flooded deep into the African continent," Yael suggested.

Tau thought on that as he took a swig from his flask, grateful for the cool water. He wondered what else Yael wanted to talk about. He wondered about her reddened eyes. They fell silent.

The smell of cooking meat wafted into the tent. One of the older camels had developed a hacking cough after the latest blow, and Tau had heard that it was to be butchered. Unable to resist the draw of fresh meat, he and Yael left the tent, following the heady smell.

The early morning that follows a night's travel was a busy time for a caravan. This was the time when friends shared meals, when families shared company, and when lovers met. Men and women sat among the tents and chatted over smoked meat and cups of diluted wine. The roasting camel drew a genial crowd, and Tau and Yael found Ulrich already feasting on a hunk of roasted meat. He grinned at Tau past greasy fingers. The dogs gnawed on the animal's thigh bones. Thor snapped a bone in half to get at the warm marrow inside.

Basi was distributing the meat. He cut Tau and Yael a generous steak. A palm frond served as an improvised plate, and Tau used a bone-handled knife to cut the meat. Even unseasoned, the fresh roasted camel was a delicacy after days of hard bread, dry dates, and smoked meat.

Tau and Yael moved away from the bustle of the camp and sat on a flat boulder that overlooked the ravine. The ground fell away before them. The place was bordered by steep cliffs banded in a dozen colors of brown, orange, and tan. A handful of small, scrubby trees had somehow found a way to survive in the rocky ground below, and their splash of green made a vivid contrast against the stark backdrop. They ate in silence.

"Was there something else you wanted to talk about?" Tau asked finally, wiping his hands on his pants.

Yael sighed. The wind caught a loose curl of her long hair. She brushed it from her face, and her brown eyes met his. "I am sad that our journey is coming to an end. This year has been the most exciting of my life. I have seen and learned so much. But after this battle...what happens then?"

Tau blinked. All his attention had been focused on the fight. Everything they worked for depended on it. He had not thought past that.

"I suppose I'll stay in Ghana. You could stay with me," Tau offered hopefully.

She gave him a sad look. That look said what he was afraid to ask. It told him that Ghana was his dream, not hers.

"Or you can go back home to Saldae," he said, his heart sinking.

She looked away. "Yes, I could go home," she said.

Her eyes were still sad when she leaned over to kiss him. Her lips were soft on his cheek, and her hair smelled faintly of lilac. She stood and walked away without another word.

Tau visited Ulrich's tent.

"Ulrich, what will you do after this campaign is over?" Tau asked.

Ulrich was finishing a hunk of meat with one hand while he held his heavy armor in the other, inspecting the rivets closely.

Ulrich chewed and swallowed before he responded. He blinked as he wiped his hand on his vest. "No idea," he grunted. He frowned, giving it intense thought. "There is no sense worrying about that now. We have to win the battle first."

Tau clapped him on the shoulder, and Ulrich grinned. He repacked his armor in its wax-lined sack, and Tau walked alone back to his tent.

CHAPTER FORTY-THREE

The last one hundred miles was marched under the watch of the enemy. The Sahel was rife with Ghanan horsemen, and they itched for battle. There were constant skirmishes between Ghanan hunting parties and Tuareg scouts, but these fights inevitably ended each time the massed Tuareg cavalry rallied. They drove back the packs of warriors, who used their horses' greater speed to escape the slower camels.

The Berber army marched in daylight, crossing rolling plains of short grass that waved in a warm breeze. Cautious for ambush, they sent scouts ever farther ahead, combing the Sahel for an organized enemy force. None appeared. All they faced for the breadth of that grassland was the scattered Ghanan pickets who stalked, skirmished, then fled before the weight of the concentrated Berber forces.

Like a lance, they pierced into enemy territory. Unlike the failed Garamante campaign that ended at the Battle of the Sahel, this attack was aimed at the heart of the enemy kingdom, and they moved with purpose. Tensions heightened as the grass grew taller. They passed into the high savanna. Soon, word came from the scouts: Koumbi Saleh was in sight.

It was Ejnar who brought news of the enemy. His camel had a reputation for speed and for biting its owner, and the beast was sweating and blowing as it raced across the undulating, grassy hills.

Tau was with Tin Hinan at the head of the column, the long convoy winding behind like a vast serpent. The desert caravan looked out of place in this new, green environment. A great army like this would normally have generated a vast cloud of dust, but the dense grass held the earth firmly in its grip, and all they left behind was a path of crushed vegetation, running like a road from the great desert.

Tau, Yael, Ulrich, and Tin Hinan watched the pirate approach. Tau suspected Ejnar had been restless, riding alone and ahead of the army's scouts. He reined in his tired mount and caught his breath.

"I have found the enemy!" He exclaimed. He was grinning as he addressed Tin Hinan.

"Where?" Tin Hinan asked.

"The Ghanan army gathers at Koumbi Saleh. Spearmen camp outside the gates, and more are arriving in droves from the south."

"How many?" Tin Hinan asked, eyes narrowing.

"From the number of tents and horses, three thousand." Ejnar sounded confident in his estimate, but then again, Tau reminded himself, Ejnar always sounded confident.

"With that many outside the city, there are likely even more within," Yael noted.

It was late evening, and Tau judged the setting sun. There was perhaps an hour of light left in the day.

Tin Hinan consulted with one of her Tuareg guides. "We are about two hours' ride from Koumbi Saleh," Tin Hinan said after a few moments of hushed conversation. She turned to Tau. "Should we press on?"

Tau looked at the caravan and the dun sea of Berber faces. The Tuareg were shrouded in tagelmust, while the Garamantes wore light-colored hoods against the blinding sun. He saw many emotions there. There was apprehension and fear, but also excitement and even optimism. On the whole, though, the army looked tired. Day after day they had traveled. They had spent a month on the backs of camels. The Tuareg and the trans-Saharan caravaneers were used to such travel, but many of the city dwelling Garamantes were fatigued and sore.

"Their scouts know that we are coming," Ejnar said. "But their army is not deployed for battle. They are encamped. If we hit them in the night, we could cause panic and confusion. We could drive them clear back to the jungle."

Tin Hinan considered. She looked to Tau for input.

"No," Tau decided. "A night attack brings confusion and chaos, and our entire strategy depends on coordination and order." He thought of Julian's victory over the Alemanni the summer before. His legions had marched twenty miles in a single morning, engaging the enemy in the middle of the day.

"We will stop here. We will make camp but keep heavy pickets through the night, so they cannot sneak up on us. We will finish this tomorrow," he said.

They made camp, eating well on fresh antelope felled by a squadron of the skilled Tuareg cavalry.

The next morning, the sun rose into a crystal blue sky. A million active insects rose from the tall grass, sending waves of living sound into the crisp morning air. Tau left his tent to find Tin Hinan and Yael talking quietly in the open space between the tents. The Tuareg queen was wearing a blue robe as she sat cross-legged on her high camel. Yael was wearing blue as well, a light blue dress that hung to her ankles. Their attention was directed south, and Tau followed their gaze.

A solitary female lion stood atop a low rise. The predator's long body was framed by the brightening sky. She gazed at the camp with placid yellow eyes. A breeze rustled the tall grass, and the lion stretched slowly, yawning as she flexed her rippling muscles. Tau watched her for a long moment, then she turned and disappeared over the ridge.

The camp woke with the morning sun. Tents were stowed, and camels were saddled for travel. Bread and smoked meat made an impromptu breakfast. Then, they moved out. Ulrich and Tau rode at the vanguard while the dogs loped alongside. They were geared for war. Ulrich's heavy steel armor gleamed in the sun, and his huge axe was strapped across his back. Tau's twin swords were strapped around his waist, and his chainmail jingled with every step.

Shields bounced from the saddles of the caravan's camels. Ahead, scattered groups of Tuareg scouts combed the countryside, while at the tail of the column, the chariots, bearing their turreted scorpions, trundled. The army moved with a restless energy.

"Another battle, friend," Tau noted.

"Yes," Ulrich responded. He rode on for another moment, face placid, then his brow furrowed in thought. He turned to look at Tau, a very serious look on his face.

"But the last one. For this war," Ulrich said.

Tau laughed. "I hope so," he said.

"It is," Ulrich affirmed gravely.

Tau grinned. "Are you sad about that?" he asked.

Ulrich thought deeply for another moment. "Will there be others?" he asked hopefully.

"Battles? Of course. There are always more battles," Tau responded.

Ulrich's broad face broke into a smile. "Then I'm not sad," he said.

"Hey, Tau," Ejnar's voice called. Tau turned see Ejnar grinning at him. Ejnar was wearing a coat of chainmail that was polished to a mirror's shine. A long cape of brilliant white was clasped at his neck. He fairly glowed in the morning sun. He rode alongside Tin Hinan and Yael.

"Come and settle a question for us," he said.

Tau slowed his camel to allow the others to catch up. Yael opened her mouth to speak, but Ejnar spoke over her.

"Yael says that the Romans have thirty different words that mean 'to kill.' Is that true?" the pirate asked.

"Thirty-three," Yael corrected him.

Tau thought for a moment. His Latin was far from perfect, but off the top of his head, he could think of at least a dozen different words that meant "to kill," mostly implying different and creative methods. There was neco, a classic, which basically meant to make dead. Then there was occido which translated into something like to slay. Suffoco meant kill by choking, perago was kill by stabbing, effligo was kill by striking and iugulo referred to killing by cutting one's throat. More came to mind, ferio, exanimo, leto, sopio, mortifico, corporo…

"There certainly are a lot," Tau answered. "If Yael says there are thirty-three, I believe her."

Tin Hinan gave Tau a sideways glance. Her face remained impassive, but her eyes looked as though they were smiling. They were deep, intelligent eyes and in such a rich shade of blue.

"I am always interested in hearing about Rome," the Tuareg queen said. "They are violent and irredeemably greedy, but they have grown so large and built so much. Perhaps when all this is over, I will go and visit them to learn more of their secrets."

"Momentum, that is all Rome is," Ejnar put in. "They are big because they are big. They grew when the world was weak, and they can field great armies because they draw taxes from so many lands, but the outside world has grown stronger over the centuries." Ejnar looked over the broad fields of the savanna, but his eyes were far away. "I have heard tales while I was rowing about the world. They say that there is trouble beyond the Danube. That there are horsemen in the East that come to smother the legions of Rome with arrows and bathe the world in blood."

King Amestan interrupted the pirate's musings. He pointed ahead with an imperious hand.

"We have arrived," the Garamante king said.

The ground fell away, revealing the great basin in which Koumbi Saleh sat. It sprawled in the circles of its strong walls. Its river, itself a trunk of the great Niger, was a ribbon of blue in the high sunlight. Cultivated fields filled the floodplain with a verdant green, and a herd of cattle grazed in pasture. The Berber army approached from the north, so the palace, with its domed roof and holy grove, abutted the walls nearest their path. There, too, was the marshalling place for the Ghanan army.

Koumbi Saleh had walls to keep out bandits and ward off surprise attacks, but the Ghanan nation had little notion of siege craft. In the kingdom's long history, victory was always won on the warrior's battlefield. So, the army waited outside the city, preparing for battle on the broad open fields. The enemy was more numerous than any had feared. Four thousand warriors paraded before the walls of the city. They were organized by tribe, the household warriors of each lord bearing the distinctive colors of their families emblazoned across their tall leather shields. The full might of an empire was arrayed for war.

Tau shivered in anticipation.

CHAPTER FORTY-FOUR

King Amestan's foot soldiers began to deploy. The Garamante infantry dismounted their camels, hefted their shields, and gathered into ranks. Teams of boys collected the camels and led them away.

The plan of deployment was simple. King Amestan organized his force into ten centuries, each led by a chosen man. These chosen men all had some kind of combat experience, and many were survivors of the testudo, having fought with Ulrich and Tau on the plain before Abalessa. Each century formed into two ranks, and Amestan furthermore divided the army into two lines, with five centuries forming the front line, and five more held in reserve.

For the Garamantes, deploying in line was fairly conventional. They had copied simple shield walls from the Romans generations before. But to the trained eye, the differences were significant. Ten ordered centuries, with gaps between them, were tactically distinct from the great, unwieldy phalanx that had collapsed at the Battle of the Sahel. Tau hoped, too, that unseen changes would tip the balance, that the weeks of disciplined training would allow these men to stand where their brothers had fallen.

Ulrich sat his camel alongside King Amestan's and watched the men form up. He said nothing; His face was impassive. The taciturn barbarian was a perfect advisor to the prickly Garamante lord, ever jealous of challenge to his authority.

Meanwhile, Ejnar and Basi each rode before a cohort of Tuareg cavalry. The cavalry wings strode forward to protect the flanks of the footmen. Basi was given the honor of taking the right, while Ejnar took the left. Five hundred camel cavalry paced the dirt, organized into ten symmetrical squadrons. Yael and Ziri's mobile artillery waited in the rear.

As Tau watched the army he had trained deploy, all he could feel was a nervous anticipation. He had imagined a hundred tactical situations and their responses, playing battle after battle in his mind, but nothing could prepare him for the actuality of war. This must have been how Julian felt at the Battle of Argentoratum. The weight of responsibility was heavier than he had supposed. He wished he could stand in the ranks again, releasing his fear on the enemy with sword and blood. Tau glanced at Tin Hinan, but her face was impassive. She leaned to speak to a messenger who turned and jogged away. Her eyes met his and there was no fear in them.

The army was ready. The enemy was in sight. The fate of three nations would be decided today.

The Ghanans were impatient. While the Garamante infantry deployed, the Ghanan army edged forward. The warriors were organized by clan, each group distinctive by color. Myriad banners rose above the milling host. Packs of cavalry on Arabian horses paced alongside the mass of spear warriors.

Most of the enemy horsemen were arrayed to the left, so Basi, recognizing the asymmetry of the enemy, sent three of his five squadrons to Ejnar. The pirate acknowledged the gift with an extravagant flourish of his long, gleaming sword. He rearranged his cavalry squadrons into a column of wedges, taking them a few paces forward as they reorganized.

That was when the bloodshed began. Ejnar's forward move unintentionally provoked the Ghanan horsemen, and they charged en masse. They outnumbered Ejnar's camel mounted Tuareg three to one, and they poured forth in a maelstrom of flying dirt and tossing manes. The bare chested Ghanan warriors gleamed with golden torques and bracelets. They brandished their spears as they raced toward Ejnar. It made a terrible sight, like a horde of demons unleashed, horses snapping at each other as they jostled at the flying gallop.

Ejnar did not panic. His men were ready, and he waited calmly. As the torrent bore down upon him, he sat and watched it come. His lone camel, just ahead of the foremost Tuareg squadron, was the focus of that flood, surely to be obliterated, swamped in a chaos of sharpened spears and warrior fury. Finally, deliberately, Ejnar raised his sword.

At Ejnar's order the first squadron of camels started forward. The squadron did not advance at the flying speed of the Ghanan horsemen, but instead moved in an ordered wedge, pacing into the maw of the swiftly closing enemy. Ejnar had timed his counterstroke perfectly. When the camels broke into a run, the Ghanan horsemen swerved aside. It was fifty Tuareg camels against a thousand Ghanan warriors, but those fifty rode knee to knee. The enemy faced an unbroken wall of spearheads, and the camels, although slow, towered over the small Arabian horses. No horse could be persuaded to charge directly into that imposing front.

So, the enemy flood parted, swarming to right and left of the tight line, seeking easier prey to devour. A few Ghanan horses failed to swerve and were ridden down. The men, trapped before the implacable Tuareg, desperately tried to twist away. The long camel spears dipped and came up red with blood. The heavy camels stomped over the bodies of fallen men and horses.

Ejnar aimed squadrons of men like arrows from a bow. As soon as the enemy swarm split, they found more wedges of Tuareg camels bearing down upon them. Ejnar sent his squadrons forward again and again, aimed to disrupt any Ghanan group that attempted to reform. The Tuareg squadrons swung back in great circles, returning to where they began before charging forward again. The herd of Ghanan horsemen was thrown into chaos, scattered about the green fields, ever pursued by the slow but tireless camels.

Tau was impressed with Ejnar's calm. The pirate betrayed no emotion as he worked his limited forces against the overwhelming enemy. Ejnar was not killing very many enemy horsemen, the faster horses scampered from the plodding camels, but he was keeping the enemy busy. Clever tactics and discipline were effectively neutralizing a much more numerous and powerful enemy. Tau was reminded of how schools of fish reacted to hunting sharks. The fish fled before the great predators, flowing, breaking formation, and attempting to regroup as the implacable beasts swam ever on, snapping up those too slow to escape.

King Amestan ordered his infantry to advance. They went at a deliberate walking pace, their focus on maintaining formation. The gap between the Ghanan and Garamante footmen closed, and Tau tried not to grind his teeth as he watched. His palms were sweaty though the air was cool, and he wiped them dry on the rough leather of his pants.

It was then that the Ghanans unleashed their trick. Tau had seen this move once before, and it made him groan. Hundreds of Berber captives were driven before of the prodding spears of the enemy front rank. Their presence had been hidden in the churning mass of the Ghanan spearmen until they were pushed, crying, stumbling, bleeding into the open space between the armies. They were women and children, held as prisoners since the great defeat that winter. As at the Battle of the Sahel, a light screen of warriors stood between the captives and freedom, stabbing sharp spears at any who tried to flee.

It was a clever tactic, albeit a despicable one. With the hostages forming a shield of bodies in front of the Ghanan army, the Garamante infantry could not advance. The Ghanan warriors would be able to throw spears into the Garamante ranks uncontested. Soon, the Ghanans would release their captives. If the Garamante ranks opened to allow the women and children sanctuary, the overwhelming Ghanan horde would follow the fugitives into the disrupted formations, tearing them apart from the inside.

There was a face in the crowd of hostages that Tau recognized, and he squinted in the bright sunlight. It was a dark face, but somehow familiar. It was a woman, and she kneeled in the dirt, roughly shoved by one of the Ghanan warriors. Tau urged his camel to a walk, his curiosity driving him forward. Tin Hinan watched him advance, her blue eyes impassive.

Tau stopped behind the rear rank of King Amestan's infantry. Ulrich was there. He had dismounted his camel and stood with axe in hand. He brooded darkly. King Amestan was in the second rank of the infantry, head bare as he stood with his men. Tau stared at the huddle of prisoners again, seeking the familiar face.

He found her. The captive woman was Newma, the healer. Tau swore. They must have discovered her secret hiding place for runaway slaves. Her punishment would be death. Her face was dark with bruises, and she looked dazed, blank eyes uncomprehending. A horse stepped forward behind her, and Tau saw his nemesis.

Kansoleh rode a tall black horse. A silver and gold headdress adorned her dark hair. Her son, Kabu, was at her side. He sat atop a small Arabian mount, his slim frame gaudy with golden jewelry. He wore a golden robe, and a jeweled knife was strapped about his waist.

It was Kansoleh who was in command of the Ghanan army, and she snarled her orders.

"Kill them," she howled, and the spears began to fly.

The Ghanans threw their spears to drop within the ranks of the Garamante infantry. This tactic had worked for them before; why should it not work again? Except that this time the Garamantes were ready for them. The heavy shields snapped up. The flying spears glanced off steel shield bosses or stuck harmlessly into stout wood. The Garamantes did not flinch. The Ghanans began taunting the prisoners, prodding them and shouting insults. Tau knew that they would release them soon, hoping that their panicked flight would sow chaos in the ordered ranks of King Amestan's army.

Instead, Yael used her weapons. Avoiding the chaos Ejnar sowed on the left, Yael led her artillery-laden chariots up the right flank while Basi screened the chariots with his remaining wings of camels. Tau heard the first thrumming report before he realized that Yael had made her move. The first heavy bolt, slashing in from the edge of Tau's vision, slammed deep into the enemy ranks. Yael had all four of her machines working. Each chariot mounted two scorpions, and each scorpion was serviced by three trained Garamante gunners. Their firing sounded like the rumble of distant thunder, echoing and rolling again and again about the verdant basin.

At this range the scorpions could not miss. They shot as fast as they could, and each missile found flesh. The unarmored Ghanan warriors had no defense against this type of warfare, and red blood splashed the ground as the artillery poured out its relentless death.

Whatever discipline was holding the Ghanan army together dissolved. The enraged enemy attacked. Hundreds of angry warriors charged toward Yael and her chariots. The scorpions turned and retreated to safety behind the Garamante lines. At the same time, the hostages, panicked, rushed toward the Garamante shield wall. Close on their heels, thousands of Ghanan warriors howled.

CHAPTER FORTY-FIVE

Unlike at the Battle of the Sahel, the Garamante infantry did not break formation to receive the women and children. As the fleeing refugees closed on them, the infantry remembered their training and stayed locked in the shield wall. They stood shoulder to shoulder; heavy shields held forward. The fugitives, seeing no safety within the walls of wood, flooded through it instead, finding the orderly gaps in the line and seeking safety behind the friendly formations. The second line of reserves came forward to shield them. The gaps closed. The Ghanan warriors were met by closed Garamante ranks and locked shields.

Ulrich grunted in satisfaction as the armies met. The women and children were safe, and the massed warriors of Ghana struck an unyielding barrier. Bare chested spearmen stabbed futilely at hard wood and metal. The Garamantes, drawing on months of rigorous drill, began to kill. Garamante spears lanced from the overlapping protection and struck down the unprotected warriors. The Ghanan light shields were useless in the claustrophobic mire of this battle. Warriors were driven forward by the weight of their enthusiastic comrades and were forced close enough to embrace their enemy. They were pushed, unwilling, onto the reddened blades of the stoic Garamante footmen.

Ghanan warriors died, and their bodies formed a rampart to trip those who came behind. The Garamantes kept killing. But those desert men showed little joy in their duty. Their faces were fixed in grimaces of exertion. Their brows were furrowed with concentration, and they breathed hard with the effort of pushing against the strong enemy that battered on their shields as they forced their bloodied spears forward again and again.

The Garamantes had been pacifists for generations. They were not warriors, yet still they fought. They fought because they had lost homes and family, because they knew they had to fight to make the war stop, and they stood because the shield brothers on their left and right depended on them. These men would not break. They would fight until they were too weary to stand.

The Garamantes began winning. Generations of warrior tradition, lifetimes of training, and the unparalleled bravery and strength of the Ghanan people were all nullified by this new way of battle. They were being defeated by a few simple months of discipline and the borrowed technology of distant Rome. The nation of Ghana howled in frustration, and its warrior men died to a reluctant race of city-building, desert folk. King Amestan stood, arms crossed, behind his men. His dispassionate face seemed to convey the feeling of his people.

"Archers," Ulrich mused. "Next time we need archers. We would kill them much faster."

Watching the slaughter of his people, Tau was suddenly glad that they had not trained any archers.

The sweating, cursing, shoving match went on. It seemed to last for hours, although Tau knew it could have been only minutes. Men could only fight with such intensity for so long before fatigue forced them to slow. Tau turned around. The Garamante reserves waited in the noonday sun. He wondered when King Amestan would order them forward.

Finally, the Ghanans seemed to relent. Realizing that they were gaining no ground, the mass of enemy took a few hesitant steps back. Those steps became more, as none of the tired men wanted to be left closest to the Garamante line. They moved away while the Garamantes caught their breath. A few steps became a dozen and then a score, and they were moving faster, and for a breathless, hopeful moment, Tau stared in disbelief as the entire Ghanan army looked on the verge of rout. Was the battle over already?

An imperious command came from the center of the Ghanan line, and Tau's heart sank as the Ghanan retreat stalled. The enemy rallied to their leader, and Tau saw Kansoleh, self-styled God-Queen of Ghana, push her horse through the mass to sit before her people.

Tau felt a hand on his leg, and he looked down to find Newma looking up at him. Tau had lost track of her in the panicked flight of the fugitives, but she had made her way to safety. Tau was suddenly very glad to see this woman who had demonstrated so much kindness and compassion. The old healer looked tired. A purpling bruise traced its way across her face, but her eyes were sharp.

Tau leapt down from his camel to embrace her.

"Are you hurt? Do you need a healer?" he asked.

"I am alright, I need no healer," she said impatiently, pushing him away. "But it is time for you to end this."

Tau opened his mouth to answer, but she hushed him.

"Do not interrupt. I am talking," she said firmly. "You already know that the people of Koumbi Saleh are unhappy, but you must realize that unhappiness extends to the warriors of Ghana as well. They fight now out of honor, but they have no love for Kansoleh. They despise her dishonorable strategies, and they loathe her abrogation of ancient tradition. They will follow you if they know you are Kayode's first son. Kayode was beloved of the people."

"But how can I show them that?" Tau asked.

"The same way your father would." Her eyes were dark and piercing. "The Ghana is a warrior first, and a king second."

Tau nodded, for he knew what he had to do. He turned to Ulrich.

"It is time to fight, friend," he said.

"Finally," Ulrich breathed, hefting his axe.

CHAPTER FORTY-SIX

Tau pushed his way to the front of the army. King Amestan saw him coming and ordered his warriors to step aside to let him pass. The Garamantes looked grim. Their faces were set with determination. The fatigue of the long march and the grinding toll of the day's fighting bore heavily upon them. They watched Tau warily as he passed by, hopeful for a turn of events that would allow this terrible day to end.

Tau stepped over the mound of corpses that marked the foot of the Garamante shield wall. The casualties had been even higher than he had expected, hundreds of black bodies were piled on the trampled grass. The Garamantes had taken almost no casualties, hard proof of the efficiency of the Roman way of war.

An uneasy truce dominated the battlefield. Fifty paces of dead ground separated the two armies. The enemy cavalry, horses blowing from their skirmish with the tireless Tuareg camels, had retired behind the Ghanan line or were scattered through the nearby fields. A fitful breeze plucked at the green pastureland, and Tau's nose closed against the stench of blood and entrails that wafted from the dead and dying.

Kansoleh, Kabu at her side, harangued her warriors. She shouted insults at them and called them cowards. She cried that the desert men were weak and should be easily defeated. Her voice was turning strident with effort. Kabu, meanwhile, fidgeted nervously with the hilt of his jeweled dagger. Both caught sight of Tau as he left the shield wall, and Kansoleh fell silent.

The world waited. All eyes watched Tau as he unclasped his

chainmail shirt. He tugged it over his head, and the padded undershirt came with it. He dropped it on the grass and drew both of his long Frisian swords. Like the warriors of Ghana, he was bare chested, clad only in his leather pants and heavy leather boots. He lifted his blades, glinting in the midday sun, and breathed deeply of the air of battle.

This was the essence of the warrior tradition of his people. Not the melee of pitched battle or the violence of a cavalry charge, but the pride of a lone warrior, coming forth to challenge the leaders of the enemy tribe. It was in just such a way that Tau's father had won renown. Before the hostile Gao, Kayode had called for the enemy's champion to stand and face him alone as, too, had Kayode's father and his father before him. The old songs spoke of such heroes. All had heard the stories as children, and all had sat in awe of the tales of the brave, of the warrior who risked everything for the glory of his people.

Tau stood alone, both swords raised high, black skin bared to the air, and called to his nemesis.

"Kabu," he bellowed. "Brother. Come and face me." Fighting Kansoleh would bring him no renown. He must shame the male heir to the throne. Then, the people would follow him.

Kabu, nervous, said nothing. His mouth hung open, and he gaped before turning to his mother. She spat.

"How dare you address the God-King of Ghana," Kansoleh demanded. "Who are you, black traitor, that you fight for these desert rats?"

Tau smiled, pride washing over him. He wished his father could have been here to see this.

"I am Tau," he announced to all of Ghana. "I am Kayode's first son and the true heir to the throne of Ghana."

Kansoleh's eyes widened. She recognized him at last. "He is no such thing. He's an imposter," she cried. Her voice was filled with fear and hate.

Newma's voice came from behind Tau, and her words were loud and clear, bearing surprising force for such a small woman.

"It is true," Newma called. "All the rumors are true. Wicked Kansoleh sold the true prince into slavery ten years ago, but now he has returned. Tau is your Ghana, not that spoiled whelp, and all warriors must swear loyalty to Tau alone."

Newma was well known in Koumbi Saleh, and her words had a profound effect. Muttering rose from the Ghanan ranks. Kansoleh, frustrated, was momentarily at a loss, and Tau used the opportunity to offer his challenge once more.

"Come and fight me, Kabu," Tau called. "Let us finish this man to man." Tau did not truly want to hurt the boy but defeating Kabu would be the quickest way to end this war. Shaming him would be enough.

Kabu was frozen with indecision. He looked from Tau to his mother then to his toy dagger and then back to Tau. His mother acted first.

Kansoleh leaned from the saddle to whisper to a priest who had hurried to her side. The priest bore the black vestments of Bida, the black snake of the Wagadu, and Tau remembered the rumors that Kansoleh had re-initiated the rites of sacrifice to that serpentine god. The priest turned and disappeared into the crowd, and a massive man stepped forth in his place.

"Makha will teach you respect, whelp," Kansoleh sneered at Tau.

Rather than fight Tau himself, a champion would be sent in Kabu's place. This was an act of cowardice, and the warriors of Ghana knew it. Throughout the Ghanan host, men shifted uncomfortably. Once again Kansoleh had misjudged her people. They would not follow her for much longer, but if Tau was to lead, he must first prove his courage.

Kansoleh's champion stalked across the open ground. He was taller than Tau and broader even than Ulrich. His skin was the rich black of the original Soninke tribes, and golden chains dangled from his neck. His shield was tall to match his massive frame. Stretched over its leather expanse was hide of the reclusive leopard. His spear was huge, its dark wood shaft was patterned with intricate carvings, and its honed iron blade gleamed like a beacon.

Despite his bulk, the warrior moved with catlike grace, evidence of the massive strength contained within the champion's rippling muscles. Tau watched him come and wondered if he could win. He gripped his swords and forced himself to walk forward.

Tau and the Ghanan champion met halfway between the two armies. Tau's heart pounded in his chest. He focused his mind. The grassy pasture was firm beneath his feet. The familiar leather-bound hilts of his swords were firm in his hands. The breeze was cool on his skin. The enemy champion had a broad, handsome face. A shadow of beard graced his sharply defined chin. Tau breathed slowly, feeling the wind fill him, revitalizing his body.

Without bothering to raise his shield, the champion lunged forward with his sharpened spear. It was a strike meant to kill quickly, aimed to puncture Tau's ribcage and drive iron into his heart. It was delivered with the effortless grace of long practice.

Tau's fear was suddenly gone. The enemy spear seemed as though it moved in slow motion. Tau stepped aside and watched the shaft pass into the empty air to his right. Slowly, ever so slowly, a look of surprise broke upon the champion's face, and Tau smiled, for the joy of battle was upon him.

Tau's rightmost sword came up, and with the speed of a dancer he drove the blade toward his opponent's chest, which had been left exposed by the warrior's still-lowered shield and extended lunge. The warrior saw it coming, and with lightning reflexes, his shield flew up to deflect Tau's sword. In the same moment, the champion spun the blade of his spear toward Tau's face. Tau ducked beneath it and stabbed his left sword at the champion's belly. The warrior blocked it with his shield, and Tau's blade cut into the shield's thick layers of hide. The man sprang back.

The champion stood a safe pace away. The man's eyes were wary, but across Tau's face a broad grin begin to spread. He faced a worthy opponent. He was enraptured in the ecstasy of battle. Tau had not had a good fight in some time, and he unleashed all his anxiety into the catharsis of violence.

Tau attacked, stabbing his dual swords like spears. He forced the Ghanan champion on the defensive. The man stepped back again and again, blocking and parrying with shield and spear. In frustration, the warrior leapt backward before pouring all his force into a thrust that took advantage of his spear's greater range over Tau's swords. Tau saw the attack coming and stepped forward, past the blade. He sliced a long splinter of wood from the shaft of the spear as it slid past and swung his other sword toward the man's face, forcing him to raise his shield. But Tau's attack was a feint, and he dropped into a crouch, swinging both swords at the warrior's unprotected legs. Both blades bit into flesh.

The warrior howled in pain, but the wounds were shallow, stopped by the hard bone of the champion's right shin. The champion swung his spear at Tau with a desperate strength, and Tau hopped back to avoid it, then the man charged. While Tau saw the tackle coming, he could do nothing to avoid it. The warrior slammed into Tau and threw him onto his back. The impact knocked the wind from Tau's lungs, and Tau looked up, feeling somewhat dazed, to see the Ghanan champion standing above him, spear in hand, triumph written in a savage grin.

Frantic, Tau rolled out of the way, losing his leftmost sword as he did. There was a splintering crack as the warrior's spear, driven with all the big man's weight into the firm ground, snapped just behind the spear blade. The man was left with a blunt shaft of wood, but in his warrior rage he pressed his advantage. Tau managed to scramble to his feet as his enemy came for him. The warrior dropped his shield to grasp the shaft of his spear in both hands. He swung the weapon like a club. Tau blocked with his sword and the shock of the impact ran up his arm. The warrior's eyes were alive with fire.

The warrior pulled back to swing again, this time in a massive overhand blow. Tau saw it coming and, instead of dodging, he allowed his shoulder to take the force of the swing as it landed. It was a glancing blow, but the shock drove a lance of pain through his body. His left arm was stunned and useless, but the enemy was defenseless now. Tau's sword came up to meet him.

The steel blade drove into the warrior's unprotected belly. It went in deep, slicing through skin and bowel and aorta before grating against the man's spine. The big man's strength ebbed, and he slumped against Tau. Tau twisted the blade and wrenched it free, unleashing a wash of blood that soaked the grassy field. Tau shrugged off the man's weight and let him thump to the earth.

Tau was breathing hard. His left arm and shoulder resonated with pain, but nothing seemed broken. He tested his range of motion, surprised to find that he was not more injured. Two more Ghanan warriors, spears held high, charged across the field. Tau spotted his other sword in the grass and forced his tingling fingers to pick it up. Tau felt a second wind fill him. The joy was upon him again as he raced forward to meet the enemy.

Yael had once asked Tau if he enjoyed fighting. At the time, they had been in a distant desert tent, on a quiet day, far from any battlefield. Tau had not been sure how to respond. He knew he was good at fighting. He knew he liked winning. But did he enjoy fighting?

It is easy to forget the joy of battle after the fight is over. There is pain and fatigue when the corpses litter the field. There is suffering when wounds gained in an instant ache for years. But that joy, that battle-joy, is still there. The sounds of the world fade and colors become vibrant and crystal clear. A great, pounding ecstasy fills the heart, and one becomes all-powerful, an invincible god, a lord of war.

Tau tore into his enemies with savage ecstasy, sure in the knowledge that he would win. The first warrior stabbed with his spear, and Tau dodged to the left. Tau's rightmost blade sliced into the spearman's neck. Tau leapt past as the warrior fell to swing his other sword at the remaining man's shield. The warrior blocked desperately, but in doing so he left himself open for Tau's other sword, the killing sword in his right hand, which slashed a cut across the man's forehead. Blood welled up, pouring into the man's eyes and blinding him. The man howled in pain as Tau's other sword flicked the man's spear out of his nerveless hand. The warrior fell to his knees, wiping at his blood-blinded eyes, and Tau kicked him hard, leaving him to whimper, curled and broken, on the grass.

Victorious, Tau turned back to his true enemy. He raised his bloodied swords and howled at Kabu, at Kansoleh, at Koumbi Saleh and all of Ghana, who watched in awe.

"I am your warlord," he howled. "Who will follow me?"

It was only then that he saw Kansoleh's wicked smile. She sat on her horse and held a leveled crossbow. The weapon was aimed directly at Tau's heart. She pulled the trigger.

CHAPTER FORTY-SEVEN

Tau should have died. He had no time to dodge, and at that close range, the maddened queen should never have missed. He watched the missile streak across the field and knew his death was coming, but somehow the shot missed its mark. Instead of piercing Tau's chest, the bolt smashed into his right leg. A lance of pain shot from his thigh, and he collapsed to the ground as his strength went. Tau looked down to see that the missile had passed clean through the flesh of his outer thigh, tearing a gash in his leather trousers. Blood welled through the jagged rent.

A distinctive thrum sounded from the Garamante right. One of Yael's ballista had shot, and the huge arrow, laid with impeccable accuracy, smashed into Kansoleh's horse. With a yelp of surprise, the queen fell into the crowd as her dying mount reared and fell.

Ulrich, with a terrible howl, charged past Tau. He attacked the enemy line alone. Kabu turned his horse and fled, forcing his way back through the densely packed crowd. Kansoleh was lost to sight. The Ghanan warriors, seeing the lone warrior come, stepped forward to meet him. Ulrich leapt the last few feet, axe swinging high. The vengeful barbarian disappeared into the fray, swamped by the horde of Ghanan warriors. Barking frantically, Thor and Loki broke free of the Garamante line. Rooster-tails of earth fountained behind the beasts as they lanced into the melee, striking like twin bolts of lightning as they strove to join their master.

Tau swore and tried to rise but made it only to hands and knees. He swore again. The wound was in the same leg that had been injured before. He sheathed his swords. Spotting the broken haft of the Ghanan champion's spear, he dragged himself to it. It became his crutch as he pulled himself to his feet.

Tau feared for his friend. Ulrich had charged into the Ghanan army alone, and the swarm had closed behind him. But the snarls of his dogs and the howls of his war cries meant he still lived. Tau limped toward where Ulrich still fought on, where one man defied the strength of a nation. A Ghanan warrior was thrown back in a spray of blood. Ulrich's reddened axe lifted and fell above the crowd.

A new sound made Tau turn. The earth rumbled. The Garamante army was advancing. Committing his reserves, King Amestan marched all his men forward in a broad line, locked shields like a moving bulwark of painted wood. Only the tops of men's heads and the toes of their boots betrayed the presence of humanity in that inhuman machine. They moved, not quickly, but in perfect order, just as they were taught.

"The Kingdom of Garama will take it from here," Amestan said as he walked past Tau. His tone was mild, but his face was cold. Centering the line, he led the advance, head held high and heavy scutum raised, steps perfectly in time with his men.

Although they wore boots and shirts rather than sandals and chainmail; though they bore simple spears instead of the fabled gladius, they attacked with the discipline of a Roman Legion. The Ghanans had no defense against this kind of fighting. The close-packed wall of shields, implacable men moving in silence, was alien and terrifying. Soldiers fought not as individuals but as cogs in a machine, and the Ghanan warriors fell in droves.

Still, the Ghanan army clung stubbornly to their enemy. They stabbed their spears futilely at close-packed shields. They scrabbled at wooden planks with their bare hands, and they pushed and shoved at the unyielding, rigid mass. Their warrior pride drove them again and again onto the reaching spears of their enemies.

As the Garamante line pushed the enemy back, Ulrich was revealed standing tall, soaked in blood and surrounded by the bodies of his foes. Thor and Loki panted, their jaws dripping red, and Tau smiled.

Ulrich lowered his axe and walked to Tau. The dogs loped behind. New dents marred Ulrich's heavy armor, but no injury slowed his steps. His face showed deep concern for his friend.

"It's just a scratch," Tau said, gesturing at his leg. Though the limb throbbed with searing pain, mercifully the wound was shallow and would heal with time.

Ulrich's nodded. "Kabu and Kansoleh got away," he said.

"That's okay," Tau said, looking up the field. "I think we will be paying them a visit very soon."

CHAPTER FORTY-EIGHT

Ejnar had performed the job he was assigned to do, but he was bored. Sitting on a slow, smelly camel ordering the desert dwellers around was pure, distilled tedium. He hated camels. They were willful and stubborn. They bit, and they spat, and no matter how often his servants scrubbed them down, the beasts exuded an unpleasant musk that permeated his fine clothes.

The camel he was riding was no better than any other he had seen. Its former Tuareg master had assured him that it was the fastest camel in the desert, but its plodding pace infuriated him. Its run was nothing like the swift, liquid gallop of a good horse. Instead, the idiot animal wandered in a manner that reminded Ejnar of the swaying passage of an overloaded river barge. He was convinced that the stupid thing bit him just as often from affection as obstinacy.

So Ejnar created his own entertainment. He hunted his own prey on the battlefield. Deep within the herd of enemy horsemen was a swift, Andalusian gray. How such an excellent horse ended up so far from its native Spain, Ejnar did not know, but he wanted that horse. It was easy to track, standing a full hand taller than the swarm of small Arabian horses. Its rider was a distinguished older man who wore an orange kente. He handled his horse skillfully but seemed reluctant to expose himself to any true danger.

Ejnar's eyes followed the man with a predatory gleam. His Tuareg camel cavalry had done an admirable job of breaking the enemy formation, effectively neutralizing the Ghanan cavalry. The Ghanan horsemen were winded, scattered over nearly a mile of rolling hills and pastures. Ejnar rallied his squadrons and dismissed all but two wings to Basi's command in support of the main Garamante offensive. Two squadron leaders rode to Ejnar's side.

The two men were Tuareg, but unlike most of Tin Hinan's people, these men claimed no loyalty to any known, respectable Tuareg families. These men were bandits. They had responded to the Blue Queen's summons for profit, not for honor. Raiding was the dark shadow of the Tuareg. Tin Hinan did not condone banditry, but most clans bore some infamy in their long history. Tuareg raiders struck in the black of night, killing, stealing, then disappearing back into the vast desert, where none could follow. In older, darker times, Roman towns along the desert's edge had suffered heavily from such men. With the Roman peace, there was a decline in nomad raids, but when a sandstorm scattered a convoy, or a scouting party never returned from an oasis, or when a caravan outpost went dark, some would fear these reviled outcasts, the condemned blue men of the Tuareg's half-buried past.

Ejnar had never bothered to learn the two men's names. They were difficult to pronounce anyway, so he simply called them Strong and Lanky. Faces hidden beneath the cloth of their enshrouding tagelmust; their eyes were no less predatory than his own.

"I want that horse," Ejnar said.

He did not bother to point. The quality of the beast was obvious, and Strong and Lanky nodded. Ejnar explained what he wanted them to do, and they understood. He dismissed them to gather their men.

Ejnar would gamble two Tuareg squadrons in pursuit of his goal. Ejnar's plan was simple, but it involved sending his two remaining squadrons deep into the enemy mass. They would be alone, with no hope of reinforcements. He drew his spatha, admiring once again the fine Roman steel of its long, straight blade.

Strong and Lanky, each with the fifty men of their respective squadrons, rode past on his right and left. They angled outwards as they passed and fanned out, forming the threads of a widening net with Ejnar at one focus. Like the alpha wolf, Ejnar had deployed his pack, but it would be he who would make the kill.

The Andalusian gray with its Ghanan rider was in the midst of the largest group of Ghanan cavalry remaining on the battlefield. Nearly five hundred quiescent Ghanan horsemen allowed their mounts to crop the lush grass. The exhausted enemy watched with apprehension as the two camel squadrons pounded past. But when those two wings suddenly wheeled and closed on the center, the Ghanan warriors snatched up their spears and prepared to fight. Nobody noticed Ejnar stalking ever closer.

The Tuareg camels drove deep into the scattered groups of Ghanan horsemen. The first moments of that battle were a slaughter, as unprepared Ghanans were crushed under the weight of the heavy hooves or impaled by the long camel-spears. Quickly though, the Ghanans woke to the attack. They brandished their own spears as they urged their tired mounts into the melee.

Ejnar's target horseman, seeing camel cavalry closing in from either side, panicked. From east, west, and south he saw Ghanan warriors going down before the camel-spears of the charging Tuareg. The only escape was north, so he galloped that way. Ejnar's prey was doing exactly as Ejnar wanted.

As the wings of Tuareg drew together, they met greater and greater resistance from the Ghanan cavalry. Unlike the earlier phases of the battle, where there had been clear lines of escape for the horsemen, camels were now closing in from both sides. Trapped, the Ghanans fought back. Tuareg camels lost momentum and were pulled down by the numerical superiority of the enemy. The tide of battle began to turn. Ejnar used the flat of his sword to whip his camel into a run.

A Ghanan warrior saw Ejnar riding alone up the field. The young warrior recalled the honor of his warrior ancestors, steeled himself to bravery, and charged.

Ejnar saw the young man come and sighed. He considered killing this unanticipated enemy with his sword but decided he did not want to risk denting the nice, clean blade. He sheathed the sword. Like the other Tuareg camels, his mount was equipped with four of the long, thin camel spears lashed along its flank. He pulled one from its bindings and leveled it, watching the man approach and hoping that the rough wood would not give him a splinter as he drove it home.

Killing the young warrior was easy. The Tuareg camel spear was an efficient weapon for such work. Its light weight allowed Ejnar to choose with precision where to plant the sharpened iron tip. The spear's long reach kept Ejnar safe from the warrior's own shorter weapon. He casually pierced his attacker through the heart. The thin spear snapped when it hit the man's spine, and Ejnar swore because, as he had feared, the crude weapon drove a wooden splinter into his palm with the shock of impact. He cursed and resolved to always wear gloves if he were to use such peasant weapons in the future. He dropped the broken stump of wood and rode on.

Ejnar raised himself up to stand on the saddle. Camels were harder to stand on than horses because of their uneven stride and swaying run, but he had practiced, and he was steady as he closed on his prey. He drew his sword with his right hand, keeping the camel's reins in his left as he guided the beast closer to the fleeing Andalusian gray and its panicked rider. He saw fear in his quarry's eyes and grinned.

Too late, the old Ghanan horseman realized his danger. He tried to swerve, but Ejnar was already upon him. Ejnar launched himself into the air, jumping from one running beast to the other. Ejnar's outstretched sword slid into the Ghanan horseman's chest, spilling red blood on the man's orange Kente. Ejnar used the sword's planted hilt to catch himself as he landed. Then, he pushed the horse's dying owner from the saddle, freeing his bloodied sword as he did so, and made himself comfortable in his place. Ejnar plucked the reins from the horse's neck and sheathed his sword. He made a mental note to clean the fine blade soon to keep the metal from rusting. He calmed the animal's panicked flight and reigned in to take stock of the situation.

About half of Ejnar's Tuareg camel riders had already died. The Ghanans were fighting back savagely. Once the camel squadrons lost their momentum, it was the Ghanan horsemen who ruled this battlefield. As Ejnar watched, a Tuareg man, tagelmust covering his face, was speared by no less than three Ghanan horsemen at once. The Tuareg man howled in pain as he was dragged from the saddle.

Ejnar sighed. He drew breath and gave a piercing whistle. Hearing it, Strong and Lanky called to their men to withdraw. Only a handful of Tuareg returned, limping and bleeding. The rest died.

Ejnar had expected the Ghanans to pursue his men, and was ready to call to Basi for reinforcements, but then he saw why the enemy held back. The Ghanan infantry was breaking. Under the disciplined assault of the Garamante shield wall, the black spearmen could not hold. The enemy fled toward the city in a great flood. The battle was over. Ejnar summoned Strong and Lanky.

"Follow me," he said.

For there was work yet to be done.

CHAPTER FORTY-NINE

Tau stood with Ulrich and watched their army win the battle for which they had been trained. The Garamante shield men were clinical and detached. They stepped forward in formation and used their spears only if the killing stroke would not break the coherence of the shield wall. They did not lunge forward; they did not lash out in rage. It was as much from their inhuman discipline as from the imperviousness of their defense that the men of Koumbi Saleh retreated. No Ghanan warrior had ever fought an enemy like this.

Basi used his cavalry conservatively. Short charges kept the infantry flanks clear of the massing enemy. Far to the left, a commotion betrayed where a skirmish raged among the mounted men. Tau assumed that Ejnar was addressing a pocket of resistance, and before long, the dust and noise of that scuffle died away too.

Yael was not using her scorpions. There were many open angles for her to lay missiles into the enemy mass, but instead, she kept her killing machines quiet. Tau understood her hesitance to use the weapons. The destructive potential of the artillery was terrifying, and Tau was not sorry to miss the ominous thrum of their wooden bows springing forward. The slaughter they could produce was industrial in scale. Yael could see that this battle was already won. Causing more death would not change the outcome.

Soon, no resistance opposed the stolid Garamante infantry. The last Ghanan warrior fled, and King Amestan could lead his soldiers to the very threshold of Koumbi Saleh.

There he stopped.

Tau walked to the open gate, limping on his crutch as Ulrich walked beside him.

"I will go no farther," Amestan announced. He lifted his voice so his close-packed soldiers could hear.

"The Ghanans have raided our cities," he said. "They have killed our women and children and taken our people as slaves. But the killing ends here. If we walk into this city, the cycle continues. If we slaughter and raze, we only invite further reprisal, further violence."

The Garamante king turned. "This is your city now, Tau. Will you bring us peace?"

Tau looked at the soldiers of Garama, and they gazed back. These small men, these city-builders of the desert, were tired. They wanted to go home. For generations, the desert had been their defense against invaders. They were a nation of engineers, farmers, and architects. When they got home, their shields would be disassembled, and the precious wood repurposed to build house-lintels and granary doors. The battle joy was not upon them. Their job was done.

A camel snorted, and Tau turned to see Tin Hinan approach on her camel. Yael and Newma walked alongside the blue queen.

"Go on," Newma said impatiently. "Ghana is defeated, and their warriors are shamed. They are ready for a new leader."

"But only if Kansoleh and Kabu are deposed," Tau said.

"Then go and do what must be done," Newma said irritably. "You know where they will be."

Tau nodded and turned away. Ulrich, axe in hand, followed. They moved to the open gates. Amestan's soldiers stood aside to let them pass.

The city streets lay silent. The fleeing warriors were nowhere to be seen. The plaster wall was painted with the gold of the palace, for it marked the boundary of the sacred grove. Tau tried to walk proudly, but his wound made him limp. He leaned on the broken spear as he followed the curve of the wall.

The gates to the palace gardens were thrown open. No guards were in sight. An unpleasant stench met Tau's nose as he entered the sacred grove. It was the smell of rotting flesh. Among the trees, in this holy place where the spirits of the ancestors wandered, corpses dangled from posts. Never had the sacred grove been so defiled. On the wooden poles were bodies of people of all ages, of men and of women. They were all black, the familiar dark hue of Ghana, evidence that Kansoleh was persecuting her own people.

Had she truly gone mad? Tau wondered what these poor souls had done to earn her ire. Their naked skin was flensed to the bone, their eyes were gouged from their heads, and their dismembered corpses hung to be picked apart by the carrion birds.

It was a short walk along the sacred path, but soon they arrived at the palace doors. Like the garden gate, the golden threshold was thrown open. The broad entryway echoed with emptiness.

Meanwhile, Ejnar lay in wait. He too was in the sacred grove. He was nonplussed by the smell. A low hedge hid him and his henchmen from Tau and Ulrich's sight. Even Thor and Loki, following close behind their master, did not notice the presence of the pirate. Behind Ejnar, a stolen cart was hitched to four stolen horses. The Andalusian gray ate grain from a sack nearby while eyes, silent and predatory, watched Tau and Ulrich enter the palace.

The palace hall was just as Tau had remembered it as a boy. Tall plaster columns rose high, joining with a domed roof intricate in patterns of purple and gold. One wall was painted with a great mural—a rich herd of antelope, resplendent on a broad savanna of yellow grass. The opposite wall bore a painting of the elusive Saharan cheetah nursing a litter of cubs. Directly in front of Tau was the great throne on its dais. The throne's marble seat was draped with golden silk and cushioned with pillows of soft down.

A large chest stood at the foot of that throne. Tau remembered it well. He went to the chest and lifted the heavy lid. As he had expected, the chest was filled to the brim with silver coins. His father had called this chest a weapon, and it was a powerful one. It collected tribute from the emperor's subjects and dispensed gifts to those who pleased the Ghana. It was proof of the unchallenged power of the emperor that the massive vessel was kept in the open and blatantly left unlocked. Tau closed the lid and moved on.

The quiet palace felt empty, but Tau knew where Kabu and Kansoleh would be. Behind the throne was a door, its thick wood edged with gleaming brass. It opened silently to Tau's hand, turning on greased hinges, and Tau and Ulrich entered the royal chambers. Tau felt as though he passed into a dream, floating between the present and a nearly forgotten past. The passageway was so familiar.

The child within closed his eyes to walk with memory alone through his long-accustomed home.

Tau found his hand on the door of his father's chamber. Emperor Kayode and Tau's mother would lie in here and laugh and hold each other. After Tau's mother died the laughter had left the palace. Invisible tears had coursed behind the emperor's dry eyes. Then Kansoleh had come.

There was a noise from the chamber, and Tau pushed the door open. His eyes met his stepmother's and registered the pure hatred they held. Slowly, Tau realized that she was covered in blood. Its sour smell filled the room. A shame, since Tau's mother had always brought the scent of fresh flowers. The blood was Kabu's. He was dead, and Kansoleh held the dagger.

Ulrich grunted and stepped forward. The dogs whimpered, but Ulrich was unfazed. He hefted his axe.

"Put the knife down," Ulrich ordered.

Kansoleh stood, brandishing the jeweled weapon. Kabu's body sullied the bed. The boy's dead eyes were wide, staring blankly at the ceiling.

"You cannot command me," Kansoleh responded. "I am descended of a god, and I will kill you both with Bida's help."

She lunged forward to stab at Ulrich. Ulrich did not bother to dodge away. The jeweled dagger scraped uselessly against his armored cuirass. She dragged the blade up to slash at his face, and Ulrich slapped the small weapon away. It landed on the bed. Tau remembered the sheets had been yellow; now they oozed with red.

Kansoleh's wrath turned on Tau, and she spat. "You are not Tau. Tau is dead. The Takrur slavers said he died. He died like his father."

"And how did my father die?" Tau asked. He felt distant and hollow.

"The gods demanded a sacrifice, and Kayode was chosen," she said.

Tau gazed at her. Too disheartened to feel any anger. "So, you killed my father, and now you killed my brother. It is over Kansoleh. I have returned, and you have lost. It is time for you to stand before your people and accept their judgement."

Tau thought of the bodies strung up in the sacred grove. Koumbi Saleh would clamor for her head.

"Never," she hissed. She went to the bed and snatched up the knife. Ulrich stood protectively in front of his friend, and the dogs growled, but Tau knew what would happen next. He watched impassively.

"When I leave this body, I will ascend to the gods. In a generation I will return and claim Ghana for my own," Kansoleh said.

Then she killed herself. The sharp point of the dagger went through her throat and severed her arteries. The warm blood pulsed into her windpipe, and she began to choke on her own blood. She collapsed on the bed, and soon her twitching stopped. Thor whimpered, and Ulrich reached down to pat the dog's head.

"She didn't need to kill Kabu," Tau mused. "I had no hatred for him. I would have liked to have known my brother."

"Come, friend," Ulrich said. "Let us leave this place."

They left the way they had come. As they passed through the throne room, Tau noticed that the chest of silver coins was missing, but he had a guess at where it might have gone. A glorious golden sunset greeted them as they stepped through the threshold.

The people of Koumbi Saleh gathered in the sacred grove. Already, the hanging corpses were being removed from their lashings. Women wept as they recovered the bodies of their children, brothers, sisters, and parents, their lives stolen by the power-mad queen. At the entrance, Tin Hinan sat upon her camel alone. Newma ascended the marble stairway.

"Is it done?" Newma asked.

"Kansoleh and Kabu are dead," Tau confirmed.

"Then you are Ghana," Newma said. "Warrior-king of Koumbi Saleh and the golden empire. The blood of Emperor Kayode runs in your veins. The people will follow you."

More townspeople arrived, and the eyes of Koumbi Saleh rose to see their new king. These were Tau's people; this was Tau's home. His inner eye saw a golden kingdom, one ruled by a benevolent leader. One whose people would flourish. One who could make a just peace with its neighbors.

And Tau, Emperor of Ghana, drew breath to address his people.

EPILOGUE

"If we give chase now, we can catch him," Ulrich said angrily. Yael fiddled with the string of her bow.

They were upset because Newma had spotted Ejnar fleeing the palace with two Tuareg, five horses, a farm cart, and the great, gilded chest of silver coins.

"He said he was moving the chest at your instructions," Newma scoffed. "But I knew that he was lying."

But she could do nothing to stop him and the pirate had escaped. The chest was full; the coins in it would be enough to buy and to crew a warship. The pirate was last seen riding west; he would be heading to the sea. Tau fought a smile.

Yael frowned. "I should have known he would betray us in the end. He was always a rogue," she said.

Tau could not keep the grin from his face. "No, we will not chase him. Let him go," he said with good humor.

Ulrich growled, and Thor and Loki bared their teeth. Newma and Yael looked confused. Tau laughed aloud.

"Come with me. I want to show you something," Tau said, and they followed.

There was another door behind the throne. This was a smaller door, camouflaged into the paneling and partially covered by a tapestry. Tau's hand felt for the secret latch, and he opened the hidden door.

A collective gasp met door's opening. The evening sunlight, slanting through the high windows of the palace, struck a blinding cascade of gold. This was the treasure room of Koumbi Saleh. Nearly as large as the audience chamber itself, this chamber was crammed with tables, shelves, and massive open crates. Golden treasure covered every surface. There were heavy gold coins, intricate golden jewelry, golden statues, and even golden lamps and chairs. There was so much treasure in this room that it was heaped in great mounds on the floor. Next to this wealth, Ejnar's stolen chest of silver was a pittance.

Tau laughed again. "I think we can let Ejnar go with his little box."

HISTORICAL NOTE

In comparison with the subject matter of my prior novel, Ulrich, which took place in Europe, not as much is known about Saharan and Sub-Saharan Africa in the third and fourth centuries. Roman historians were aware of the Garamantes and Gaetuli, and the Ghanan empire left us some of their own records and oral histories, but the exact events that may or may not have taken place in a given time are mostly lost to history. So I took the opportunity, when writing this book, to take my fair share of liberties with the specifics, but the general setting and the cultures described were very much real.

By the middle of the fourth century A.D., the Roman colonial cities along the African coast flourished much as they had for hundreds of years. Sophisticated cosmopolitan centers, the African colonies maintained a high level of productivity and generated much of the grain that was exported to European Rome. The war with the Sassanid Empire had drained some of the Empire's resources, which allowed the resurgence of Greek piracy in the Mediterranean, but otherwise the African provinces remained, for a long while, some of the Empire's most valuable holdings.

The Gaetuli, making their home in the Atlas Mountains, were descendants of the fabled horsemen of Numidia. From a Roman perspective, the Numidians were made most famous as the powerful cavalry first wielded by Hannibal of Carthage, some five hundred years earlier. By the fourth century A.D., the Gaetuli, disenchanted with empires, had retreated to the southern slopes of the Atlas. They raised some of the best horses in the world and mostly kept to themselves. The great Atlas elephant and Barbary lion seen in this book have, sadly, since gone extinct.

Meanwhile, in the depths of the Sahara Desert, hundreds or even thousands of miles from the next nearest society, lived an extremely technologically advanced civilization, which has since been swallowed by the desert sands. When the ruins of great Garamante cities and foggara were rediscovered by archaeologists in the twentieth century, the construction and architectural techniques were so impressive that it was thought that they could only be Roman. The truth is far stranger. For more than a millennium, a unique empire flourished here. Vast caravans, each boasting between one thousand and ten thousand camels, carried the desert trade. Prosperous cities of concrete and stone were surrounded by verdant fields of wheat and groves of date palms. The Garamantes quenched their thirst with mineral water mined deep beneath the mountains. The water was carried to the cities and agricultural fields with extensive, underground aqueducts. However, mineral water, much like mineral oil, is a non-renewable resource, and the final well eventually went dry, resulting in the extinction of the entire Garamante culture somewhere between 600 A.D. to 700 A.D.

Also deep in the Sahara Desert lived the Tuareg. Ethnically they were Berbers, like the Gaetuli to the north and their city-building Garamante brethren. They were known as the "blue men of the desert" for the indigo dye which colored their clothes and stained their skin. The men wore cloaks about their faces called tagelmust, and they were famous camel-riders and feared raiders. Like the Garamantes, they managed to live and travel within the great Sahara but, nomadic and elusive, they seemed not inclined toward a city-building, sedentary lifestyle. It is unknown how they interacted with the Garamantes, with whom they must have shared much territory. They famously gathered under Tin Hinan, the first Queen of the Tuareg, in the fourth century. Her tomb can be found built within an old Roman fort just beyond the town of Abalessa in southern Algeria. Of all the cultures exhibited in this novel, only the Tuareg persist to this day.

Ghana was called the Empire of Gold. This Ghanan Empire is historically distinct and geographically a great distance to the northwest of the modern-day nation of Ghana. The date of Ghana's founding has been lost to history, but it was well described by Arab historians in the eighth century, and oral tradition dates its existence to at least the fourth century A.D. Its true names were Awkar or Wagadu, but it was often called Ghana after the title of its king. Ethnically Soninke, they forged the greatest Sub-Saharan empire yet seen, built on great gold mines and trade with the trans-Saharan camel caravans. They boasted a powerful warrior culture and a vibrant, unique theology. Ghana's capital city of Koumbi Saleh was said to be a place of great beauty, although its once verdant grassland has since been swallowed by arid desert as the Sahara has expanded. Ghana became an Islamic state after the Muslim conquests of the Maghreb in the seventh and eighth centuries, and later was subsumed into the Empire of Mali in 1240 A.D.

By the mid- fourth century A.D., a Western historian's eye would be invariably drawn back to the tribulations of Rome. Barbarians ravened at the gates, dissention and corruption rotted at the core of Empire, and the Sassanids to the east grew ever stronger and more dangerous. The Frankish tribes laid the groundwork for the systems that would define feudal Europe, and from the far Eurasian steppe, a people known as the Huns continued their fateful trek westward.

Printed in Great Britain
by Amazon